P9-BYK-106

Fallen Lake

Fallen Lake

Laird Harrison

with thanks

Laird Harrison

VERDANT BOOKS

47 Hazel Street

Rutland, Vermont 05701

Copyright © Laird Harrison 2012

All rights reserved. No part of this book may
be reproduced in any form or by any means without
the prior written consent of the copyright holder,
excepting brief quotes used in reviews.

ISBN 978-0-615-55085-5

Library of Congress Control Number 2012931792

Cover and design by Pattie Lee

The list of people I have to acknowledge
for this book begins with Rachele, Dashiell and Trevor,
who suffered the most for my labors.
Anastasia Hobbet, Terry Shames and Robert Luhn
offered invaluable suggestions that led to its improvement.
David Frauenfelder was there from the beginning, and
Adeline Holsing gave me early encouragement.

Chapter One

HIRAM knows he will always remember Laura's hair—its copper glint in the last of the sunlight, and the way she laughs when the ball slips under her bat as she swings so wildly she falls. He will remember that the sun off her teeth, off her hair, enters from his eyes to his chest, his groin. It's probably too late for him now. Laura sees him seeing her, and she smiles, as if they are alone. At that moment, he can't think of his wife and his daughters any more than a drowning man thinks of his wallet.

No. That's wrong. He knows Sibyl is watching him even as he is watching Laura. Smooth and straight, Sibyl isn't missing a single detail, there, to the left through the chain-link backstop, her deepest brown comprehending. For twelve years, there hasn't been a step he could take without her knowing the consequences. She has predicted his pain and impulses, engineered his joys, prevented his disasters.

He's been Sibyl's life work, and he feels treacherous until he notices also that Leif, Laura's husband, has rested a long hand on Sibyl's shoulder. Leif has seen Sibyl watching Hiram desiring Laura. And as she gets to her feet at home plate, Laura also turns to notice Leif's hand on Sibyl. The quartet is complete.

***

Oh Sibyl. Her hair is so light, her fingertips so cool when Hiram gets into bed with her that night. She has filled the water glass on his bedside table and neatly stacked his books there. This bedroom is furnished in Scandinavian simplicity; a headless pine bed frame, white-painted built-in drawers with half-moon handles, one straight-backed chair. Sibyl vacuums the beige carpet twice a week. If love can be expressed through order, there is none greater. Is it possible that she will find, in her infinitely organizing mind, some path through the morass he fears to the exaltation he has glimpsed?

"Sibyl."

She turns in bed. Her gaze falls like mist on his face.

"What did you think?" he asks. "Of the day."

"It was nice." Her expression is impenetrable. "Nice weather till the fog came in. Some people came out that we hadn't seen in a while."

"But I mean, shouldn't we talk about it? I saw Leif put his hand on your shoulder."

"And you and Laura have been making eyes at each other for months." She lets her tone creep up a half step.

"Yes!" He tries not to sound eager. "That, too. What do you think? Are we in danger here?"

She sighs. "No. No, because I trust you, Hiram. We've been together long enough I know you're not going to screw up what we've got. And I'm not going to, either."

"Okay." He swallows. Sibyl is always right on these things.

It's black night when he wakes from an urgency stronger than he has felt in years, a longing that surges from his chest to his thighs. His touch on Sibyl's arm summons her. She starts to shrug him off but through the dimness seems to sense his desperation. She can do the drill half asleep by now and she does: flicks on the bedside lamp to squeeze goop on the diaphragm, positions it, flicks the light off, rolls onto her back. He's in. She doesn't move beneath him.

***

When the doorbell rings, Hiram flings it open as if to greet the sun. Laura's body shifts inside a buttercup summer dress, her hair blazes its brassy iridescence once again in the slanting rays of dusk, and freckles jig under joking eyes. But you can't look too long at the sun, and Hiram doesn't want to be obvious so he turns at once to Leif and grasps his hand, that same smooth and long-boned hand. Leif's grip is soft, like a woman's; not because he's effeminate, Hiram intuits, but because of his self-confidence. His hair is black and straight and full. His slim smile gives nothing away, only lightens the lean face under a thin Clark Gable mustache. Behind this couple, the two sons, Ivor and Matt, repress prepubescent energy. But Darby, junior hostess, leads them back to the kitchen where she and Adrienne serve lemonade they have made that afternoon with lemons from the tree in the backyard. Then Sibyl shoos them outside to play.

Hiram leads Leif and Laura into the living room to show them the furniture he has made.

∗∗∗

When she first heard the Wrightsons were coming, Darby wondered if she could get herself invited to a friend's house. She barely knew these boys. But then she thought, *at least there are kids,* because after all, it might have been a boring grownup party completely. Matt is the same age as Adrienne and Ivor is the same age as Darby, and Darby had seen Ivor around school enough to know he is fine. His jeans are hip tight, and he holds himself like David Gates but with hair almost to his shoulders and a smile that you want to photograph. Matt is actually a little weird, just in the way he stares at you through those hexagonal glasses, as if he is totally unaware that people don't like being stared at, as if he never gets that feeling that you get when your eyes meet someone else's and you want to look away. He is also skinny as a stick.

Sibyl comes into the kitchen to fill the Wrightsons' drink orders. "Why don't you four go outside and play?"

Darby rolls her eyes, but Adrienne says "let's do kick the can."

"Kick what?" asks Matt.

"The can," Darby says. "It's a game you play outside. In the street."

"We can get Tony and Sarah and Rachel to play, too." Adrienne is already bouncing out the front door, followed by Ivor and Matt. "They live next door." And Sibyl heads for the living room with the grownups' drinks on a tray.

Darby's eyes trail her mother out the kitchen door. Her motions metered in split seconds, she twists off the vodka cap, splashes a cupful into her lemonade tumbler, and replaces the bottle exactly where Sibyl left it. She turns to join the kids outside.

***

When Sibyl brings Leif his scotch, he follows her back to the kitchen.

"That was some game this week," he says.

"How so?"

For a moment, he talks to her as if she were a man, analyzing the softball game: the long ball hit unexpectedly by Sam, Eileen's strength as a fielder, her own great save at third base. Before he gets to the moment in the game when he, Leif, hit two consecutive grand-slams he stops himself.

Sibyl looks up from tossing the salad. "What's wrong?"

He picks up a corkscrew from the counter and studies it like an archeological artifact. "Nothing." His eyes slide to her and his teeth glint below his mustache. "You should do this more often."

"Do what?"

"Hiram says you have a wine bottle that needs opening?"

"There." She nodded to the cabernet Hiram brought out from his cellar earlier.

In three hard twists Leif sinks the screw to its haft. Grasping the bottle by the neck with his left hand, he draws the cork out with his right in a single motion. Not a drop spills. It's a contrast to the way Hiram, even with his carpenter's shoulders, has to hold the bottle between his thighs and strain.

"Do what?" Sibyl repeats.

"Have us over."

"Well. If you behave yourselves—" but without waiting to hear her answer, he leaves the kitchen again.

It's well that he does, because Sibyl doesn't want anything to happen between them. For the past six weeks, Hiram has dogged after Laura. On an afternoon when the ball cracked off Larry's bat and soared down the invisible line that separated left and center fields, Laura and Hiram, outfielders, collided, fell to the ground and rolled over each other. In the meantime, Leif was everywhere that Sibyl went, offering her statistics or a quotation from Erik Erikson. Worse, she couldn't close her eyes without seeing him swing his bat.

It was to dispel these images, and not to enliven them, that she invited Leif and Laura over for dinner. Until now, the softball group seemed the safe place because so many people were watching. But as the attraction among the four of them escalated, it became clear that she had to make a change. If Sibyl could bring the other couple into her house, the four might reach that point in getting acquainted when you bang your shins against something so disagreeable (they whip their children, or take drugs) that you can't overlook it. Or more likely you simply find there just isn't anything *there*.

A few minutes later, the Eisenbergs' spinet comes alive. The instrument has abided, lonely and reproachful, in the basement since Darby rebelled against her lessons over a year ago. If it weren't for Adrienne's possible future lessons, Sibyl would have sold the instrument, because every time she passes it on the way to the laundry room it reminds her of Hiram's profligacy (Sibyl argued for renting) and of the family's failure to be musical. It is so forgotten that Sibyl thinks first of a radio or television before realizing she is listening to something created in the bowels of her own home. She doesn't know what led Leif to wander down there, where he has no business; she has never mentioned the piano to him.

Sibyl goes down. The room isn't exactly a concert hall; its floor is a coconut vinyl which Sibyl has planned to change since the day they bought the house. And even in daytime, almost no light comes in through the one high window. A massive ochre hand-me-down sofa bed, legacy of the Eisenbergs' first conjugal apartment, offers the only seating. On the third door, opposite from the stairs, the washer and dryer and their plumbing are the reason Sibyl long ago gave up trying to make this room homey. But there's no place else in the house to put a piano. And now, as Chopin's Opus 9, No. 2 aches from its strings, there is no place more beautiful.

Leif, playing from memory, doesn't acknowledge when she comes in. It's typical of him that he has never mentioned he could do this. But his hands themselves call for her attention. Like form-changing sea creatures, long fingers arch, spread, trip, tap and slide their way across the keys. They tense, strike, then suddenly soften. They know what emotion they will splash into the room. Only after they still, holding down their final chord, and after Hiram's loud clapping takes the place of their music, does Sibyl realize that he and Laura have come down to join her in the audience. And only then does she notice the kitchen timer calling plaintively.

Dinner proves so successful—the steak au poivre so *en point*, the soufflé so airy, the crêpes suzette flambées so dramatic, the Wrightsons so amazed—that Sibyl has to admit to herself she was trying to impress. The conversation never pauses. And then as the four of them sit in the living room sipping Courvoisier, the sound of children's laughter cascades down to them.

"Well, they seem to like each other," says Hiram, as if answering the main question before them.

"What were they playing earlier?" Laura asks. "Kick the can? It's so nice to see them doing something besides watch TV." She and Leif cuddle on the beanbag right at the feet of Hiram and Sibyl.

"We're all so isolated now, from one another," says Leif. "Remember when we grew up? Everyone played in the street all afternoon. There was more of a sense of community. Kids need that."

"Adults, too," Hiram suggests. He begins talking about the vineyard, his dream. Laura and Leif fix their eyes on him as he measures out the scent of mud, the rush of rain, the surge of little buds. "It's so pretty up there in Napa," he struggles. "And it seems more like what people are meant to do. Real work. To grow something."

***

Sibyl wakes up. The window is open over the bed, and night feels like a cool hand. On her shoulder. On her breast.

During the day, Leif only amuses her: his self-conscious self-assurance, abashed majesty, apologetic athleticism. In the night, he stands in her mirror. She can sense him, like her male shadow, because she has not only seen, but felt those hands. A touch, only on a shoulder, as he and she watched Laura through the backstop, but the shoulder, with its sleeveless shirt, felt his skin. He was smooth, unused by the tools that have calloused her husband, and he went through her. More than the cool, more than the eloquence in the slenderness, it was the confidence that knew its way into her pores. A certainty that Hiram never had. And so it has been impossible for Sibyl not to imagine the hands moving from her shoulder to caress her cheek, to run through her hair, to span her breasts, enumerate her fingers, circle her navel. To release her own nocturne.

Now Sibyl reaches beneath her underwear. Her quick, silent motions won't awaken Hiram, but from across the still city they might awaken the other, whose hair is black and whose teeth shine. He could take her, if he were here now, could walk away with her. Her back arcs. For a long time after her breath slows again, she looks into the dimness, unable to shut her eyes.

Then excitement fades to ashes on her tongue. A shiver ripples through her, and her skin becomes goose flesh. Turning suddenly to a half-sit, she bangs the window shut.

***

Laura serves an ace to Leif's backhand. She can't help laughing as the ball whisks under his racquet which slips from his hand and flies across the asphalt. "Wow!" Leif chuckles as he lopes over the court to pick it up. Laura doesn't remember when she first met him. In a town like Buford, Nebraska, you don't meet people any more than you meet streets or buildings or the sky; they're just there. Over the years, Leif gradually loomed larger and larger: Leif Wrightson sets the Buford High School record in the 100-yard dash. Leif Wrightson wins the Central Bank Essay Contest. Valedictorian. Captain of the baseball team. He was expected to marry someone like Pat Cathaway, with her dimples and cashmere sweaters. Why did he call Laura?

Look at him now: still sculpted like Jack Lalanne, his shirt tight around those hard-edged biceps. How was it you could live with a man, sleep with a man, eat with him every day, and then one day look at him across a tennis court and see a stranger? He smacks her next serve low over the net so she has to practically dive for it. The ball twangs weakly off her outstretched racquet, and Leif slaps it into the opposite corner of her court, far from her reach.

The imprint of Hiram's lips still tingles on her cheek, his farewell from last night. What does he want? This is an honest man. She could sense that immediately. He faithfully shows up for work every day. He doesn't miss a daughter's birthday or a recital or school play. There was a moment at the Eisenbergs' when Leif went to get something from Sibyl in the kitchen, and Hiram got up to show Laura the rocking chair he'd made himself in the shaker style, how the joints were fitted without nails. She looked at him bending over the chair, square and sandy-haired, his head and shoulders smoothed by the stream of years, and realized for the first time that most women would not find him attractive, but that she did, and that this made him hers, like a secret hiding place. He stood up and returned her look. His smile made his wide lips sensual. His eyes, the color of a Mediterranean sky, could see all the filth in the world and still believe easily that a little hard work will take care of it soon enough, that you can laugh about almost anything over a glass of good chardonnay. They stood there, filling their eyes with each other, until Leif started showing off on the piano downstairs.

Laura wouldn't mind, at this point in her life, a glass of chardonnay. But she knows this can't be, isn't done, goes against everything they were both brought up to believe.

Zing. Leif hits an ace. While she was distracted with her daydreams of Hiram and everything else, Leif has focused, with the result that he has won nearly every point after her ace, and the game. Now he eases up, returning her serves with drifty lobs. Irritated by the condescension she slams the next one back at him. He laughs.

"Let's take a break," she says. They towel off on the bench, side by side, with a half hour or so before they have to drive Ivor to a soccer game. It's nice here, on the new municipal courts with the lively scent of new tennis balls and the sun on the park lawns, the thock-thock of other players' racquets on balls. It seems as good a time as any to open her mouth. "What do you think of the Eisenbergs?"

He glances toward her, puzzled. "I like them. What do you think?"

This is important enough, she has to try. "I like them, too. But I mean... Well, Sibyl. Are you attracted to her?"

Another couple has taken Leif and Laura's place on the court. Leif's gaze follows them. "She's attractive. Of course. But I find lots of women attractive. I find Raquel Welch attractive. There's nothing going on between us." As he speaks, he realizes that he is lying, that it's the first time he has ever truly lied to Laura, that he has been caught, because in fact he has never felt this way before.

"Would you mind if we didn't see them anymore?"

"Why should we not see them anymore?"

"I'd just be happier."

"Are you attracted to Hiram?"

"Yes."

Leif stands his racquet on its head, folds his hands on its grip and looks into the distance over the back of the tennis courts. He reminds Laura of pictures she's seen from the middle ages of knights who clasped their hands on their swords as crosses before which they knelt and prayed. "So," he says finally. "All right. Let's not see them anymore."

***

"I do trust you." Sibyl folds the front section of the newspaper and stacks it together with the local and business sections. She even pulls the Sporting Green from Hiram and folds that, too, adding it to the pile. "I trust you to stop now before anyone gets into trouble."

Hiram snorts and pushes his chair back from the table. As long as they've been married, he has allowed Sibyl to lead him around because it's easy and comforting and because she convinced him she knew what was best. Now, for the first time, he sees that he has chosen the life of a cow. He slams the door to the garage, revs the engine of the Rambler, and pulls out so abruptly that the tailpipe scrapes on the driveway.

As she rinses Hiram's plate and slips it into the dishwasher, Sibyl tries to throw off the dour costume he always dresses her in. One of these days, she would like to trade places with him. She'd like to be the one who dreams up childish projects. She'd like to let him think of the practical reasons they can't happen. To go away with the Wrightsons to the mountains for two weeks is a ridiculous notion, and Hiram knows that. He only suggests it because he knows Sibyl will say no, and then he can blame her for disappointments that are beyond either one of them, disappointments that are just part of life.

Over the course of the day, Sibyl calls three other families, but men can't get away from their jobs on such short notice. By the next morning she has seen that the way out is actually very simple. The Wrightsons are bound to be no exception. Just in order to stop thinking about it, she picks up the phone.

Only as it's ringing does she realize her mistake. The Wrightsons might, in fact, be available. Unlike everyone else in the Eisenbergs' circle, Leif, on the academic calendar, makes his own schedule over the summer.

Laura pauses so long in response to Sibyl's proposition, that Sibyl wonders if she's lost the connection. "Laura?"

"It sounds wonderful. But we have plans already. A car trip. In Utah and Nevada. But thanks. Some other time."

"Some other time, then," Sibyl repeats. It's as she expected. Even if the Wrightsons were available, Laura would never agree to this. She can see what might happen.

Setting the receiver in its cradle, Laura flushes with righteousness. In truth, she hasn't made a single reservation for the month-long desert car trip to which she long ago assented. The idea of all those freeway miles, the endless Howard Johnsons and Best Westerns, offers no appeal. Leif, too, has said so little about the plan since suggesting it, Laura can tell he's nearly forgotten the whole idea. And now she must choose it, prefer it, say this is what she wants. She must choose asphalt sliding endlessly underneath the rubber tires, the bored boys slapping at each other in the back seat, when she could have the mountains, rivers, trees and Hiram. To select condescension over conversation, numbness instead of release. It required all her fortitude, but Laura has passed the test.

And now she wants to celebrate. Dinner was going to be simple tonight, but instead she begins planning a repast that will as closely as possible resemble the duck *a l'orange* that she and Leif had the night he proposed to her at Tartuffe's in Kansas City. She has to drive all the way to Berkeley to get duckling and Seville oranges, and when she gets back, Ivor, cruising through the kitchen in search of sweets, looks aghast. "You're putting orange peel in it?" He makes a gagging noise and points a finger into his open mouth.

Still, she savors the surprise as she experiments with deglazing. At 5:30, it occurs to her to call and check what time Leif will be getting home. He doesn't answer, but that's not unusual since he's less likely to be in his office at any given time than in class, at a faculty meeting, in the library, the computer lab. And he hasn't been terribly good about calling lately. So she busies herself sculpting little flower canapés with strips of green pepper pressed into cream cheese for the stems, slices of stuffed olive for the flowers and pickles cut lengthwise to make leaves.

Matt comes in promptly at 6 p.m. for his ritual hamburger, rice and peas. The deal they've worked out long ago is that he can have this meal, the one he has every night, if he fixes it for himself. By the time the duck is out of the oven, Laura has eaten several of her own canapés. Ivor wanders in soon after, and Laura has no good argument to dissuade him from making three PB&J sandwiches for himself. Laura would like to join him.

The phone finally rings. "Laura, I'm going to be a little late coming home."

"A *little* late?"

"Yes." He sounds impatient. "A little later than I planned. The symposium ran long."

Now it comes back to her, something that Leif mentioned in passing maybe six weeks ago and that he obviously expected her to immediately inscribe on the family calendar. "Oh. Right."

"Remember? Anyway, what I wanted to tell you is not to wait up for me or anything. I might have drinks with David Dinkelston afterwards."

Whoever that is.

"What's wrong?"

"Nothing. I made dinner for you." She laughs, a soft ironic hiss. "Duck *a l'orange.*"

"Sounds yummy. I'll take some in my lunch tomorrow."

Laura hangs up the phone, steps into the dining room and blows out the candles. Then she stands over them, letting the waxy smoke twist into her face and hurt her lungs, ten seconds, thirty, maybe a minute until she coughs and rivulets trickle down both cheeks. In the kitchen, Laura decides she'll leave the sauce pans, which cover almost every inch of counter space, for Leif to deal with. She picks up the phone, flipping through her address book.

Chapter Two

AFTER dinner every night, Hiram watches Laura's face flicker across the campfire. In bed, he hears her laugh from her tent not thirty yards away. And every day, she grows in his esteem—how she's game for chess, for pinecone baseball or rock climbing, how she can wrap a finger in her filament hair and comment as intelligently on sedimentary formations as on John Updike. Now, swifter than he hoped, comes a glimpse of her nude and irresistible flesh.

Instead, Hiram tries to focus on his wife. Sibyl is doing the breast stroke, and the water darkens her hair from yellow to tawny between her delicate shoulder blades. Now she turns. Her resilient small breasts appear, and he senses the elegant proportions of her legs. A dark triangle precisely delineates their meeting.

Sibyl is, objectively, beautiful. Hiram has never forgotten this. But she seems as angular and ungenerous to his eyes this moment as the Scandinavian couch in their living room at home, whose thin cushions barely pad its polished pine. Contrast that—he shouldn't but he can't help it, can't help a sideways glance and then another—to Laura's embracing form: the fecund hips and generous thighs, pouting nipples on soft and doughty breasts, the innocent curl of that pubic patch, counterpoint of her normally brassy, now dampened hair. It all seems an extension of the promise in her smile.

Thou shalt not. Thou shalt not. Unless… Over there, Leif rises from the lake, his torso as majestic as Poseidon's. That straight-lipped amusement he always wears is heightened by the occasion, and there's no mistaking the direction of his gaze. Obviously, he has interpreted the rules even more liberally than Hiram; he thinks the right to strip is also the right to stare. Sibyl catches his ravaging look and dives to hide.

Hiram is not handicapped; his body still does what he needs it to, reaching shelves, ambling down the sidewalk. But there's a pinch in the spine, a twinge in the knee. He can no longer slide home ahead of the first-baseman's throw. He doubts he could swim to the other side, as he did once, right here in Fallen Lake, when he was nineteen. He can look forward in life to nothing but what he's got now, only slower, grayer, stiffer. He imagines he can feel the weight of flesh on his flanks. Leif, barely two years younger, has maintained a stomach of sheet metal.

But, of course, it's not a competition.

Someone grabs Hiram's ankle under water, making him start. There's a flash of pink in the swirling mud below him, and a moment later, almost simultaneously, Sibyl's and Laura's heads appear ten feet away, both giggling, and he doesn't know which of them touched him. He dives after them.

***

Matt shrugs. It's so obvious: you know how many cards there are in each suit, you know what's in your hand, you keep track of what's been played, and you can guess what's left in your opponent's hand. Especially with only two people playing a game like *Hearts*. It's not cheating, it's just thinking. What's he supposed to do, pretend not to know? "You want me to show you how?"

The air is warm and smells of pine and earth and the canvas of the tent. Mosquitoes have gathered on the netting, silently waiting.

"I'm sick of cards." Adrienne scatters her tricks in a heap on the floor of the tent.

"Okay." Adrienne's sick of cards; Matt's sick of Adrienne. In fact, he prefers games like chess where the element of chance is removed, but still, he has played this game according to the rules and won every hand the way you're supposed to win. Her anger makes no sense. He pushes himself upright and unzips the netting.

"Hey, you're letting the mosquitoes in!"

Matt doesn't answer, zipping behind him. Nothing moves in the camp. He listens a moment for the older kids, but hears nothing. Ivor may be practicing his sprints on the straight stretch of trail a quarter mile below the camp. And Darby has been so grumpy the past few days, she doesn't like being with anyone. So Matt turns to one of his pastimes: identifying trees. In the first couple of days of this trip, relying on *The Field Guide to North American Trees*, Matt learned to recognize the firs, pines, and spruce that dominate the Sierra forests along with an occasional redwood. A much greater challenge has been to master the identification of a fragment using bark, a cone, a broken branch. Now he strolls a few meters behind the tent to investigate a fallen log with most of the bark eaten by termites. The trunk lies straight and cylindrical, and very long, which suggests *Pseudotsuga menziesii*, the common Douglas fir. Then he finds a branch with a cone still clinging to it, the needles brown. *Pseudotsuga* cones are pendulous. This tight, erect strobile looks more like *Abies alba*, or silver fir. He confirms his identification with a narrow patch of bark: ashy white, rather than grayish.

Next Matt turns his attention to a section of the tree where the trunk broke and some rings are revealed. There aren't enough to count directly, but if he had a measuring tape he could average the widths of the exposed rings and approximate the tree's age. Perhaps he can also determine the cause of death. Matt crouches, opens the main blade of his Swiss Army knife and scrapes at the wood to ascertain whether the insect invasion began before or after the fall.

"What are you *doing?*"

Intent in his autopsy, Matt didn't notice that Adrienne followed him out of the tent. It seems hopeless to try to explain dendrochronology to someone who won't count cards. "Nothing," he tells her, not looking up.

"Why are you picking at that tree?"

"I'm not picking, I'm doing a vivisection."

"Vivisection?"

"I'm figuring out why it fell down and how long ago, okay?"

"Why?"

Matt doesn't respond, hoping if he ignores her, Adrienne will wander off.

She doesn't. "You think you're so smart."

The accusation hits him as it always does, like a blow to the chest. Why does everyone hold it against him if he's interested in science and math? If he's better at them than other kids? He closes his eyes and tries to regulate his breath. Calm, calm, he must remain calm or sometimes he can't exhale. Mom always wants to know why he doesn't invite kids over to the house, why he never gets invited. If she heard this conversation, maybe she'd understand. Should he pretend to be dumber than he is just so people will like him? Even when he tries to play cards, this happens. He clamps his teeth together, bracing for the next word out of Adrienne's mouth which will be "four-eyes." Or "egghead," "bookworm," or "nerd."

Instead she shuffles away.

Relieved, Matt opens his eyes and returns to his scraping.

Five minutes later, she's back. "Okay, show me."

"Show you what?" He turns to look at her. Adrienne is tall and thin: about 10 centimeters taller than Matt, which would make her 150 centimeters. That's 13 percent taller than normal for a 10-year-old girl, according to a chart Matt studied when he visited his doctor last fall. She has exaggerated her height further by wearing hot pants, which give the illusion of even longer legs. On the other hand, her weight is about average, maybe 32 kilograms. Her hair is blond, like her mother's, and hangs a good meter down her back. Somehow here in the backcountry she has managed to keep it silky clean. Her movements are quick and abrupt, as when she threw down the cards. Her complexion is light, except where slightly sunburned. She is frowning at Matt now, with an expression of impatience. But there is also a softness about the dark eyes under their thick brown eyebrows that appeals to him.

"Show me how to count cards," she says.

Matt sighs and folds his knife back up. Back in the orange tent, he runs through the basics: number of suits, number of cards in each suit, number of people playing, the importance of playing high cards early. He tries to take it slowly, but no matter how he explains it, Adrienne can't seem to keep track. After 10 minutes she lets her cards sag in her hand and lies back on her sleeping bag. She gazes at him.

"What?" He stares back.

"Have you ever kissed a girl?"

Matt blushes. "What do you mean?" It's the first time anyone has every asked him this question and it brings up all kinds of images of lovers on TV, and also a glimpse he got of Ivor with a girlfriend, Cindy, six months ago in the living room when Mom and Dad were away. Matt knows all about the functioning of reproductive organs in plants and animals, how intercourse is practiced among various species, including *Homo sapiens*. Reading about this, thinking about this, sometimes excites him. Still, there's something vast and unsettling about the subject when he tries to apply it to anyone he really knows. Especially himself. Only a couple of years ago he can remember kids teasing each other: "Eew! Ben has a girlfriend!" Since last year, when he started going to Emerson for fourth grade, he hasn't heard that kind of taunt. In fact, for kids Ivor's age, it's clearly cool to have a girlfriend or boyfriend, though what that means, what you actually *do* with a girlfriend, isn't completely clear. Ivor's glad enough to tell stories, but with Ivor you never know what's truth and what's exaggeration.

"You don't know what a kiss is?" There's a teasing note in Adrienne's voice now. She has noticed his confusion and is happy to have found a subject where she is at an advantage.

"Well, yeah. But do you mean a kiss on the cheek a kiss on the lips or what?"

"On the lips."

"No."

"Do you want to?" she asks.

"Now? You?"

"Yeah."

Matt likes his innocence, doesn't want to give it up now, so suddenly, but to refuse an offer is no longer a lack of experience, it is a lack of fortitude. And rejecting the offer might hurt her feelings. Besides, he is impelled by curiosity and by the gentleness of Adrienne's face, the softness there which, without realizing it, he has wanted to touch. "Okay." He leans over her.

"Wait." Adrienne holds up a hand to stop him in mid lean. "Here." She finds lemon drop wrapper on a mat in the tent and covers her mouth with it. She sits up. "Okay," she says through the plastic.

Matt presses his bare lips onto her covered ones. He can feel only a hint of her warmth, and smells just a wisp of her breath as her nose brushes his. It's a kiss wrapped in plastic. It lasts as long as the two can hold their positions, then Adrienne bursts into giggles.

Relieved and disappointed, Matt laughs, too. They both fall back onto their sleeping bags.

A moment of quiet. Then Adrienne looks over at him. "Do you want to be my boyfriend?"

"What would I have to do?"

"Kiss me, like that. Hold my hand. Go to movies with me. Stuff like that."

Matt swallows. One kiss was fine. Being a boyfriend though, sounds like a lot of responsibility, especially since he's not confident that Adrienne has given him a full job description. He would like time to think the question over, to consult with Ivor and possibly with Mom, but Adrienne's brown eyes seem to expect an immediate response. Her impatient mouth is twisting into a pout, as if he has already insulted her.

"I guess so." He figures he can back out later.

The frown disappears and her eyes widen. "You should give me a ring or something."

"I don't have a ring."

"Oh." Adrienne frowns in thought. "It's too bad we didn't bring any soda, we could use the pop top. How 'bout a piece of string? Or… I know! Come on!" Adrienne hops up and unzips the tent. Over by the campfire circle, in a bag of garbage from previous meals, she finds an aluminum foil package that once contained hot chocolate mix. Humming to herself as Matt watches, she rips the package into a long sheet, washes off the cocoa residue with water from the lake, and rolls the foil into a shiny little bar. She bends the bar into a circle and twists the ends together to make a ring.

"Here." She hands it to him. And when he doesn't move, she prods, "Put it on my finger," and holds out her left hand.

He's not sure which is the correct digit, so he slips it over her forefinger. She seems content with that and holds it up to admire.

***

After the kids are asleep, Hiram throws a few sticks onto the fire, a signal to the adults that the evening isn't over. Then from a pocket of his denim jacket, he pulls out a Ziplock bag, brandishing it in the beam of his flashlight for a moment.

"Hiram!" Sibyl gasps. "Where did you get that?"

Laura laughs in surprise.

Leif nods, lips pursed, as if this is exactly what he expected. "You have rolling papers?"

Hiram shakes his head, remembering. "I brought my pipe." He gets up again to search in his and Sibyl's tent for the meerschaum he used for only six pretentious weeks in college. He finds it wrapped in a rag at the bottom of his duffle bag.

The pipe is too big for the job, as Leif explains from knowledge acquired at parties during graduate school days. But by thrusting a burning stick into the bowl and then sucking furiously on the mouthpiece, Hiram proves he can get a reasonable lung of smoke. "Try it," he sputters, eyes watering. He hands the stick and the pipe over to Leif.

Leif, nonchalant, takes a long slow drag. Wordlessly he passes the implements on to Laura. It's not the first time for her, either, having attended some of the same University of Chicago parties. She has to light the stick again in the campfire and gets as much wood as pot in her first puff. She leans back, tossing long auburn hair behind her shoulder.

Then it's Sibyl's turn. Although they went to Berkeley, she and Hiram both graduated more than a decade ago, before colleges became hotbeds of the counterculture. She has never actually seen a reefer. She grimaces for a moment, exactly the same expression she had on the hike up when the trail turned into a mud puddle. Then she sucks tentatively and coughs behind her hand. Hiram is about to apologize for putting her through all this when she hands the pipe and stick back to him. He takes another puff.

The pipe makes another circuit, gets a refill, continues around. Leif tells about a grad student party that involved two bongs and a hookah and ended up on the roof of married student housing. "Everyone took turns reading passages from *Winnie the Pooh*. We all thought it was the most profound thing we'd ever heard."

Sibyl titters. "I don't feel anything," she says. "Do you?"

Hiram's throat burns. He shakes his head.

Across the campfire, Laura's got a blissful smile, and Leif looks sublimely pleased. Hiram feels a gush of warmth toward them. It's less than a year since they met, but the two couples have become the closest of friends. He and Sibyl could share anything with Leif and Laura.

"Half the people went home with someone other than the person they came with," Leif says. "Even some of the married couples."

"To do what?" Sibyl asks. "Play Pooh sticks?"

"Married couples?" Hiram repeats.

"To have some honey," says Leif.

Giggles bubble out of Laura. "Not Leif and I, though."

Hiram looks for her eyes in the orange light. "Why not?"

Laura turns to Leif. "Why not?"

Leif takes the pipe from Hiram and draws thoughtfully. Everyone waits for him to release—ten seconds, twenty, almost a minute. Then he blows a thick, narrow stream toward the fire. "Never found the right couple."

"Describe them," Hiram says. "The right couple."

"Discreet," says Leif. "And…"

"Sexy," says Laura.

"Honest," Leif says. "More than anything."

Laura offers the pipe to Sibyl, but she passes it on to Hiram and asks, "Why honest more than anything?"

"What about you guys," Laura says. "Have you ever?"

"Not so far," says Hiram.

"Not so far?!" Sibyl shakes her head.

"Meaning," says Leif, "that you would?"

Hiram forgets about the pipe in his hand. "Under what circumstances?"

"You tell me."

This is the question Hiram has spent so much time thinking about. "I never really thought about it," he says. "But we'd have to be clear ahead of time about the, uh, parameters. Everybody would have to want to. And everybody would have to agree it was a one-time-only thing."

Sibyl squawks, "Hiram!"

"So it would be a switch for one night only," Leif says, "and then in the morning the spouses are back together." It's as if only the details needed to be settled. As if by leaving the city, they've left behind all the rules.

"If anybody got cold feet they could call it off," Hiram goes on.

"And everybody agrees it's confidential," says Leif. "Just among the four people involved."

After a few minutes of silence, the fire pops, and a burning limb rolls from the center of the flames onto the edge of the fire ring. Leif picks up a stick and pokes it back.

"So what are we talking about here?" Laura asks.

Everyone is avoiding everyone else's eyes. "Okay…" Hiram rubs his hands on his jeans. "We're all adults, right? Let's say for the sake of argument I'm attracted to Laura. Okay?" A smile escapes Laura before she looks away. "That doesn't say anything about Sibyl. I'm attracted to her, too." Sibyl's head is down, unreadable in the flicker of shadows. "I find you both incredibly foxy. And say this isn't just me. Say the attraction goes both ways. Four ways. I don't think there's anything wrong with that. It's a normal part of being a human being. So the question then would be, 'What do we do about it?'"

No one speaks.

"Okay," Hiram continues. "Three possibilities: One, we could all go to our respective tents and wake up every morning for the rest of our lives denying that we ever had those feelings. Two, we could sneak around having secret affairs, feeling shitty about ourselves and mad at each other. Or…" Hiram thanks the darkness for hiding his blush.

"Swap," Laura says.

Hiram searches for Sibyl's face. She could have headed this off. She had every opportunity. Since she didn't, she must want it to happen. They need it, both of them. He gets up and positions a couple of fresh branches in the fire. "If we're all agreed," he says. "We just try it once, and then if we don't like it, that's it."

"I'm game." Leif folds his hands behind his head and sits up straight on his log, as if he had just anted up in a poker game.

"Me, too." Laura's voice is quiet and so velvet that Hiram feels it in his thighs.

Now everyone turns to Sibyl, who is staring into the fire. "Sibyl?" Laura prompts.

Hiram's shirt is wrinkled, stained and dusty; even in the firelight, Sibyl can make that out. Ironed shirts, mildew-free tile grout and gleaming kitchen linoleum are simply too ordinary for Hiram to re-mark on; the efforts required to achieve them are beyond his ken. Sibyl suspects this may be the reason Hiram delights in camping trips. For her, dirt is an indefatigable enemy. For him, it's a charming novelty.

He actually enjoys walking in it, sitting in it and having an excuse not to wash it off.

Why didn't Sibyl prevent the situation she finds herself in now, with the fire crackling, Hiram's round face lit up in nervous anticipation? Even a year ago, his attraction to Laura was as obvious as a puppy's attraction to a hamburger, but Sibyl believed that she could call him off, that with a couple of words, she could awaken his good upbringing, his obligation to her and to the girls.

In their thirteen years of marriage, he has never given her cause to question his fidelity. Maybe that's what made her overconfident. She believed she could control this camping trip because she knew she would be with Hiram twenty-four hours a day. Everything would be literally out in the open.

But she left someone out of her calculations.

Leif's confident face has found her; through the heavy shadows she senses his body, hale, expectant and long. Across the space between them, she feels his hand on her shoulder, as if he were Magellan, wordlessly inviting her to circumnavigate.

***

Hiram's flashlight beam gropes the inside of Laura's tent. The circle of light climbs and descends the mounds of her sleeping bag and finds her sitting. He enters, and turns to zip the mosquito netting behind him. He sits where Leif must usually sit.

At last! He plays the beam along the denim of her leg, onto the white and brown fleece of her Icelandic sweater, stops short of her face. How strange to be doing this in the darkness. For so many months, he has only had the sight of her. He has created her touch and taste in his mind. Now he'll have touch and taste and not see her at all. Of the person he actually knows, he will have only the voice.

"Hi," she says. No, even the voice is changed, made husky by smoke. *Hi*, she says. As if they are running into each other by chance.

He switches off the flashlight and darkness snaps in. He could be anywhere, imagining this moment. Grabbing might make her vanish altogether. He hears her breath. Hesitate too long, and her resolve might fade, or his. He feels for her hand, pulls it to his mouth, kisses.

"Hiram?"

"Yes."

"Are you sure you want to do this?"

"Yes." He doesn't want to ask, but he must. "Are you?"

There's a heartbeat of uncertainty, then she also answers, "Yes."

No more talking, or they'll talk themselves out of it. He moves closer, finds the back of her head with his hand, finds her mouth.

He has always known she will be generous, the abundance of her taking all of him. But what's most wonderful about a new lover are the differences you don't expect, the coarseness of her hair, her hand clenched on his buttock, the caress of a foot on his calf. He didn't anticipate the small way she has of tugging—tugging his tongue with hers, tugging his shirt over his head, pulling him with muscles inside her that he didn't know women had. In his whole life, he has only made love to one quiet person. He never knew what it would be like to fall on the hot stomach of a woman expressing wants. Her hands take him everywhere, clutch, snatch. At the base of his neck he feels her teeth. In her invisible regard, Hiram finds true what he believed; everything he gives, she takes. He delights in her explosions.

***

Sibyl doesn't speak. She switches off her flashlight. Leif can hear her moving, fabric rustling over the sound of the breeze outside. Then she stops.

"Sibyl?"

"Yes?"

Leif's uncertain hand finds her naked chest. It finds her thigh, also bare. And under the tips of his fingers, he can feel her goose flesh raised against the mountain chill. Nude, cold, stretched out on her sleeping bag, she is waiting—waiting with the surrender of her body and the resistance of her mind. Oddly this opposition, the steel closure, releases *him* and the passion to awaken *her*. And so he moves slowly. His finger on her toe. His lips on her forehead. He caresses an ankle, kisses a cheek, *accidentally* brushes against a breast. *Incidentally* entwines a forefinger in her fringe, then wanders away, only to return, a little deeper, then skitter along the inside of a thigh, to trace an areola, to hint with his tongue along the edge of a lobe. And all the time, she doesn't move until his hand finally strays across the labial border. She flinches. By an effort of will she relaxes again, but it is enough, he draws back.

The breeze picks up, branches slide against each other. From the other side of the campground, Leif thinks he can hear Laura's voice raised and he imagines them, the other two, pressed together. The wind settles again, Sibyl breathes. Leif feels her hand searching for his in the darkness. She finds it, takes it, returns it to her mons. He feels how moist she has become. His middle finger makes gentle circles. Still she says nothing. He closes his eyes in concentration, the will to give pleasure. Her breath quickens. The rhythm moves her buttocks against the nylon of the sleeping bag. Her skin gives off a new scent. Her breath catches. "Oh!" she says. Then: "Oh, god." She shivers. She pushes his hand away.

So reticent! She doesn't offer anything to him, doesn't touch him where he is swelling for her, doesn't seem even to acknowledge him! But after they both creep into their sleeping bags, Sibyl in hers, Leif in Hiram's, she rolls up against him, puts her arm around him.

***

Before sunrise, Hiram weeps with his face away from Laura. She turns his head with her hand. "What is it? What's wrong?"

He can't tell her what he's thinking: that they will have to pay some terrible price for this pleasure.

"Is it Sibyl?"

"Yes. No. I'm just afraid we won't be able to do this again. That this will be the last, the only time."

And she laughs. "But Hiram," she asks him, "why? Sibyl and Leif are in the other tent. They did exactly what we did. You're not cheating on her. She agreed. And anyway, you and I, we're free. Everyone is. We can do this again and again if we want. And I want to."

"Me too, more than anything."

"So we will."

But Hiram—as happy as he is with Laura's hot, moist leg lying on his and her breath still intoxicating him—can't escape the fear that every gram of joy is purchased with a gram of misery, that he is now deeply, horribly in debt.

Pale predawn illuminates the inside of the tent, revealing what he couldn't make out in the night. Lots of Laura's things: a cotton shirt hung to dry, a hairbrush marking the place in a paperback, *Stranger in a Strange Land*. But it's Leif's possessions that dominate. An extra-large flannel shirt asserts itself in bold red plaid. His massive, Vibram-soled hiking boots look as though he could walk on molten lava in them. His toothbrush protrudes from a plastic bag. And there, on Hiram's wrist, lies a coarse, straight black hair that can't have come from Laura's tawniness or from Hiram's own curly brown head. Right now, a few yards away, Leif might be looking around Hiram and Laura's tent, noticing the things of Hiram.

Hiram sits up.

"What?" Laura asks.

"The kids." Soon they'll be stirring, wandering out of their tent. Hiram doesn't want them to see him coming out of the Wrightsons' tent.

"Oh, yeah. *Them!*"

"I can't, I don't want to have to explain. You know?" Hiram slips on his clothes from the night before, unzips the door and exits, zipping behind him. Outside that atmosphere so full of last night's breath, the air tastes full of pine. Birds and squirrels are doing their morning warm-ups. Hiram runs a hand over his disheveled head. The campfire's dead, and he should start it up for coffee, but he needs to get away for a moment and think. He walks down by the lake. The water is still and slate blue this time of the morning. Only an occasional fish grabbing at a mosquito stirs the water.

Hiram sits down in a different body from before, a body cleaned out, soothed, relaxed and at the same time trembling. The fear and exaltation are so overwhelming he almost cries again. He has finally gotten a drink after a lifetime of drought. He'll need more of this, and more. He can't go back to the way it was and yet, to proceed, what will that do to Sibyl, to Darby, to Adrienne?

A rock tumbles down the bank to plop into the lake. Hiram looks up into the face of his wife. Instantly, framed in the sheets of her clean straw hair, he sees scenery that's never been there before. My god! And here's her hand on the back of his.

***

When Leif wakes, Sibyl is gone. Hiram's green mummy bag, full of Hiram's chummy sweat-and-wine smell, confines him. He finds his sneakers and gets to his feet. Outside, the campfire is cold, the other tent silent. He hesitates. Should he speak? Peer inside? Then someone talks down by the lake. He follows the sound to find Sibyl and Hiram, in their matching denim jackets, both sitting with their knees drawn up, looking over the flinty water. He doesn't want to interrupt them, husband and wife, and is about to return and find Laura, when Hiram turns, then Sibyl. When she sees him, she stands. She does not smile, but her face reddens to the ears, and he realizes she is expressing herself more directly than she ever has before. "Hiram," she says, turning back to her husband.

"Go ahead." Hiram meets Leif's eyes and smiles. A wave of his hand encourages Sibyl, and she goes to Leif. He reaches his hands to hers and their fingers flutter awkwardly at each other. They are afraid. But Leif feels himself return to explosive, ruttish, outlandish arousal. He can see the sky reflected in her eyes. Then Sibyl shifts her gaze. Behind him, he feels the presence of his wife.

Laura laughs. "So a good time was had by all."

***

Darby climbs through the forest, higher, higher above the lake. The other three are playing *Hearts* in the kids' tent, card after card, and she wants to get away from Matt and Adrienne giggling, Ivor looking at her all the time. It's depressing her, they all depress her, the camping trip, the whole thing. The dirt. Last night she woke up from some kind of dream and though she couldn't remember it, she was crying. She bit into her makeshift sweater-pillow, so the others wouldn't hear.

What she needs most right now is a good stiff drink. With the kids hanging around in camp all the time, she rarely gets a chance to take a hit from the Scotch. At home, it's much easier. There are so many bottles to choose from—vodka and brandy, tequila and rum, each with its quirks and virtues, they've become like a cast of friends. Plus you can easily water them down when no one is looking. Now it's been two days, and she can't stop thinking how a quick swallow would warm her throat, blunt this sadness.

She can't stand to talk to anybody; at dinner last night she took her chocolate pudding out of everyone's sight. It was the only dish she could stand. How many times can you have Rice-a-roni in one week? It's making her sick; a couple of days ago she had a pain in the stomach, like nothing she's ever felt before. And Mom said it was gas! Please.

She wants to climb away and read "Love Story." Roxanne said it was the best book she'd ever read, way better than the movie, that it made her cry so hard her mother made her stay home from school. Darby wishes she could talk to Roxanne right now, about the dream, about the weird stomach ache, about Ivor. But Roxanne is a couple hundred miles away, probably lying on her bed listening to "Best of Bread." They should have phones in the forest for when you *have* to talk to someone.

The sketchy trail that Darby's been following fades into a patch of bent grass stems and a widening between trees. Something smells sweet and Darby recognizes a tree that Daddy calls a "banana pine." She breaks off a piece of bark to smell it and gets pitch on her fingers.

Daddy's so excited to be camping. What is it about trees and lakes that makes him so happy? He's almost too happy; his laughter woke her up last night. Even Mom is strangely dizzy. When Darby complained she had no clean underwear, Mom got this stupid grin on her face and said, "So go without for a day." Like she's really going to walk around with no underwear in front of Ivor and Matt and Leif?

The adults stay up every night now, whispering, laughing. They think the kids are too dumb to know something's going on, but Darby has seen them all skinny dipping together. They think they're just so super cool to be running around naked in the forest, white butts flashing through the leaves, boobs and dicks bobbing, like middle-aged hippies. Back to nature.

She can't hear any of them now, so maybe she's hiked far enough. She sits down in this clearing in a sunny patch of the grass and leans her back on a log. She opens her book, and for a good fifteen minutes gets lost in this incredibly sad romance. Darby needs love like this: so absolute, so enormous, so *endless* you could die.

The fumbling boys at Pleasant Valley Junior High School with their peach fuzz and skateboards make her long for someone more beautiful (long hair, probably a gold chain with her name in cursive letters, slim; and he likes Simon and Garfunkel, rose gardens and sandalwood incense). Darby knows she could love this guy more and better than any eighteen-year-old college girl. She could make him happy, could sing to him and cook for him and comb his long hair, and read to him from Khalil Gibran.

Darby reads on. The only distractions are an occasional mosquito whining at her face and huge ants she has to keep brushing off her bare knees. Then the roughness of the log starts to hurt her back, and she thinks she'll lie on the ground. But as she shifts her legs, there's a sticky wetness on the back of her thighs. And when she crouches to look at where she's been sitting, she gasps. A reddish brown spot stains the dirt. It's not mud or water, but blood! Unzipping her shorts, Darby pulls down her panties to get a better look and almost faints. Blood! It has soaked through her panties and out her cutoffs and now an intrigued fly buzzes to the scene. Oh shit! Oh gross! She's got her period!

This is something she has read about in books by Judy Bloom and in the *AMA Encyclopedia*, and it is one of her regular conversation topics with Roxanne: how it would happen, what it would look like, how it would feel, what it would mean. It would be like getting boobs, only more sudden, more dramatic.

It would be a time for celebration, and Darby would take it calmly. More than a year ago she swiped a package of tampons from Roxanne's mother's bathroom, and now she keeps them in the back of her underwear drawer so she won't be humiliated by having to ask Mom. She and Roxanne have promised that whoever gets her period first will call the other one immediately. But there's no way to call and Darby is alarmed. The blood's so brown and thick and starting to smell a little like something you'd find in the back of a refrigerator. What if it's not menstruation at all? What if she's bleeding to death from a rare mountain disease?

Mom. This is just too big a question to keep to herself. Darby tears off a couple of leaves, wipes the insides of her thigh as best she can, zips up her shorts, snatches up her book and hurries back down the trail. It didn't seem like a long way up, but now there are so many rocks to skip over in her second-best tennis shoes, too many roots that want to trip her and branches slapping at her face. She crashes her way through thick manzanita, calves scratched, until she finally recognizes the orange tent and even hears Adrienne's silly tittering.

Coming around a tree, she almost runs into Ivor who is zipping up his jeans. He must have just peed, and he looks startled at first, then recovers and gives her his "big-foot" grin: cross-eyed, tongue sticking out one side of his mouth. Ivor is tall and bony with brown hair cut raggedly below his ears and there's something about this big-foot face that's so right-on it usually cracks her up. Now she doesn't have time for it.

"What's wrong with you?" he says.

She just keeps on until she's in the middle of the camp, looking around. "Mom?"

"They're in the tents," says Ivor, who has followed. "They don't want to be disturbed."

Darby walks over to her parents' tent, careful now, afraid the blood is going to trickle down her legs again for everyone to see. "Mom!"

"I'll be out in a minute, Darby." Mom sounds drowsy.

"I need to talk to you."

"What is it?"

Darby doesn't want to shout for Ivor and everyone else to hear, so she lifts the flap, unzips the fly.

"Darby, wait!" shouts Mom, but it's too late, Darby has seen. In the dim, bluish light that filters through the canvas, Mom is lying nude on her sleeping bag. A man's arm crosses her chest just below her boobs, and this arm isn't connected to Daddy. It belongs to the muscular body of Leif, bluish and naked also, stretched out next to Mom. He turns, raises his sharp, amused face to stare at Darby.

"Darby," Mom says in an apologetic voice. But Darby's seen enough, she zips the tent up again and steps backward. Her thoughts are shouting so loud she can't hear anything except, *why? why? why? What about Daddy?* And *Not now, Mom. Not now.*

"I told you," says Ivor from behind her.

She's too dazed to respond. Instead she wobbles past him and opens the door to the kids' tent. She has to get cleaned and changed, but obviously not inside, not in front of Matt and Adrienne, blood splattering all over. "Adrienne," she hisses.

Darby's little sister looks up from the hand of cards she's playing against Matt.

"Push me my duffle bag."

Adrienne starts something sarcastic, but then catches Darby's expression and, for once, just obeys. From the bag that Adrienne shoves across the tent floor, Darby fishes out a shirt and a pair of jeans. She grabs the roll of toilet paper from its place by the door, and a pair of her underwear from the clothes line. She runs back around the tent, avoiding Ivor.

Thankfully, he doesn't follow her as she heads away from the camp again, along the fishing trail that circles the lake. The problem with lakes is that you can see across them; from most spots along the shore you can survey most other spots. But after a few minutes' walk, Darby finds a huge boulder by the water that blocks most of the view from the camp.

Removing only her shoes, she wades out. The lake feeds on snow, and even under the late afternoon sun, the water hurts. Darby forces herself out farther and deeper until, squatting, she's up to her neck. Now she undoes her cutoffs and pulls them free, her underwear as well. She rinses everything: shorts, panties, vagina in the freezing mountain water, twisting, wringing, dunking her clothes, rubbing herself raw. Finally she can't stand the cold anymore and picks her way ashore over the hard rocks of the lake floor, skin tightened with goose-flesh, nipples hardened to knots on the plank of her chest. She grabs her towel and wraps it around her tightly, shivering.

***

Leif has wanted to make love to Sibyl on Red Mountain since he first stared at the bold, bald peak from below. And now they hike, Leif and another man's wife. Back in the camp, his wife is with another man. *Monogamy is an artifact.* He wrote that fifteen years ago in his dissertation. He has spent hours elaborating a theory of what could take the place of one man and one woman. But the meaning of it didn't touch his life. He's kept the separation and never thought he'd be doing This. This? He'd better not think of it as "This." It isn't a "This," not yet. It's Sibyl, the woman with her hand in his hand, her little brown leather boots keeping time across the alpine grass. And there above is the hard, dark rock, suddenly visible when they break out from a stand of conifer into granite and grass.

He always assumed it would be Laura, just Laura, and in her hills and valleys he would be lost. To touch Laura was to wander in a countryside of remorse. What will he and she say to each other now? There's no taking this anywhere. The theory was only a theory. All the

time he and Sibyl spent flirting at softball games, through an odd meeting in the library, the dinner at her house, even when the conversation
turned to swapping, he never really believed it would happen.

*With the advent of birth control, labor-saving devices and antibiotics, love has
been liberated from monogamy.*

What is he thinking? Is he about to quote to this woman, this gift
from the gods, from his own Ph.D. dissertation? He must stop these
thoughts before they bubble to his lips, because they have nothing to
do with what's happening now. And why talk at all when Sibyl is so
quiet, so content simply to walk beside him and to hold his hand?

The trail takes them across a meadow, and Leif feels through his
Vibram soles the softness of soil soaked by a nearby stream. The pale
grass, the lupine and columbine, delicate against so much rock, make
everything seem possible. The trail disappears in a landscape of fissured boulders. Struggling pines can still find enough soil to grow
short, twisted trunks and brushes of fragrant needles, and the moss
and lichen coat flanks of stone, but there isn't enough dirt for boots to
leave an impression. To find the path now, Leif and Sibyl must search
for little cairns of three or four stones—"ducks," Hiram called them—
that someone has stacked at intervals of a dozen yards.

He thought Sibyl would want to talk. You don't walk for thirty seconds with Laura without getting a conversation, and there's so much
they have to figure out at this moment. But when he said to Sibyl,
"How are you feeling?" she answered, "Let's just walk for a minute."
So they've gone on in silence, so much silence after last night's silence
that he's starting to wonder if that's how it is to be with her, a deaf
mute affair. Finally she says, "God, it's beautiful up here."

And he answers vehemently, "Yes! Yes, it is!"

The stream splashing its way down the mountain and the scrape
of their boots make the only noise. Nothing else moves. Through the
thin air the sun keeps parching them, so they stop to drink in the gray-
blue of Disappointment Lake. A swath of snow still clings to the bank
a dozen yards from where Sibyl squats over the canteen she's filling.

Leif maneuvers behind her, packs a loose ball and tosses it underhand to splat on her head.

"Hey!" She scoops up what's left of the ball and hurls it back at him, a near miss.

He's got all the ammunition and tosses ball after ball down at her until she rushes him, her teeth showing white between wind burned cheeks and hits him with both hands in the chest, knocking him on his butt. He turns her on her back in the snow patch, and kisses her. His fingers start to work on her buttons but she pushes them away. "Not here."

He follows her eyes up the mountain.

A few hundred feet up they reach the saddle called Hell For Sure Pass. Red Mountain, a heap of ruddy scoria, towers just another thousand feet from the spot. They're really climbing now, not walking; the trail's so steep they use their hands almost as much as their feet, gripping stems of stunted bushes, hoisting themselves with handholds on jagged rock. Sibyl breathes roughly.

Leif pauses. "Do you want to rest?"

But she shakes her head and pushes on, as if it's some contest between them, passing him up the mountainside. A few more yards and they run out of boulder. They're slogging up a slope of pure slag, slipping and causing miniature landslides below them, a little afraid they'll be carried down the mountain. Still they make headway until they're on solid rock again, and finally scramble to the summit, a brick-colored knife ridge. Now the Sierra lies revealed. From their feet the ground plunges in every direction to jade canyons and shadowy half-hidden lakes, then bubbles up on the other side in gray rock mounds, dipping and rising until it reaches the horizon in a white-speckled, saw-toothed range of peaks a hundred miles off. Up from the vastness around them whacks a biting wind. Leif's sweat seems to freeze on his skin.

He takes Sibyl in a victory embrace. She hugs back and he smells her salt through her dampened T-shirt. He bends his head to taste her. Then, just as Leif imagined, they strip, teeth chattering. He lies on the igneous, with Sibyl stretching onto him, lithe, hard, squeezing in a way that Laura never could. He will carry the scratches and scrapes on his back and butt and legs for days.

***

Matt and Adrienne are boyfriend and girlfriend. After dinner, she washes his plate, fork and cup. She makes s'mores for him, and only him, using up most of the marshmallows and all the chocolate bars. She moves everyone's things around so that her sleeping bag is right next to his in the kids' tent. He helps her to win at *Hearts* against Darby and Ivor. He shares with her his wildflowers, ant lions and hollow trees.

They hold hands at the campfire. Late into the night she whispers secrets: That Darby just got her period. That, at home, Darby sometimes spends an hour in front of the mirror examining her breasts. That she, Adrienne, recently shoplifted a lipstick from Penny's. She tells him stories about the house she and he could have when they grow up, with a tower and stables.

Ivor and Darby sneer, but there is a trace of envy in Ivor's voice when he talks about "Matt's new babe." And Adrienne explains to Matt that Ivor tried once to kiss Darby, up on the hill above the latrine, and that Darby pushed him away.

On the third day, all four of them—Matt, Adrienne, Ivor and Darby—sit in the kids' tent. Everybody's sick of *Hearts* now, nobody feels like swimming or fishing or Frisbee and the grownups are gone.

"Where?" asks Darby, disheveled. She slept so late they were gone when she woke up.

"I think Mom and Dad went hiking up to Hell For Sure pass again and Hiram and Sibyl went to swim at Lower Indian Lake," says Matt.

"Hah!" Ivor snorts. "You guys don't know."

Darby smiles.

"Know what?" Adrienne demands.

"Hiram and Mom went to the lake. Dad and Sibyl went hiking," says Ivor.

"So?" Matt says.

"You kids are so dense," Ivor chortles.

"What do you mean?" Adrienne's eyebrows push together.

"Daddy and Laura are sleeping together and Mom and Leif are sleeping together," Darby says.

"But…" Adrienne twists a hand in her long hair, tugging in a way that looks painful. "Why? Why are they doing that? Don't Mom and Daddy…? Do they still…?"

"Don't ask *me*." Darby shrugs, then shakes her head. "They didn't get *my* permission."

Ivor cackles and throws himself backward onto his sleeping bag.

Adrienne stands up, almost stumbles, and unzips the mosquito netting. She slips out of the tent. Matt starts to follow her and say something. But say what? Do what? He doesn't understand what this means, so instead he questions Darby and Ivor. They tell what they know: that Dad has been sleeping in Hiram and Sibyl's tent, and Hiram has been sleeping in Laura and Leif's tent. It's gone on for the last three nights, and sometimes also the afternoons. None of the adults has said anything about it. Darby and Ivor don't know what it could mean, where it could lead.

It's either innocuous, so trivial that the grownups just haven't bothered to mention it, or else it's shameful, so disgusting that they've been trying to hide it. Whatever it is, Matt would rather ignore it. He will just go along as he's been going, as if nothing has happened. Unless Mom or Dad tells him otherwise, there's no reason to assume anything has changed.

Matt goes looking for her later that afternoon because he's found a grouse's nest. He finds her, after 45 minutes of searching, in a clearing he showed her the day before. If you lie on your back, you can see all the way to the top of a redwood that towers over the tallest fir. She's not looking at the trees, though. Sitting on a fallen log, long hair draped over her face, shaking, she doesn't notice him at first.

She looks up. Her face is shiny. "What?" she asks.

"Are you okay?"

She doesn't answer, so he sits next to her. "Is it the thing about the grownups?" he asks.

She turns her head away from him. She takes a long, tattered breath and her right hand clutches at her left and hands him something. The ring! But it's not a ring anymore; it's squished into a ball. Adrienne stands and walks away.

Matt stares blinking after her. He sticks the foil into his pocket and starts to get up, when suddenly he can't breathe. He sits down again, gasping, straining, fighting the panic. He's in the middle of the forest, where no one can see if he chokes to death, and a hundred miles from a hospital. His whole body screams for oxygen. His face reddens with fear, he digs his nails into the bark beside him.

And then he notices that the bark is orange-red and roughly fissured. *Abies magnifica*. He's never seen such a large specimen so recently fallen. He exhales.

Chapter Three

THERE'S a kind of vertigo in waking up not knowing what bed you're in, or who is sleeping next to you. Laura keeps her eyes closed for a second and tries to measure the breathing, to suss the scents. Hiram? Or Leif? Even after six weeks of sleeping with Hiram every Sunday night, she still wakes up disoriented. Then the memory trickles back into her consciousness of Sibyl's beef burgundy, a long funny conversation among the four of them until after midnight, and then sinking into bed with Hiram, almost too tired to make love.

She opens her eyes. Yes, there's Sibyl's spotless nightstand. And on the other side of Laura is Hiram, looking as if he'd gotten up hours ago just to admire her sleeping. The damp-earth scent of last night's sex drifts from between the sheets, and Laura imagines that Sibyl will change the bed as soon as she gets home that day. Hiram says Sibyl has done that every time so far in the months since they returned from camping, and Laura can understand that impulse. More than once after getting into her bed at home, Laura has smelled Sibyl welling up around her and buried her face in Hiram's neck.

"Oh, it's you!" She touches his thigh beneath the covers. "For a moment I didn't know where I was."

"Hmmm, I know what you mean," Hiram says dreamily. "It's nice."

"Nice?"

"Yeah, because in that instant that I can't remember where I am,

I don't worry. Whether it's you or Sibyl, I know there's love."

Laura twists in the bed. It's a sweet sentiment, she supposes. Part of what makes Hiram adorable is that he sees everything from the happiest possible perspective. "But I… Well, I hope I'm not breaking the rules if I say I'm glad when I wake up and find out it's you." It's hard enough to love two children the same way. Laura doubts whether it's really possible to love two men equally.

Now Hiram's stubby fingers close around Laura's beneath the covers. "And I'm glad it's you," he says. "Anyway, there are no rules that I know about. We're making this up as we go along. I just like the feeling of evenness. That we all love each other."

"I just wish it could be *more* even. One night a week with you doesn't really seem fair. It should be at least fifty-fifty. I don't want to have to pack an overnight bag every time I come to see you, and forget my underwear, like last week. I want to be… just around you more."

Hiram doesn't answer at first, so Laura worries that maybe she has broken some unwritten rule. Then when he speaks, his voice breaks out of its pillow-talk whisper into the volume of normal conversation. "Would you like to live in one house? All of us together?"

"I…" Laura hesitates before one more whirl into the crazy unknown. "What would that be like for the kids? We haven't explained it to them. In the mountains we said we'd wait until we got back here. And then we said we'd wait until we figured out what we were going to do."

"So let's figure it out. Hiram says. "Kids can't be happy if their parents aren't happy. And they'd have everything this way—both sets of parents and live-in friends. They have a great time playing together. We could move to the country. Plant a vineyard. Have a… a kind of community together. I've been thinking that for a long time, but I haven't said anything because it seemed too soon, too fast to be talking about a next step like that. Just in the last few days, though, I don't know why, it's seemed to make more sense all of a sudden. What do you think? Would you want to?"

Laura takes another leap onto the merry-go-round, because in a strange way it's the only idea that makes sense, the only way to keep everything. "Yes. I do," she says.

They laugh.

"I mean, 'I would.'"

***

For Sibyl's job interview, she stretches a girdle over her hips, then skin-tone nylons and a bra, firming everything. Over the girdle she pulls a white silk slip and a Lincoln-green wool skirt. The hem's too low to be fashionable; she refuses to be cowed into a miniskirt under any circumstances. However, the knee-high silver boots, which match her blouse, show she's not square, and she loves the playfulness of their cut and color. Yesterday she curled her hair; this morning a touch of her comb restores that shape, and she holds it with a coat of spray. A matching silver silk scarf completes the effect.

As she parks the station wagon in a downtown San Francisco lot, there's a Donovan song jangling through her mind, an up-tempo, self-confident sort of guitar thing, and Sibyl enjoys the feeling that she is living in her times. Her ebullience carries her up the elevator of the high-rise offices of the General Services Administration.

It is Leif, more than anyone, who has made it possible for Sibyl to return to work. "When the kids are older," Hiram always said to her. "When I've got a few more big projects under my belt."

"Are you having trouble?" her mother asked. "Do you need a loan?"

Even Sibyl's friends didn't understand. "I just couldn't take proper care of my kids," was Nora Brower's reaction.

But Leif said, "What's stopping you? The kids are old enough to be alone or go to their piano lessons or ballet or whatever. Let them come to our house after school. With the money you make, hire someone to vacuum your rug and scrub your toilet." Sibyl stared at him, this stranger lying naked on her bed. What gave him the right? Who was he to reach inside her, to pull away the pile of rocks everyone had heaped on her aspiration? Eyes wide, she kissed him full on. Then a week later, he called to tell her that Sam Brower was looking for people.

It should have been Hiram who told Sibyl about the job. Sam Brower is an old frat brother of Hiram's. He, more than anyone, convinced his frat brothers to let Hiram, the first Jew, into Alpha Delta Mu. The two played in intramural tennis matches. So Hiram must have known about the opening Sam has for a new trainer at the General Services Administration. And yet he said nothing. It obviously never occurred to him that Sibyl might work here. She has been talking about going back to work for years. But for all his eagerness to launch into this group marriage, Hiram remains old-fashioned in odd ways. He still carries a handkerchief. He still dresses in white when playing tennis. He still refers to his fifty-seven-year-old secretary—the woman who essentially runs his business—as a girl.

"Kids driving you up the wall?" A flicker of amusement crosses Sam's lipless mouth. Older than Hiram by a couple of years, Sam has kept up with the times. A couple of years ago, he expanded his consulting business by offering video cameras to give feedback, helping people see how they come across in meetings and speaking engagements. He has furnished his office in impeccably modern restraint, a Jackson Pollack-style paint-splashed canvas on one wall. His phone has push buttons instead of a dial. And instead of a jacket and tie, he's wearing a turtleneck. Still his full head of prematurely gray hair and his sharp-chinned triangular face give him a look of authority. Even in college, everyone listened to him.

"I love my children. I just feel ready to…" The truth is that the kids hardly need her anymore. Darby, the young sophisticate, knows more about the world than Sibyl did when she was in college. Even Adrienne is plenty old enough to make herself a snack when she gets home, and she practically never needs help with her homework. "I just think I could…"

She spent the weekend typing and retyping her resume, playing out the interview in her mind, but now he doesn't even ask to see it.

"Let me show you to your desk." As an independent contractor, he has discretionary money for his own staff and doesn't have to run her hiring by anyone. They reach a bare cubicle. "Tina will get you set up with a W-4 form, Rolodex, typewriter, whatnot."

"I don't know anything about video cameras," Sibyl says.

"Nobody does. That's the great thing about new technology. We're all equally stupid."

Heading home that night, she realizes she has no idea what she'll be paid. It almost doesn't matter. The strangeness, the newness races through her veins. To be working, *working* with people on something as cutting-edge as video cameras has charged her up like nothing in her life. Well, almost nothing. That this could happen on top of Leif defies all belief and expectation. But in fact, it has happened *because* of Leif, and finally she sees what a miracle has come into her life.

***

The air in the house feels heavy when Darby comes home, thick and still; the faint scents of coffee, of toast, of the shampoo and deodorant and breaths of four people, have hung undisturbed since breakfast. "Hello?" she calls out. But all Darby hears is the low hum of the refrigerator. So it's really true. Mom is at work.

She drops her book bag in the kitchen and heads upstairs to Mom and Daddy's room, with its odor of carpet cleaner and dry cleaning. The closet door is ajar, and a pair of Daddy's shoes sit outside it. Mom must have left for work in a hurry. Darby has always defended her right to leave her own bed unmade, to drop her clothes wherever they fall on the floor of her own room. But somehow the hint of chaos in her parents' room disturbs her. She carefully positions Daddy's shoes along the back of the closet door and shuts the door.

In Adrienne's room, plastic horses line the windowsill. A God's Eye made of popsicle sticks and yarn hangs in the window. Puffy and Brownbear rest their backs against Adrienne's pillow, gazing paternally over the other stuffed animals. Darby feels an unexpected pang. By the time she was Adrienne's age, Darby had given up on kid stuff.

And she never got into the dance and music that Adrienne performs to please the grownups. Ballet. That's where Adrienne is now, which mean's Darby has just about an hour to do what she's been craving to do.

She never had such a full selection and so much time to deliberate. Even on nights when they go out, Darby has had to tiptoe around Adrienne. Usually, she grabs the first bottle she can when the grownups' backs are turned. Now she pulls out the vodka, unscrews and inhales. Not very interesting. The scotch, on the other hand, wafts a worldly, cynical aroma, while the orange liqueur smells childish. There are so many cocktails she has wanted to try. She could mix a gin and tonic, or a martini. What goes into a mint julep? But there isn't much time, and she can't take too much from any one bottle without risking notice.

Dust has settled on the shoulders of the schnapps bottle, which means it's been so long since anyone touched it, they probably won't remember how full it was. Darby pours herself half a glass and settles down in front of the television. TV, too, is against the rules, since she hasn't done her homework, but she has always been able to pull off a B or C without much studying. Besides, a girl has to have a moment of relaxation.

She's seen "My Favorite Martian" too many times. "The Flintstones" is just goofy. Does anyone really watch cooking shows? A few sips of the overpowering schnapps tell her why it's sat so long neglected. Her mouth tastes like a peppermint bomb exploded inside. But a little water helps it go down, and now *finally* Darby can relax. She's had a brutal day, after all, yelled at by teachers for not finishing various assignments, ignored by Rolf Peterson, embarrassed by a bottle of fingernail polish coming open in her book bag. And now, a vacant house.

Darby looks into her empty glass. Maybe it's time to try a screwdriver. She's only had a couple of sips before a key turns in the latch. Adrienne with her waist-length perfect hair, her book bag over her back and her ballet slippers in her hands, radiates such sweet innocence that Darby feels a gush of affection. She switches off the TV and goes to meet her sister with a hug.

"So Mom's really not here?" says Adrienne.

"Just you and me." Darby takes a swallow.

"Oh, can I have some orange juice, too?"

***

Sibyl yawns. Compared to a day of housework, working with video cameras and editing machines shouldn't be so exhausting, but somehow it is. "Mind if I lie down?" she asks Hiram, and he obligingly scoots to the other end of the couch. "Barnaby Jones" is hardly the most riveting program she's ever watched. She feels herself drifting when she becomes aware of Hiram's hands on her feet. He's never done this before; she's never asked him. He's rubbed her shoulders in the past, but the squeamishness that structures their marriage has prevented even something as simple as this, and she finds her body, lately accustomed to pleasure, relaxing in a new way. Hiram has stronger fingers than Leif, and though they seemed crude to her in the past, she feels now that they are more able to release the knots.

When Leif came into her tent that night at Fallen Lake, Sibyl didn't expect much.

Even though he had visited her in so many dreams, she still thought sex belonged to men. Hiram, arching over her body at night, vanished into his own male pleasure world about a thousand lightyears from any place she'd ever been. A woman's orgasm was something she provided for herself. If Sibyl trembled when Leif unzipped the mosquito netting, it was because she knew they were being bad. If she smiled, it was from embarrassment.

How strange and how glorious to be proven wrong by Leif! He knew her body better than she did. He knew where to touch. Afterward, lying with Leif's lean shape against her in the darkness, she started to hate Hiram because of all he had held back from her. Then, just as quickly, she saw that he'd been as hopelessly lost as she had. They'd been two kids whose parents all together hadn't said a dozen words about sex. And Hiram, like Sibyl, always understood it was something to be ashamed of. Like an illness. A physiological weakness. After Leif made love to her, she wanted to laugh, because she suddenly saw it wasn't *what* she did, but *how*, that made sex powerful.

She had accepted the simple message of her family, her church, all her teachers that marriage was meant to contain sex. If sex ever overflowed this tidy and scrupulously maintained dam, it would smash through American civilization, overrunning its edifices and flooding its gardens. Now Leif has proven her parents right, sex can change everything, and it does want to spread. The full wonder of what's happening now, however, is that it can spread in any direction; having seeped out of Hiram and Sibyl's marriage to fill up and overflow the beds of Sybil and Leif, Hiram and Laura, it now splashes back. She is surprised Hiram can touch her this way, surprised he knows how, surprised she wants him to.

Barnaby has wrapped up the case now, cornered the villain and the credits roll slowly down the screen. "You about ready?" Hiram clears his throat. "To turn in?"

Upstairs, his hands show their new life, roaming her body to knead out stiffness. Always before, she's felt like his receptacle; to become his oeuvre now inspires her. She closes her eyes, breathes slowly, absorbs the changes Laura has made. Then without warning, she turns on *him*, touches *him*, pushes *him* backward on the bed. She takes him.

***

Waking one night, Hiram hears Laura's moan. There's no sound like it, the helpless, desperate, low-throated call that starts deep in her chest and surges beyond her control. No matter whether the kids are awake, it's the middle of the afternoon or there's only a thin tent-wall between her and the other couple, she can't stop herself when Hiram does certain things to her. Now he feels a hot flush of anger. She does it for Hiram only. That's what she's told him, several times. It belongs to *him*.

Sibyl sleeps here, beside Hiram, her lips pressed together, silent breaths barely stirring the blankets over her. That sound again. It belongs to him! He sits upright. Leif has no right to do this, Hiram is the one, Hiram! When you have to compare yourself to a man like Leif every day, you take refuge in whatever points of superiority you can find. It's a failing, Hiram has schooled himself against it, and yet in moments like this, when the night makes him honest, Hiram knows how much he cherishes these facts:

- He knows more about wine than Leif does.
- He knows more about carpentry.
- He can throw a slightly better screwball.
- He can make Laura jump out of her skin.

The moan again. Again! Hiram throws of his covers and stands for a moment in his boxer shorts beside the bed, ready to… what? It's not a ballroom; you can't cut in on the other guy in mid fuck. "Excuse me sir, I believe that's my moan."

Slowly he sinks back to the side of the bed, turns on his side, covers his head with his pillow. Then, blessedly, Sibyl stirs.

"Sibyl?"

"They're sure making a racket aren't they?"

"It's driving me crazy."

She laughs. "You're not jealous?"

"It's just keeping me *up*."

"Hmm…" Sibyl turns, groping in the bed. "You mean this?"

***

Out of nowhere, Hiram challenges Leif to one-on-one basketball. The proposition causes Leif to raise an eyebrow. He hasn't known Hiram to play basketball with anyone. Their game is tennis; when Hiram can focus, he can hit some powerful serves and has even beaten Leif in a set or two.

"Right now. Tonight." Hiram spits the words out as if they disgusted him.

The mature route would be to decline, to take Hiram aside calmly and ask what's behind these lines bunching on his forehead. But Leif finds himself nodding. He wants to see, rather than hear, what Hiram has to express.

Out on the asphalt, their shoes squeak, the ball slaps pavement, and the two men grunt with mounting exertion. Suddenly as he drives to the hoop, Hiram bashes a big shoulder into Leif. On a jump shot, Hiram's head smacks Leif's nose. Still Leif says nothing until Hiram, trying for a layup, jabs an elbow into Leif's rib cage. "What the fuck, Hiram?"

"What's the matter?"

"Just... take it easy."

"Take it easy yourself."

Leif spreads his hands, searching for words, and Hiram takes advantage of the distraction to shoot and score. That puts him up by four points. Now Leif's face flushes as he takes the ball out. Old moves from high school come back to him; he feints left, stutter-steps, and pirouettes right around Hiram to back-spin the ball up and in.

Hiram scowls. And when he gets the ball, he lowers his big head, dribbles once, twice, then snatches it up like a running back heading for the line of scrimmage. Leif stands his ground, and Hiram plows full into him. As he falls, Leif's uprooted legs tangle Hiram's feet, so he, too, flies headlong.

For a moment the two sprawl silently. Leif's hip and shoulder blades sting. Slowly he raises one arm to study a scrape that is beginning to ooze.

Hiram groans. "Shit!"

"You fucker!" Leif closes his eyes. "You complete asshole."

When he opens them again, Hiram is standing over him reaching a broad, bloodied hand down to pull Leif to his feet.

Chapter Four

THERE'S a moment this Sunday afternoon when the juice runs thick from Hiram's press and the air loads up on the heavy scent of crushed fruit; when pulp and seed spatter, yet the flies haven't yet gathered; when an October shaft of sun hits the back lawn; when Hiram sees he's done it. Escaped. Scot-free. And as beautiful as this moment may feel, more will follow and more after that, so that he doesn't even have to fear the fall of night because what's to come is already contained in this moment.

"You've got the easy job," says Leif, trudging up from the car where he and Sibyl and Laura are unloading lugs of grapes they've bought and picked that weekend.

"You wanna try it?"

Leif grabs the lever of the grape press and yanks. He examines the sweet gush of sauvignon blanc. "I like this," he says, "the whole thing: picking grapes, pressing them. There's something very basic about it, very concrete. It makes me realize how little I work with my hands. How little I create that you can actually feel and smell and taste."

Hiram puts his hands on the crank as well, joining his strength to Leif's. "How'd you like to do it full-time?" he asks when they pause for breath.

"I don't know. It's satisfying to actually make something. More satisfying than grading papers about demand stimulation. But I suppose like most jobs, it's fun until your livelihood depends on it, then it turns into hard work."

"Because I was thinking…" Hiram hadn't planned to bring up his idea yet, but it seems to come naturally into the moment. "You know this fantasy of mine that I've talked about—buying a couple hundred acres in the wine country? Putting in some vines? People are catching on to good wine in this country; there's more of a demand. You can really make a living at it. Producing something. Growing something."

Leif purses his lips. "So?"

"Well, I was thinking we could go in together, the two families. We could do most of the work ourselves. And living in the country would be good for the kids, you know. Where there's plenty of space. Trees and grass. Less crime."

Leif's jaw tightens with intensity as he focuses on what Hiram's describing. "What does Sibyl say?"

"Nothing, yet. We haven't really talked about it."

"I don't know, Hi," Leif says. "It's a hell of a big step. We'd be living a completely different life. Completely different."

"Right." Hiram feels a strange tingle as the two men fall silent again, watching the press, and Hiram realizes that a bond has broken, that his marriage will never be the same. According to the normal protocol, he should have spoken to Sibyl before anyone else about something so enormous. Now Sibyl has lost her monopoly.

This idea he just broached has been gestating in his mind since even before Fallen Lake, since that softball game when this all started. Impulsively, Hiram grabs Leif's bicep below the sleeve of his skin-tight T-shirt.

For once, Leif's whole face gets involved in his grin, eyes wrinkling, nostrils flaring, mustache twisted by mirth. And he grabs Hiram's arm in return, like the secret handshake from some fraternal order of their fathers' generation.

***

The devotion of two men to her physical pleasure, the power of their sheer attention is like a drug. But what is the price? Sibyl wonders as Leif kneels behind her where she sits in front of the Eisenbergs' fireplace, working his fingers into the muscles around her neck. The first rain of the season patters on the bay window and the Kingston Trio croons softly on the hi-fi. In front of her Hiram sprawls on the beanbag, his wide lips half open in satisfaction. Laura sits Indian-style by the fire. This is where they hold their powwows. Going around the circle, it quickly becomes obvious that Hiram has talked to Laura, Laura has talked to Leif. Hiram has even spoken to Leif about it, this commune idea. Sibyl can't remember anyone bringing it up before except as a kind of joke and now it seems to have become an assumption.

Laura and Hiram are rhapsodizing.

"I just think the kids will have such a good time. We could have horses, chickens, pigs."

"You can see the stars at night. You can hear the wind."

"Square dances in the barn."

"The earth beneath your feet."

Sibyl tries to inject a note of realism. "I just wonder about the kids, moving away from all their friends."

"But Sibyl," Hiram says, "the schools are so much safer up there. In Pleasant Valley you're always hearing about the drugs."

Sibyl flails. "Farming is really hard work."

Laura's eyes nearly close with amusement. "My boys have never had to do a day of manual labor in their lives. It's going to be a shock to them at first. But over time, they'll adjust. And I think in the long run it's going to do them a lot of good to understand what real work is. You couldn't get away from that in Buford."

Isn't that why you left? Sibyl wants to ask her, but doesn't for fear of turning this into a fight. She twists to see Leif's face behind her. But he's on their side, too: "The last few months have been fantastic, really incredible," he says. "And I think we'd all agree that this shuttling back and forth to each other's houses can't go on forever. It's too contrived. We need to move toward something more organic, more day-to-day."

Sibyl pictures herself in overalls milking a big cow, somewhere about a hundred miles from The City, from Sam Brower and his computers and video cameras. Just when her life had been getting perfect, this comes up, and she wants to jump to her feet, kick the fire apart and send everyone home. And then she realizes the cold that would fill the room, the emptiness. She sees herself returning home from work, wearing a business suit, suitcase in her hand, to a vacant house. Casting about she finally settles on the only possible allies she has left. "Let's see what the kids say."

***

Ivor's walls are brown painted plaster and you can see a couple of places where he wrote on them and then his parents made him wash it off. On his dresser, there's a GI Joe with the head of a teddy bear stuck on. Over his bed, the model airplane is like any other model airplane until you look closer and see that the back part is blown off by a firecracker and a melted green army man has oozed halfway out of the cockpit.

Darby brought *The Game of Life* with her because the Eisenbergs don't have it, and she wanted to play something that Matt couldn't figure out. Last week they played *Clue*. It was fun for a while because Ivor put on this great British accent for Colonel Mustard, just like James Mason, and Darby was Miss Scarlett. Colonel Mustard kept following Miss Scarlett around from the kitchen to the ballroom to the conservatory and saying he was in love with her. What ruined it is that Matt had already solved the mystery before anybody else made a decent guess.

Life, on the other hand, is luck. Darby can see Matt's brain whirring and flashing in back of those glasses like a computer that's been given some kind of trick question. She knows he was dying to become a doctor or scientist, but instead he had to settle for policeman. It's his turn now and he flicks the spinner.

Everyone giggles as they watch his little plastic car land on "Getting Married."

"Who's the lucky girl?" Ivor asks him.

"Karen Mortimer," says Adrienne. Karen is the squarest girl at

Pleasant Valley Junior High, and it's funny to think of her with Matt, both of them wearing their glasses, looking at a test tube or something. Adrienne is lying on her stomach, and her hair falls on the board. Darby would like to take scissors to it.

Matt turns red, but doesn't say anything. Then, next turn, he gets a baby boy. And a couple of turns later, he gets twins, and another girl after that so that his little convertible is overflowing with pegs that fall out as he moves it around the board.

"Matt, Matt, Matt!" says Ivor. "Haven't you ever heard of rubbers?"

"He's can't control himself," says Adrienne. "He's a myna... what was it, Darby?"

"Nymphomaniac. But you can't say that about a guy."

"What do you call it if it's a guy?"

"A guy."

"I feel sorry for the kids," says Ivor. "Can't you just imagine Matt telling them they have to wear green T-shirts to school every day?"

Matt takes his hand off the little car and sits on his haunches. His blinking eyes remind Darby less of a computer now, more of the ticking of a time bomb. Adrienne sits up and sweeps a tress behind her shoulder. "I think Matt will be a very good father," she says, feeling sorry.

"Matt?!" Ivor's eyes widen.

"He's a lot more responsible than some people."

"Hey, kids!" It's Laura calling from downstairs. "Dinner!"

For once, Darby is having fun with the whole Eisenberg-Wright son mixup. In fact, being with Ivor and Matt has begun to feel natural, not like boys from school but more like cousins. She realizes she has actually come to look forward to the Sunday nights when the two families get together. Let the grownups eat by themselves. She smiles at Ivor. "Your turn," she says.

But Adrienne, ever obedient, hops to her feet. And Matt, too, has automatically risen. Downstairs sits Laura's infamous tuna casserole with the potato chip topping. The first time she saw it, Darby was shocked. Now, since they've had so many dinners together, it seems almost normal. Same thing with Miracle Whip instead of mayonnaise, margarine instead of butter. Darby has even stopped gagging at Leif's Richard Nixon habit of mixing ketchup and cottage cheese. But the way the grownups are now, as soon as you're used to one thing, they come up with something else hard to swallow. Another one's coming right now, Darby senses when the plates are cleared. It's ominous the way Daddy straightens his back and clears his throat. "Adrienne, Darby, Matt, Ivor. We have something we want to talk to you guys about."

Ivor picks up his plate and heads out of the room.

"Ivor, get back in here," Leif says.

Ivor sits down again, grinning. "Sorry, I just wanted to avoid talking about whatever you guys want to talk about."

Laura says, "Don't be Mr. Smarty Pants."

"I think you're going to want to hear this," says Daddy. "Because it concerns you. It concerns all of us."

Why does Darby feel like she's riding in a car that just had a blowout?

"We've been talking, the four of us grownups. All of us enjoy spending time together. And so we've been thinking it would be fun to have a farm, somewhere in the country, where we could all live."

Laura smiles brightly. "And we want to hear what you guys think about the idea!"

Live on a farm? Darby would rather drive a nail through her skull. "You mean like some adorable little town with one main street and a general store and everybody knows each other?" she asks.

Daddy frowns at her. "Well, sort of…"

"And the guys all wear straw hats and go fishing and the sheriff is a fat old fart but it's okay because there are no robbers?"

"Watch your language," Sibyl says.

Darby fixes Daddy with her best sarcastic smile. "I don't think so.

But thanks for asking."

Daddy shifts around in his chair. "There's really a lot that you might like about living in the country."

Darby strikes a tone of exaggerated politeness. "Undoubtedly, Father. Like for instance?"

"Well," Laura says, "we were thinking we could get some horses. You like to ride, don't you?" She glances at Adrienne, the horse fanatic, when she says it. It's total bribery and pandering. Darby has no interest in a horse. But for a moment she waits and listens, in case a similar offer is in store for each of the other four kids (possibly something a person could actually use, such as a car?)

But at that moment Ivor cuts in with a loud "Yeehaw!" sounding so much like Hoss from *Bonanza* that the spell breaks. Even the grownups have to smile in an annoyed way.

***

Pale, flaxen-haired Jane Jummel always throws weak pitches, but they're surprisingly hard to hit, because she either puts a screwy, accidental back-spin on them or throws them so high they're falling almost vertically when they reach the plate. This time, though, the ball floats directly into Leif's strike zone, big and slow as a watermelon. From first base, Hiram can see what's coming from home plate where Leif's jaw sets, his hands tighten on the grip of the bat, his elbows rise and... WHACK! A white streak soars over center field, looping, looping above Sam Brower, who back-pedals hopelessly with his neck craned to watch the ball pass six feet above him. By then, Leif has touched first base. "Home, home, home, home!" chants Helen Palac from behind the backstop. Leif gazes downfield, sees Sam sitting on his butt and slows to a jog.

Big mistake.

Somehow, Sam has come up with the ball. He launches a mighty lob to the long-limbed single woman, Blair Fischer, who is new to the group but quick as a pro. She has raced halfway back for the relay. She snags Sam's throw and, in the same motion, spins and fires at Sibyl, the catcher. Leif, rounding third base, realizes his danger and charges, head down like a rutting moose. Crack! The ball hits the backstop over Sibyl's head. She scrambles in the dirt, grabs it, and steps dangerously in front of the madly steaming Leif. Hiram sucks in a breath. But instead of smashing her to pieces, Leif slows and grins. He snatches Sibyl in his long hands and lofts her like a Raggedy Ann, allowing himself to cruise unobstructed over the plate.

A clamor of protest rises from Sibyl's teammates as she kicks in his hands. Past the point where, by the conventions of normal clowning, he should have returned her to her feet, Leif holds her at the length of his bulging arms, until finally she stops struggling, and he lowers her to him. He kisses her then, in full view of the entire group—not a lingering, tongue exchange, but enough of a smooch that no one can see it as a joke. "Whew!" shouts Helen, wagging a freckled hand by way of emphasis, and Bob Eidler whistles.

"Hey, guys," shouts Paul Jummel, "Can't it wait till after dinner?"

Watching from first base, Hiram feels something pass over the field like the shadow of a falling jetliner. Of course, all this may not be news to the group. The tide of teasing has risen in recent months, the snickers when Hiram, for example, was standing behind Laura, arms around her to show her a smoother swing with the bat. There was whispering when she gave him a hug after his home run last month. But no one has said anything; everyone has waited, it seems, for some kind of announcement. It's made Hiram more careful, in fact, to keep his distance from Laura during the games. He swallows and thinks how odd it is, how unexpected that Leif has let the cloak fall this way, because Hiram expected to be the one. Now Leif, without consulting anyone, has decided to go public, and Hiram feels the group turning on them.

"Oh, no, I'm not playing catcher," says Helen Palac in the next inning. "Not with Leif at bat."

"Better not let Hiram put his hands on a bat this evening. I think he's a little pissed."

"Let's put Sibyl on first. She really knows how to tag the runner."

"*Certain* runners!"

"Hey, what does it take, Sibyl?"

"Something Hiram doesn't have."

Dinner is at the Browers this time. "I can't believe he did that," Hiram tells Sibyl in the Rambler on the way over from the park. And when she doesn't answer, lost in reverie, he repeats, "I can't believe he did that. What was he trying to do?"

Sibyl shakes her head. "I don't know."

She's embarrassed, of course, Hiram knows this. To have everyone suddenly see something she didn't mean to reveal is horribly painful for Sibyl. It's something he's always respected about her, this sense of decorum. But suddenly it just irritates him. At least here in the privacy of their car, she could say something, criticize Leif or even defend him. "What a dick!"

It's not the way he normally talks, and Sibyl turns sharply to him. "Hiram!"

"Well, what was he trying to do?"

"Look. It was going to happen sooner or later. We couldn't keep it a secret forever. Especially if we're all going to move in together."

"All right, so let's tell people, but not like this. I mean what's everyone going to think?" He stops the car a little more abruptly than he has to and backs into a parking spot near the Browers' driveway.

"Don't ask me, Hiram. It wasn't my idea."

"What wasn't your idea?"

"None of this... stuff."

Hiram's about to remind her she could have stopped it at any point, but Sibyl's already getting out of the car.

Leif and Laura are a little late getting to dinner, and Hiram wonders if they've stopped somewhere to chat in the car. Maybe Laura is reading Leif the riot act, or is crying. Whatever it is, Hiram hopes that she makes him see what a rash thing he's done.

Nora Brower has set an electric deep-fryer bubbling in the

middle of the dining room table, cut sirloin into cubes and laid out two-pronged fondue forks. It's a very sociable way to have a meal, and in the fun and novelty of it, Leif's indiscretion seems to slip from everybody's mind. Nora is demonstrating how to tell when a beef cube has cooked enough at the end of the fork, and hardly anyone even looks up when the Wrightsons finally arrive, both of them frowning.

They might have taken their places quietly, but at the last minute, Bob Eidler, who has a divorce in his own recent past, calls out, "Hey, Leif, over here!" He scrambles up from his chair, grins widely and gestures that Leif should sit there, next to Sibyl. A couple of people laugh nervously. Leif blinks, deciding what to do, then sits down in one of the two empty chairs on the other side of the table. Laura sits beside him. "Thanks, Bob, I'm fine here," Leif says.

Bob leans over the table toward Leif. "Are you sure about that?"

"Bob," says Sam Brower, "I think your beef is burning."

Nora changes the topic: "Does anybody here honestly think these wire-taps made any difference in who got elected?" The conversation latches onto Erlichman and Haldeman, Liddy and McCord, but Hiram feels Bob's question lingering on everyone's mind. To douse the annoyance of it, he drinks a couple of glasses of his own '69 Gewurztraminer too quickly. All this accomplishes is to fog his mind so that he launches into a ridiculous defense of the president. When that wears out, he leads a discussion about the Oakland A's, whose pitching staff looks unstoppable this year. He hears his voice rise and fall with a kind of desperate cheer.

Hiram has made some of his best friends in this group and has brought in others, people who have helped each other's careers, introduced each other to lifetime mates, minded each other's kids. Always, barring some major holiday, they get together weekly, and there's something fine about the regularity of it, the rhythm of meeting every seven days so that the friends become like family. A clan.

Now Hiram senses all this is in jeopardy, and he tries through the best of his wit and charm to fan away the smoke that started with that kiss, because he knows he's as culpable as Leif. More culpable, because he and Sibyl have been coming here so long, while Laura and Leif are relative newcomers, and because he wanted Laura so very much. But why should it be wrong, this love of four? Why should it threaten? So while he pours wine for his friends, touches their arms and shoulders and laughs hilariously—as if one person could restore the group's fellowship by sheer force of conviviality—he feels a contradicting pressure build inside him.

A memory surfaces. Hiram and Sam Brower were sitting in a bar. In a gray flannel suit, no one looks more Brahmin than Sam. Even wearing the white T-shirt slightly moistened from the tennis match they've just played, Sam carried power in his criss-crossed forehead, his gray sideburns, and once again Hiram found himself hanging on all pronouncements from the small and lipless mouth. "It may seem like we're a wild and crazy bunch," Sam said. "But the truth is we live by the Tenth Commandment. Thou shalt not covet thy neighbor's wife." They'd been talking about Blair Fischer at the time, how Bob Fidler kept ogling her. That was different. And yet Hiram can't shake the memory of Sam's forefinger raised to make a point.

It's only 8:15 when Hiram notices Laura and Leif heading for the door, and he bounces from his seat, unable to restrain himself anymore. "Leaving so soon?" he asks loudly enough for everyone to hear.

Leif nods, tight-lipped.

"Well, good night, Laura. I'll see *you* on Sunday." Hiram fastens his right arm around her shoulders, and when she turns to him, he kisses her full on. Their mouths lock while the heat from their faces seems to bathe the room. She doesn't hold back, and a shiver rattles through him when she finally steps away.

"Goodbye." She lets Leif tug her out the door.

Hiram stands with his eyes closed because this is the only way he can keep holding her smell and taste, until Sibyl nudges him. She has collected their jackets.

***

They don't match in very many other dimensions—Darby is thicker around the hips and has shorter arms and legs—but she and Sibyl wear exactly the same shoe size. Which means Sibyl must go hunting periodically for some of her favorite pumps. They're not in the mess on Darby's half of the girls' bedroom, and not in her closet either. But stooping to look under the bed, Sibyl finds the pumps—and something else that glints in the dimness. She reaches into the shadows and pulls out a crumpled Coors can. Chill flows up her arm and into her brain. This is exactly the sort of thing she feared could happen with all the changes going on in the household. She corners her daughter late that night when Darby finally gets back from one of Roxanne's parties.

"It was Daddy." Darby's wide eyes stare straight into her mother's face.

"Your father was drinking beer in your bedroom?"

"He came in to help me with some homework and finished his beer while he was sitting on my bed. What's the big deal?" It's not out of the question. Sibyl can easily picture Hiram opening a beer in the kitchen, then trailing after Darby when she asked him for help. Still she can't suppress the nagging fear. And Hiram, when Sibyl gets him aside, is of no help.

"Maybe." He shrugs. "How would I remember?"

"I need your help with this, Hiram. It might be nothing, but we have to be on guard."

"What if she has a drink now and then?"

"Hiram! She's twelve years old!"

Hiram shakes his head. "Relax. If you make it forbidden fruit, she'll just go drinking away from home. Let her do it here where we can keep an eye on her."

Sibyl wants to take Hiram by his wide lapels and shake.

***

In the middle of the night, beside his wife, Leif cannot shut his eyes. There's a faint whistle when Laura exhales. Now her back is to him, the copper cascade pouring over her pillow, her face half sub-merged in one generous arm. Beneath the sheets lie the gracious mounds of her hips, the jiggling undisciplined mass of her cheeks. They have sometimes coolly filled his hands and he has sometimes buried his pelvis into them.

Leif breathes her sweet, dusty scent, like fading honeysuckle. He smells her now in a way he hasn't for a dozen years because his senses are heightened from Sibyl's freshness. Sibyl's air of balsam and lime, fast lines, sharp shoulder blades, her white undimpled skin, the prod of a bone in her elbow or hip contrast so much with Laura's sweet-ness. Sleeping with his wife on a Monday after Sunday with Sibyl, Leif feels as he did when he returned to America after a semester in Japan. Everything startles him. The familiar becomes strange.

This strangeness ebbs and flows in Leif's life now. At times in the classrooms of Stephens Hall, it's as if nothing has changed and he's at his old routine again. And then at other times, like now, he's filled with the mystery and the unreality of it. By four o'clock he's given up trying to sleep. He quietly dresses himself, hops in the Plymouth and drives to his office on campus where he can turn on a light at his hand-me-down cherry wood desk and try to analyze the situation.

There's a sheet of paper rolled into his typewriter from last week. At the top of it are typed the words, "TOWARD A NEW VIEW OF FAMILY ECONOMICS," and then nothing underneath—a manifes-to which he has felt incapable of writing. In his head, the links in the chain are so clearly thought through, they seem obvious. Birth control, labor-saving devices, antibiotics, the rise of the welfare state—they've all changed the circumstances that made monogamy useful. So the circle of love and intimacy could, and should, widen. It should be clear to anyone reading the newspaper, to anyone who is breathing the air these days.

But no one admits it. At least no one in academia. Economists in particular are so obsessed with minutiae they can't look up from their adding machines to see what's going on around them. Long ago, soon after his dissertation in fact, it became clear that Leif wasn't going to survive in academia if he continued the visionary thinking that originally attracted him to the field. He'd have to find a way of expressing himself in mathematics if he wanted to get a job. The one article he tried, in a spasm of sincerity two years ago (but it feels longer) was rejected everywhere he sent it. And so there the ideas have sat, in the back of his desk drawer. Until this summer. Surely, it's no coincidence. If Leif hadn't prepared his mind for this change in reality, he would never have allowed himself or Laura to fall into it. At the very least, he would have put a stop to it before things got this far. And yet the ideas are so abstract, so theoretical that it's still hard to connect them to the reality he finds himself living. Even the phrase he invented four years ago, "extended marriage," seems so far from the experience he is now living that it tastes metallic in his mouth. He's a paleontologist riding a live Tyrannosaurus, a microbiologist swimming with the amoebas.

Last week as Leif was collecting a stack of mimeographs in the departmental office, Herb Firth asked how many spouses he would be bringing to the Christmas party. That drew a great guffaw from Al Pincherman, who stood picking up his mail nearby, and titters from the department secretary, Carol Lunka, typing at her desk. Leif's mind quickly pawed through the branches of the grapevine. Several people in the softball group had affiliations with the university. Helen Palac, for example, worked part time as some sort of administrative secretary in the chemistry department. The softball group was all abuzz about the foursome now, but still Leif was amazed at the speed with which the news had gotten around.

So it doesn't surprise him much when, at ten o'clock that morning while he's still hunched over his desk, typewriter untouched, a knock sounds, and Trent Hilderbrand's big, bearded face pokes in. It's probably the first time the department chair has ever entered Leif's office, but it now seems to Leif inevitable, expected. "Hey ho," says Trent. "Could you stop by my office around one?"

Leif frets as never before until he's in Hilderbrand's book-lined office with its Rothko original. Hilderbrand has been the department head for seven years, steadily accumulating power in a position no one took very seriously before him. Now he's recreating the department slowly in his own image, forcing his Keynesian textbooks into courses where they hardly belong, meting out sabbaticals to his cronies and punishing resisters with heavy lecture-hall loads. With Leif's mentor, Jacques Villiers—the man who brought him to Pleasant Valley—departed for Yale, Leif's known enough to toe the line in his teaching, and as a result Trent hasn't bothered about Leif's eccentric line of research.

Trent starts by innocently asking Leif about his family. "Laura's liking her classes?" He has an infallible memory for personal detail.

"Very much."

"Matthew and Ivor are bearing up?"

"Bearing up?" Leif squints at Trent. "They're fine. Matt just tested at the college level in math."

"Excellent. So, what I want to say to you, Leif, is, I'm sure you're aware of all the rumors swirling around your personal life."

Leif shrugs. Denial is pointless.

"Of course I would never think of probing into your private affairs. You do what you want. However, as the senior faculty member in this department, I do wish to offer some advice. If this wife swap is in the nature of an experiment... I mean, if you're considering it in the light of research—Well, you can't possibly hope to publish anything on it, do you know?"

Leif does know. He knows plenty of tenured faculty whose careers seem actually to benefit from their steamy reputations. A rumor of extramarital high jinks suggests virility. A whisper of perverse predilections gives a man the air of Old World sophistication. It's not the sex that his colleagues, headed here by Hilderbrand, condemn. It's not even the particular arrangement. It's his passion. Anthropologists aren't supposed to go native. Lawyers aren't supposed to represent themselves. And economists are supposed to calculate mathematical models of reality, not slide their hands into its pungent darkness.

And so Leif shakes his head. "Of course not." There's a moment of silence into which, he imagines, Trent would like him to add something like, "This has nothing to do with my research." But of course that's not true. This has everything to do with the ideas he's played with in his head for so long. He is, in fact, finally moving out of contradiction with himself, and this is the one thing his colleagues never could forgive.

As Trent rolls a ballpoint between his thumb and forefinger, Leif searches for an answer that will satisfy everyone. To defend himself, he'll have to separate his life from his work. He will have to convince Hilderbrand and the others that the extended marriage has nothing to do with what he's thinking. Just his own little, ha, ha, peccadillo, and that in fact he's just about to come out with a statistical formula for Mises's theory of marginal utility. He will have to convince them, in short, that he doesn't care.

"You do what you'd like, Leif," Trent goes on. "I'd never dream of trying to impose a direction of research, let alone a… a standard of morality, on anyone in this department. You've had your very interesting perspective all along, and I've never suggested you should change anything about it. But as chairman, one of my responsibilities is to the department's reputation."

"I see."

"No, I'm not sure you do see." Hilderbrand sighs the patient sigh of a teenager's parent. "You've been here, what, three years? You only caught the tail of the '60s. The Free Speech Movement. Students for a Democratic Whatever. Students taking drugs, students copulating in the hallways. And not only students. It's utterly changed the way people think about PVSU. It's cost us tremendous credibility. We can't afford to lose any more now, to be seen as anything other than serious scholars. If what you're doing now, this communal thing, is to be your major emphasis… Let me put it this way, I don't want any personal essays cropping up anywhere, or any newspaper articles. I don't want any how-to manuals or philosophical treatises, any California State University Economics Professor Leif Wrightson's Guide to Cohabitation coming out of this. Do you see what I mean?"

Leif wants to smash the Rothko on Hilderbrand's hairy head. Intellectual curiosity, he wants to bellow. Freedom of speech! Truth! Now Leif can see his future written on the department head's fatuous forehead. He may continue teaching a year or several years longer as long as there's a need for someone to indoctrinate the endless ranks of freshmen according to Hilderbrand's approved syllabus, Hilderbrand's approved texts. Hilderbrand's approved ideas. "Thanks for the warning," Leif says, pushing himself abruptly up from his chair.

"Leif?"

"Yeah?"

"From now on, why don't you run by me anything you intend to publish? Just for a little friendly review." Hilderbrand smiles thinly. "Also any calls from news reporters. About anything. They go to me."

This last bit is outrageous, and Leif feels his tongue swell out of his mouth. "There's still such a thing as academic freedom, I think."

"Sure." Hilderbrand nods slowly in pretended equanimity. "People who earn it, have academic freedom. Almost complete academic freedom, in fact."

The implication is clear. Leif doesn't have tenure and won't get it as long as Hilderbrand has anything to say. "So let me just see if I understand. What you're saying is I can't express anything about my life, my work, or my thoughts in public."

"All right, let me spell it out. Your little fetish has nothing to do with any kind of economic theory or any serious theory about anything. If you had any sense of our field, of our discipline, you'd have realized that a long time ago."

The fury has Leif's whole head vibrating now. "I suppose you're right. As long as people like you have anything to do with it, there won't be any new ideas about anything." Watching his words explode like red rockets in Hilderbrand's face, he feels a stab of instant regret.

"People like me? It's people like me who keep people like you employed. I think you'd better think long and hard about whether you want to stay that way."

Laura's worried face comes into Leif's view. He opens his mouth, closes it again. "Of course. I didn't mean to... I'm grateful for my position here."

Hilderbrand waits, eyebrows raised, for something more. For Leif to grovel! It's Leif's only hope now, but he can't force himself. Stiffly he turns and leaves the room.

Only a week later comes the notice that Leif's contract will not be renewed after fall; his next semester will be his last. Staring at the terse paragraph of bureaucratese, Leif plots a mutiny. Hilderbrand doesn't have the authority to fire him, all on his own. Leif will gather together his colleagues, put together a petition. He can go to the Dean of Social Sciences, the Provost for Academic Affairs. But the faces of the other professors appear in his mind's eye. Pincherman could be sitting where Hilderbrand is and saying the same things. Saarberg is too beaten down, too cynical to speak in Leif's behalf. All the tenured faculty either share Hilderbrand's Keynesian tunnel vision or are completely passive. They're all so grateful to Hilderbrand for taking on the administrative tasks—leaving them free to do their research—nobody ever challenges him on anything. Besides that, Leif's thoughts are too fresh, too original for anyone who takes their orders from the *American Journal of Sociological Economics*. He thinks of calling a lawyer, but what would be his charge? Employers get away with this kind of censorship all the time. Academic tradition doesn't have the force of law.

But my god! Leif's face falls into his hands. What is he going to do? Four lives depend on this income. It's pointless to even apply elsewhere in the CSU system; all the department chairs know Hilderbrand. Is it too late? Could he still slither back down the corridor to beg?

Anything would be better. Teaching high school. Selling hotdogs. Mopping restrooms. And there is a better possibility. Leafy, laden grapevines shimmer in the future that Hiram has painted. No, Leif is finished here. It isn't rational. It isn't sensible. But what Leif saw in the firelight, what he felt on Red Mountain, was that rational and sensible no longer mean right and good.

Chapter Five

HIRAM and Sibyl used to go out for lunch when their marriage was young. But it's been over a year now, so Sibyl feels surprised when he asks her to meet him at the new place, Asparagus Dreams, one of the businesses that recently started in a converted warehouse over by the university. Its stained glass windows depict vegetables; natural wood covers the walls and floor; potted ferns hang from the exposed rafters. Hiram says, "I think you should try the lentil-walnut burger."

"Why don't you try the lentil-walnut burger?" Sibyl says.

"Because you're the adventurous one."

"Me?"

"When it comes to food."

Hiram settles on a tuna sandwich, the most recognizable item on the menu. Sibyl orders miso soup and green salad with lemon-tahini dressing.

"Okay," says Hiram, "about Leif quitting his job…"

Sibyl frowns. "That idiot! Why couldn't he keep his mouth shut, at least until he found another job? I could have punched him when he told me."

"They're going to have a lot of rent to pay and no income."

Sibyl lets out a long breath. Now it's clear why Hiram wanted to eat with her, instead of with Laura. "Hiram, I'm not ready to move to the country."

"Me either."

"You're not?"

Hiram bites into his sandwich and grimaces. He lifts a slice of dense whole-wheat bread to investigate. "What is this?"

"Alfalfa sprouts."

"The stuff they feed horses?"

"It's supposed to be very nutritious."

"Tastes like dirt." Hiram picks the green mound from his tuna. "No. If we're going to do it, we have to find the right place. We have to line up financing. It's going to be a long time before we make any money on it. Then what happens to Jancorum? I can't run a business here and a business there at the same time, not very easily. I'm already so distracted I was late submitting a bid last month."

Sibyl feels a trickle of relief to hear Hiram talking practically. "I think Leif understands that. And Laura. It's just too big a step for all of us."

"But in the meantime, they have all this rent. They have no income. And we have a pretty big house."

Sibyl freezes with her spoon stretched toward the tahini dressing. "You want them to move in with us?"

"Think of it as a tryout. All of us living together. We can see whether it works out on a day-to-day basis."

Sibyl wouldn't mind being able to snuggle up to Leif in the evening. To wake up with him in a leisurely way, not having to dash to work. After half a year of back-and-forthing, she'd be glad to dispense with the overnight bags, the mix-ups about which car is where. And she's happy to hear Hiram giving practical reasons to do something instead of fantastically romantic ones. If the other three are really serious about staking their futures on a place in the country, it really does make sense to do a kind of trial first, like so many ordinary couples are doing these days, living together before getting married. But after the way the vineyard idea crept up the last time, she can't help a twinge of suspicion. "Is this something you and Laura cooked up?"

Hiram takes a bite of sandwich and washes it down with his jasmine tea. "We batted it around briefly."

"The girls aren't going to be thrilled."

"They love Matt and Ivor. You've seen how they play together. The four of them will have a ball conspiring against the grownups."

Sibyl smiles at the thought. Then she pictures her house crammed to the rafters. "Adrienne will have to move back in with Darby. And they may have… They may get teased at school."

"Why should they? Communes are everywhere now. What's his name—Alvin Toffler—said group marriage is the wave of the future. And kids are better off this way. You remember that article that Leif showed us the other day, about that study that showed kids are healthier and smarter and everything the more adults they have in their lives? It's like a return to the old extended family. More people to watch out for them. More role models. They may grumble, but in the long run they'll be happier."

Hiram doesn't really understand. Having been a teenage girl herself, Sibyl knows how much her daughters cherish their privacy. They require it. Shoved into one room every night, they may strangle each other. And in the turmoil of adolescence, they need their home life to be predictable, solid, stable.

But what Hiram is really telling her is that it's too late for that. Back at Fallen Lake Sibyl saw what Laura had already done to him. The truth is, Sibyl has lost her exclusive hold. This may be the only way the girls can keep their family together.

Hiram cocks his head. "What's wrong?"

"Why?"

"You grimaced."

"Just chewing."

"Sibyl, I swear. I will go along with whatever you decide."

Meaning that Hiram and Laura have already made up their minds. But Sibyl can't let that get to her. The right way to look at this, the positive way, is that Hiram still wants to be with her. And she knows that Leif does, too. Sibyl must see it their way: as more for everyone. "Okay."

"Okay what? You'll consider it?"

"Okay let's invite them to move in."

When they get up from the table, Hiram kisses her deeply, embarrassing her in front of their waiter. And she feels a rush of the pleasure she's always gotten from granting him a boon.

But driving home, she sees that what had seemed like a choice is now taking on the dimensions of obligation. By the time she parks in the driveway, Hiram has already phoned Laura from his office, and Laura has spoken to Leif, and as Sibyl opens the front door Leif calls out to her, grateful and joyous.

***

Matt is lying on the top bunk in his bedroom, immersed in *Ants from Close Up* when his mother appears in the doorway.

"You need to start packing, Matt," she says softly.

He stares. "Why?"

"We have to have everything packed today, so we can be ready tomorrow when Dad gets the truck."

Of course, they've told him it would happen, but he didn't pay attention. They've come up with so many crazy ideas in the last two years. Many of them, like living on a farm, never happened. So he's stopped believing in it. He has tried, as much as possible to go on with his life as if all this didn't concern him. He's gone along to the Wrightsons' house every week, or they've come to his, he's played *Sorry* and *Life* and *Hearts* with Adrienne and Darby, and then he's gone back to his work. So when Mom set a pile of cardboard boxes on the floor of his room, he stepped around them.

"Come on, I'll help you," Mom offers. "But I can't do it all. You have to decide what you want to bring and what you want to give to the Goodwill."

Descending from his bunk, Matt is a three-toed sloth from a Bolivian Cecropia. He half-heartedly folds a pair of pajama pants.

"Let's get going on this, Matt," Mom urges. "We have to get everything packed up by tomorrow."

"Why are we moving?"

"We've been over this before. We're moving because Dad quit his job. We need to save money on rent. And because we want to be with the Eisenbergs. You and Ivor have a lot of fun with Adrienne and Darby. I know it's a big change, and it's going to require an adjustment from all of us, but, you know, life is full of changes."

The boxes and the changes and the fun, fun, fun. Matt leans backward till he's lying on the floor and not paying attention anymore. The spots on the acoustical ceiling wall look like the honeycomb of fire ants' nests in the Congolese rain forest. If you were on an expedition to Africa, a scientific expedition, you could forget everything but the specimens you're gathering and the observations you're noting.

Mom piles all of Matt's clothes into boxes, angrily telling him he has to take responsibility, can't just dream his world away. Finally she leaves, saying that whatever isn't packed in a box by the time Dad comes with the truck tomorrow will be donated to Goodwill.

A few minutes after she leaves, Matt begins with his books, stacking them carefully; first geology on the bottom layer, then paleontology and zoology on top of that. On the shelf, they're arranged alphabetically, and when he can't fit all of zoology into the box with the other natural science books, he has to stop and reconsider. Either he can subdivide by alphabet, A-L in this box, and M-Z in the other box. Or he can break zoology into vertebrates and invertebrates, or perhaps into mammals, reptiles, amphibians? His microscope takes a half hour to properly prepare, padded in his underwear and socks, and his telescope and binoculars require almost as much attention. Then it's on to nets, glassware, specimen jars.

In the end, he has to break his Polystyrene stegosaurus skeleton into sections; it will take hours to restore. Down comes the periodic table of elements. Down comes the poster of Mars. The Natural Science Foundation Scholastic Achievement awards. Three hours later he sits exhausted in the middle of his room, staring at the empty shelves, the tape-scarred walls, the balls of dust.

***

"You should obey Laura and Leif just as you would me or Mom," Daddy says. It's eight o'clock and they've barely cleared the remains of a rushed dinner: omelet, toast and frozen peas. Mom and Daddy have a lot of work, they say, to get ready for the Wrightsons.

"Do whatever they ask you to do," Mom agrees. "They've told the same thing to Ivor and Matt."

"Oh, really?" Darby asks.

"Really," says Daddy. "We mean it, and you'd better do it, because we're going to back them up 100 percent."

Darby cocks her head at him. Are she and Adrienne supposed to pretend they have four parents? Is she supposed to listen to Leif with his hard smile as much as to Daddy, who has read to her, smoothed her hair, kissed her forehead for twelve years? Is she supposed to crawl into Laura's arms as if they were the same arms that had picked her up off the sidewalk, nursed her, changed her diapers, for Christ's sake?

Do they think that Darby, at thirteen years old, will actually *obey* anyone? If they knew half the things she does, the drinks she's had, the boys she's fooled around with or the classes she's cut, they'd realize how ridiculous it is to imagine she's going to take orders from a set of fake parents. Don't they understand that she goes along with her own parents (*when* she does) only because she feels like after feeding, clothing and housing her for twelve years they've earned her respect? You can't transfer love like money between bank accounts.

That night, as Leif staggers into the living room, arms stretched to hold a large dresser, Darby stands in his way for a moment, just to provoke him into giving her his first order.

Instead he sets the dresser down, a smile flickering. "Is this civil disobedience?"

Caught, Darby can't think of a comeback.

"Look," says Leif. "I know this is going to take some getting used to. But I promise to make it as little like an invasion as I can, and as much like a…" Now he's the one searching for a word.

"Party?" she suggests.

"Well, maybe not a party every day, but a step in that direction."

He sounds so sincere, Darby has to remind herself not to be sucked in. "Woo hoo!" She twirls one finger in the air, then turns her back on him to drift upstairs. She has work to do there: building some kind of barrier to separate her side of the room from Adrienne's. Pushing her desk and hi-fi cabinet around doesn't seem to help much, though. She has lost all her privacy and half her space.

At bedtime, Sibyl strokes Darby's cheek. "It's only for a while."

"Only a while until what?" Darby asks.

And Sibyl realizes that she doesn't know the answer to that. Back at Fallen Lake, when Leif crawled into her tent, she had convinced herself that this was only a test. They said to each other and to themselves that if they didn't like it, they could call it off. They didn't say what would happen if they liked it.

And Sibyl isn't the only one feeling dazed. Hiram has been unable to sleep past four in the morning for the past six weeks. Leif, finishing out his last semester at PVSU, keeps losing his lecture notes. Last Thursday as Sibyl was putting on her sneakers for the softball game, Laura called to ask if Sibyl could bring some mayonnaise to dinner afterwards. "You mean to the Palacs' house?" Sibyl asked.

"No, to my house."

"But the Palacs are hosting," Sibyl said. "Don't you remember you switched with them because you were going to be too busy packing?"

There was a long pause and then came Laura's laughter with a squeaky edge that Sibyl had never heard in it before. "I just made dinner for sixteen people who aren't coming over!"

Sibyl runs her fingers through Darby's hair, which is so like her own in color, so like Hiram's in texture, but aromatic from that shampoo she and Adrienne have been using lately—Herbal Essence. "I don't know, Darby," she says now. "I don't know. We're just taking this one step at a time."

The book Leif has been urging everyone to read, *Future Shock*, sits on Sibyl's nightstand. She hasn't gotten much past the introduction, but the term "dizzying disorientation" has stayed with her. She can feel it in her stomach now, the acceleration of a rocket ship toward some barely charted planet inhabited by creatures who may or not speak, build buildings, drink water, breathe air.

***

Three manila folders wait on Hiram's desk. The top one holds the June Jancorum sales figures. The next two are specifications, one for houses here in Pleasant Valley, another for a high rise in Oakland. He opens the first folder and pulls out the ledger, but his eyes see undifferentiated gray. The air smells of carbon paper and Whiteout. He works his finger under the knot of his tie to pull it looser. He shuts the first folder and opens the second, sits up straighter, punches figures into his adding machine, loses his train of thought.

The other day he watched as a troupe of bulldozers cut into the former ranchland that would become a new subdivision in Contra Costa County, land where for a hundred years cattle had grazed, and before that, deer. Asphalt will cover it, his own company will pour concrete foundations and raise four-by-fours cut from hundred-year-old redwoods. At his orders, parking lots and streets will sweep across the pastures.

Hiram wants no more of this. He wants to plunge his own hands into the loam, to cover himself, to submerge a vine in the breast of earth and watch it root, watch its pale fronds unfurl in sunlight, feel its fruit heavy in his palm. He wants rain on his back, mud on his boots, sweat in his hair, wants his muscles to ache again like they used to swinging a hammer, only this time opening, instead of sealing, the earth.

The door opens and he looks up to see his secretary, Greta Dalminger, standing in front of him. Tall already, she creates the impression of towering with her out-of-fashion beehive hairdo. Greta uses that hauteur to intimidate guniters and joiners, and after thirty-one years, she can still make Hiram uneasy. She hands him a contract, and Hiram signs and initials without pausing to read because he knows if Greta is bringing it to him, it must be good. She has been with Jancorum since Sibyl's dad started it. She could run this company. She does run this company. Knows the developers, the regulations, the suppliers. Everyone agrees it doesn't make sense for Hiram to go out and supervise crews anymore, especially since he broke his knee, but half the time it seems all that's left to him is martinis and slaps on the back. He would as soon let Greta do that, too. And now it's time to drive across town and meet big James Quist for lunch.

"You might want to take his offer," Greta says.

"What?"

"James. He wants to buy Jancorum."

"You're shitting me." You can talk to Greta almost the way you would to a man. "How do you know that?"

"Hi." Greta puts her hands on her hips. "Word gets around. You'd have known it too, if you weren't so..."

He cocks his head.

"Look, Hi. Everybody knows everybody in this business. People are starting to talk about you and Sibyl and that other family living in your house."

He feels heat in his face. The ripples of gossip have spread farther than he realized.

"It's not just that," Greta continues. "I can do a lot, but I can't do everything. We could have gotten the Castro Valley project if we had gotten the bid in a week earlier. And when was the last time you went to a Builders' Alliance meeting?"

Hiram's eyes flicker to his desk calendar, but he already knows the answer.

"If you don't want to be in this business, step aside for someone who does."

"Greta!" No secretary should be able to talk to her boss like that. But she has already turned on her three-inch heels.

***

To meet the nude body of a woman, your mother, not your mother, your father's wife, slim-hipped, emerging from the bathroom, smelling of Prell, hot water and warm flesh, your father's wife, not his wife, his lover, can snap something inside you. In a half second you take in her hair, black with water, the nipples on neat pillows, and your eyes involuntarily shift over the small stomach with precise navel, to where the slender legs meet, the dark arrow pointing down. More than her body, naked, white, what gets you is the calm with which she looks you in the eyes.

Only six or seven years ago your own mother told you to pull up your pants, you can't walk around with your penis out. Also don't touch it in front of other people; that's private. There are rules. But now they've changed. There has been a Sex Revolution and a Generation Gap. The younger generation has stopped following the restrictions of the older generation, the uptight older generation, and has proven that sex is free. Should be free, because what's natural is good. So you wonder, which generation do you belong to?

Sibyl's smile says, "This is normal, this is natural, that you should see my body." And back there, at Fallen Lake, Dad laughed and said, "You kids are so prudish!" because you and Matt and Adrienne and Darby didn't want to go skinny dipping together. Now Sibyl passes you in the hall, on the way to her bedroom, your parents' bedroom, someone's bedroom, without saying anything more. No bathrobe, be- cause it's plenty warm enough in the house to walk from a bedroom to a shower and back again and to cover yourself only for the sake of covering yourself is silly, like those statues with the leaves. It's natural, it's normal and it feels like snow in the face, because you looked, and you looked not only because you ran into her—there she was and you didn't have time to avoid her—but also because you wanted to see. Of course it's interesting to see any woman naked. Though you would not want her to see you naked.

Would you?

There's only one bathroom on the ground floor, and it's in Matt and Ivor's bedroom, so Adrienne and Darby have to come through. The other day, Matt was undressing, when Adrienne came in. He saw her eyes take him in. "I knocked," she said.

He pulled his underwear on. "You're supposed to wait for an answer."

***

In the end it's not Laura's folks, with their supposed small-town small-mindedness (they've got the gift to dismiss everything that happens in California as faddish nonsense), it's not Leif's self-righteous brother (he has too many other ogres to battle at present), it's not Sibyl's uptight WASP Republican parents (their sense of propriety keeps them silent). Rather it's Saul and Rose Eisenberg who decide that someone has to throw cold water on this *mishegass*.

They come from Anaheim finally to see for themselves. Like Sibyl's parents, they squint at the bed in the dining room, but unlike Sibyl's folks, they don't abstain from questioning until finally they pester the outlines of the story from Hiram. "Ay!" Saul Eisenberg keeps exclaiming, and Rose cries into a handkerchief. "You think this can work?" Saul keeps asking. Then they return to Anaheim and, Hiram thinks, into resignation. But a month later, they drive all the way back to Pleasant Valley again to corner their first-born and his wife at the Imperial Palace restaurant.

"It's okay for you, but think about the kids!" says Saul.

"This is not a normal way to grow up," adds Rose.

"What are they thinking about your behavior?" says Saul. "Do their friends at school, their teachers, know that their parents are hopping in and out of each other's beds?"

Hiram's chopsticks, squeezing too tightly, bisect a dumpling halfway to his mouth and the two halves flop messily into his lap.

"Use a fork," says Rose. "It's easier."

Saul turns to Sibyl. "I hope you don't mind that I speak frankly." He has Hiram's big dome, but not his kind eyes (those obviously belong to Rose), and the creases that bracket his mouth run so deep they give him the severity of a nutcracker. "It's because we're concerned about you."

Sibyl hasn't touched the sweet-and-sour pork that Rose heaped onto her plate. She doesn't feel the least bit hungry, and when she thinks about it, she realizes the reason; she knows Saul will insist on paying the restaurant bill. Swallowing his food feels too much like swallowing his advice.

When she first met Hiram's parents, Sibyl was afraid of them. She'd heard about Saul's temper, the shouting that famously drove one neighbor to move away. She'd heard about Rose's tears. At that first dinner, in their house in Anaheim, Sibyl barely opened her mouth, afraid of provoking someone. But there were no scenes that night, no yelling or sobbing. Only solicitous questions, lots of wine, food, advice, more questions and more food, followed by kisses. She began to feel embraced in a way she never had by her own family. When the tantrums did roll in a year or two later, she could almost surf in them, appreciating the display of emotion as a kind of spectator.

"Well, thanks," she begins.

"And about Darby and Adrienne," Rose interrupts. Small and hunched, she peers at Sibyl through thick lenses from beneath a remarkable pile of dyed auburn curls. "It's confusing enough to be a teenager with all that's going on in the world. Especially in the Bay Area. You have drugs, homosexuals, Black Panthers."

"Protesters," Saul says. "Pushers."

"Hell's Angels."

"Hippies."

"Homosexuals."

"I said that."

"You have to add this to your kids' lives?"

If Sibyl weren't here now, Hiram could just agree with his parents and then go on with his life as if the conversation never took place. But Sibyl takes these family conversations literally. Whatever he says, she will remember and quote to him verbatim six weeks from now.

"What you do in the privacy of your bedroom is your business," Saul says. "You're adults. You experiment. It's not to my taste, but it's not my business. I just ask, 'Have you thought about your children?'"

Hiram finally stirs. "Dad, you don't have to…" But he doesn't know where to go with his sentence. The truth is that he's as touched by their meddling as he is annoyed. He wants to say something reassuring, but what can he possibly offer that will make sense to them? How can he placate them without insulting Sibyl?

Hearing Hiram trail off, Sibyl steps into the void. "I think about my children every minute of every day. Darby and Adrienne are fine. Adrienne got straight A's last semester; Darby is on the swim team. They are not taking drugs. They are not joining motorcycle gangs."

"Sibyl." Rose's shrunken, warm hand clasps Sibyl's fist next to her plate. "We don't mean you aren't good, caring parents."

"We didn't drive here from Anaheim to criticize," Saul says. He takes off his own black-rimmed glasses for the first time in the conversation, which suddenly softens his face.

"You didn't?" says Sibyl.

"We came to help," says Rose.

"Help?" Hiram sits up.

"We'd like to bring Darby and Adrienne back to stay with us for a while," Saul explains.

"Just until you've gotten though this… time," says Rose.

Hiram and Sibyl glance at each other's surprised faces. "This *time?*" Sibyl says. "You make it sound like someone's sick!"

Saul raises both his hands. "Before you take offense at us, listen to what we're proposing."

"It would be fun for us," says Rose. "With you living so far away, we don't get to see them so often. We would like to get to know them better. And they would have a good time. We have Disneyland."

"Hollywood," adds Saul. "Sunshine."

"Beaches that are warm," says Rose. "Not cold, like the beaches you have here."

"You want to take my children away?" Sibyl's face has tightened.

Hiram sees that he has to head off a confrontation. "Mother," he says, loudly enough to talk down Rose's protestations. "Dad. It's very nice of you to be so concerned. But it's not as if we haven't thought about Darby and Adrienne. We think that ultimately what we are doing will be the best thing we could do for them."

Saul holds out his palms in exasperated supplication.

"We know what we're doing is different from what you're used to," Hiram pushes on. "We know it's hard to accept. But we're not just screwing around. We're trying to build something. Something that might actually be better than what most families have."

There's a painful silence as the realization sinks into Saul and Rose that their son is in much, much deeper than they suspected. "Oy!" is all Saul can say. Rose searches in her purse for her handkerchief.

Chapter Six

HIRAM has read about the thousands of hippies fanning out into the countryside these days, kids in their patchwork jeans settling on old farms and ranches, pushing seeds into the dark dirt. Less knowledgeable than the pilgrims who almost starved at Plymouth Rock and as blind in their faith, they shun all the advances of chemistry. The carrots are stunted. The bugs eat the lettuce; there isn't enough water; the rows are too close together. The outhouse is too close to the main house. The hippies get hepatitis; they collect food stamps; they beg for money from Mom and Dad.

Hiram, Leif, Sibyl and Laura won't make these kinds of mistakes. Hiram not only has made wine in his backyard for fifteen years, with plenty of trips to vineyards, he has run a business for almost as long. Together with Leif, he's learning about soil tests and microclimates, about integrated pest management, drainage, water tables, rootstocks. They follow the markets. They interview winemakers, vintners, sunburned third-generation Italian-American farmers, North Coast real estate agents. More and more they are convinced what they're planning will work.

Three properties in Napa County, a half dozen in Sonoma and Mendocino, and suddenly he finds the spot. He has no question in his mind when he sees it, and he can't wait to take the others, all eight of them, up to see it in the van. They pile out in front of a 1940s ranch house halfway up a hillside furred in golden grass. Big hay fields stretch in most directions from the house. A Mrs. Shulman greets them with a black poodle-retriever panting at her side and lets them take their tour. Hiram leads them eagerly to creeks named Austin and Poney, which converge on the property, their banks supported by junked cars and overgrown with blackberries. "The Shulmans said they'd clear the cars off if we buy it," Hiram says with a wave. "Look out for poison oak." Splashing across rocks and mud, the eight of them arrive at another expanse of hay. Down a back road there are yet another eighty-two arable acres for a total of 302, plus another ninety-three of oak-forested hills.

A shambling barn of corrugated aluminum leans against a hill, as beaten as a war refugee. "We can tear it down," Hiram says, "build our house there. What's important is the land. This is some of the best soil in the state, the lab guy said. And this coastal climate is perfect for grapes. It's like Bordeaux; rarely freezes, not too hot in the summer. You can grow anything here, really, if you've got the water. And we've got two creeks. Everyone around here's getting into grapes. We're lucky to have found this when we did." He points across a distant fence where spindly young vines file across a field. Dairy farms are being sold, prune orchards ripped out, as California wines make their international reputation. Here in Mendocino, the climate, the soil, are every bit as good as in Napa, but the property values haven't climbed that high. There's just enough time now to get in on the good of it.

While he talks, Sibyl smells the dry, hot wind that ruffles the hay fields. Ivor throws a foxtail at Darby, and she turns on him like a wounded panther, curling her lip. Matt cranes his head back, watching buzzards make slow circles in the sky. Adrienne disappears into a hideout she makes by flattening the tall amber grass.

On the way back, they pass a little corral with some palominos, but when Adrienne asks, "How many horses will we have?" everyone is silent. Sibyl can't bear to tell her there is no money now for horses and might not be for years.

Passing through the town of Shultzville, Darby murmurs, "Nowheresville." Adrienne says its little clapboard houses are cute, but Darby points out that it only has a gas station, a Safeway and a hamburger place. "There's no way to get into town unless you can drive a car, and once you get there, there's not even a movie theater or anything to do if you live here, no one to talk to but the farm kids."

But Hiram ignores her, bubbling about a modern, solar-heated house that will rise up from the acres of well-kept, organically fertilized fields. Laura and Leif chime in as well. There's a swimming pool in the dream, maybe a tennis court, but everything in its time; get the vines in first so the place can start producing income. They'll buy a tractor, till and harrow, the whole group coming up to plant on weekends and vacations, until the house is finished, maybe in a year. Ten miles outside Shultzville, it's clear the group will make an offer on the property. No one notices Sibyl's silence as she counts the miles ticking out between this place and her job.

"Oh great," says Darby, "every weekend and vacation for two years. Should I jump out of the car now or should I wait till we get home and slit my wrists?"

Hiram, Leif and Laura just laugh, but Sibyl turns in her seat to take in Darby's misery. "Oh, Darby," she says, reaching around to touch her daughter's hand on the seat back. "There's a lot to do in the country, it's just different. Walks and things. You saw how pretty it was. Anyway, we won't be moving for a year or two and then we can visit Pleasant Valley or San Francisco as much as we want. You'll like it. You just have to be open-minded."

***

Sibyl sits by herself when the rat trap goes off in the broom closet. Three months after buying this farmhouse, the Eisenbergs and Wrightsons still haven't been able to rid it of vermin. Sibyl wishes she had asked Hiram to unset the trap before he went back to Pleasant Valley to deal with a crisis at Jancorum. Laura and Matt have the flu. Leif is caring for them and won't come until tomorrow. Everyone seems to have a reason to be in Pleasant Valley this weekend except Sibyl.

Sibyl has never set a trap before, even for a mouse and certainly never had to face the consequences. She's sitting quietly in the living room, the lights dim, reading *Games People Play*—which Sam recommended as something they might use in seminars—dozing off, really, and suddenly a sharp bang sounds from the kitchen making her eyes snap open. She knows instantly what it is, and wonders if she can just leave it until Hiram or Leif get back. Then there's a rattle and she realizes the poor animal must still be in its death throes.

More than death throes, it turns out, as the rattle turns into a panicked crashing. It must be throwing its trapped body in agony against the brooms, the walls, the mop handles and dust pans, trying to work itself loose. Maybe it's only caught by the tail. Silence for a moment allows her to imagine it has finally expired, and then the thrashing resumes with a desperate squeak of pain.

Sibyl dials Hiram in Pleasant Valley. "Yeah, I know," he says cheerfully. "Those traps don't work as well for rats as for mice. We used to use them at the warehouse. It usually doesn't finish the job, and a lot of times the rat works its way free. I still think it's better than poison; you don't want the rat to crawl into the wall and die where you can't reach it. Anyway, you'd better go in and get it."

"Go in and get it?" Sibyl's heart pumps desperately as a renewed banging resounds in the closet. She imagines that she can see the closet door shaking with the impact. Any moment it might burst open, the bloody animal flopping itself onto the kitchen floor.

"Right. I've used a kitchen mitt. Or a good barbecue glove might be better. We have some in the top drawer by the stove, I think."

"Then what do I do?"

"Well, you could drown it in the toilet. But hitting it with a hammer is probably more humane. You know, on the head. It's quicker."

Sibyl swallows. "Maybe I'll just leave it for tomorrow. When you get back."

Hiram sighs. "The problem is the rat might get away. If it hasn't already. Then it'll be wise to the trap. You'd better kill it now. I'm sorry I'm not there, or I'd do it, but that's part of living in the country, you know."

"Right. Of course." Sibyl hangs up, furious at Hiram for set-ting a trap and then running off, furious at him for wanting to live in the country and at herself for going along with the whole proposal. A voice in her head says this is a man's job and she shouldn't have to deal with it. She knows whose voice it is, and she's furious at her mother for bringing her up that way, and at Hiram for putting her into a position where she feels like a hypocrite. If women ran the world, these problems wouldn't even come up, right? You would just live and let live. Just ignore the little beast, let him have a handful of Cheerios every day, or whatever he wants. But no. She could never stand for that—rats multiplying, becoming ever bolder, dashing across the table to snatch food from their plates, chewing Sibyl's clothing in the dresser and scattering their droppings in the backs of drawers. Biting the kids.

There's a tool chest by the back door, and Sibyl picks out the heavi-est of the two claw hammers she finds. She slips the barbecue mitts on her hands and faces the closet door. Silence. The rat has either died or escaped. Minutes tick by without a sound and Sibyl's heartbeat finally slows. Should she have a look? Throw away the little corpse, or reset the trap? Nothing. Slowly she opens the closet door until the light from the kitchen falls on a round gray body protruding from the overturned yellow rectangle of wood.

"Squeak ack!" As the light hits it, the rat comes alive, its hind legs scratching frantically at the trap. These squeaks, Sibyl realizes, are its instinctive screams, warnings to any other rats in the neighborhood that death is at hand. Or pleas for clemency. But Sibyl doesn't know how to save this animal. And when the rat flips itself over, so that the triangular head is revealed, neck held firmly by the bar of the trap, Sibyl's hammer comes instantly down. Bang. And bang again. Smash-ing over and over, long beyond the point when the little rat's brains can serve any function, she hits until the head is flat, eyes popped, trap bloody. She hits again, again, again, again.

***

Darby's parents can make her ride with Laura, but they can't make her talk. For the past half hour of this drive up to the property, Darby

has answered Laura's questions with a grunt, and ignored her comments. She has focused out the window, watching the houses peter out,
and the cows peter in. She has not even let this woman into her gaze.

Darby is supposed to be grateful that she got to stay over Friday
night in Pleasant Valley. Of course, Laura dragged Darby out of bed
at 9 a.m. this morning, when the rest of the world (or at least everyone who went to Roxanne's party) was still cozily sleeping. And then
Laura insisted Darby should eat breakfast, which she couldn't because
her stomach was upset from the vodka. At the party, Roxanne's boyfriend, Mike, secreted flasks everywhere in his clothes—in all his pants
pockets, his jacket, his shirt— even one in the hood of his sweatshirt.
Remembering, Darby chuckles.

"What?" Laura asks.

"Nothing."

Laura huffs a big sigh and flips on the radio. Drums, guitar and
Carly Simon's melodious jeer: "I'll bet you think this song is about you.
Don't you? Don't you?"

Laura taps her finger on the steering wheel and bobs her head in
time to the music. She sings. "I had some dreams they were clouds in
my coffee. Clouds in my coffee."

Darby stares. "You like this song?" To hear Laura's voice producing words that Darby danced to the night before is just too weird.
It's true the grownups have Beatles and Grateful Dead records, but
Darby always assumed their tastes ended with the '60s: peace, love, and
understanding, blah, blah.

Laura nods. "Well, you're where you should be all the time. And
when you're not, you're with some underworld spy or the wife of a
close friend. Wife of a close friend." Suddenly she stops, letting Carly
finish alone.

"What do you like about him so much?" Darby asks. She's not sure
herself where the question came from. She certainly has no intention
of starting a conversation.

"Who? Hiram?"

"Yeah."

This time, Laura's sigh sounds contented. "He just makes me feel so... so good about myself."

"Daddy?" Darby thinks of her father as a little self-centered—able to come up with the occasional great Christmas present or funny bedtime story, and usually amiable, but generally not aware of other people's needs. "How?"

"Because he loves me. And he tells me that. But it's not just that." Laura glances over at Darby, assessing. "Okay, you really want to know?"

Darby shrugs, wondering if Laura is going to divulge something juicy about their sex life. She's not sure she wants to hear it.

"He believes in me. He just takes it for granted I can do anything. It's the most flattering thing in the world. I mean, Leif always told me I could go back to college, right? But he said it in a way that made me feel like he wasn't sure. It's almost like I let him down by marrying him and having kids. He loves me, too. I know that. But somehow he became almost like a parent rather than a partner." She peers at Darby again. "I probably shouldn't be telling you this."

"No you should." For once Darby feels she has gotten a glimpse into what's going on. "I mean, it's okay. If you want to."

Laura smiles. "So by contrast, Hiram just started talking about which classes I would be taking. We were looking over the course catalog one day, and the next day I was sending in my application. Leif had been telling me to do it for years, nagging me. You know how sometimes you refuse to do something, just because somebody is forcing it on you?"

"Yep."

"But with Hiram, it just happened. He just asked me what I would do if I could do anything. I said maybe I'd teach English. And the next thing I knew we were stopping by the admissions office at PVSU. And I have to tell you, it's the most wonderful thing."

"It is?"

"When you're in junior high school, four years more school doesn't exactly sound tantalizing, I know. But the stuff I'm studying now—it's blowing my mind. Did you know the most famous poet in ancient

Greece was a lesbian?"

"Umm. Sappho?"

"Okay, so you did know." Laura brushes back a strand of auburn hair. "But did you know that before people invented farming, when they were still nomadic, men and women were equal? I mean think of that. Everything we take for granted about men dominating society only goes back a few thousand years. Before that there were *tens* of thousands of years when we were all equal."

"So are you sure you want to plant a vineyard?"

Laura laughs. "Good point. Let's become nomads. I'm going to tell Leif what we really should do is sell the property in Mendocino and the house in Pleasant Valley and just travel around the country in the van."

"How about we just go back to what we were doing. Two regular families in two regular houses." Laura fixes her eyes on the road for a moment. "Look, I know this must be hard on you, having us cram into your house. All these weekends in the country. The plans to move. I'm sure this is messing up your social life."

"Uh. You could say that." *Totally destroying* Darby's social life would be a better way to put it. It's nice to hear one of the adults admit fault.

"I'm sorry." Laura bit her lip. "I'm not going to just say, 'Be patient, you'll meet new friends in Shultzville.'"

"Thank you."

"Matt and Ivor aren't exactly thrilled either. I guess Adrienne probably feels the same way you do."

"Adrienne? Buy her a horse. She'll be happy."

There is something pleasing about Laura's laughter—how quickly, how naturally it splashes out, as if she is so filled with humor that a tiny joke is enough to make some overflow. For a split second, Darby glimpses what has attracted her father. "Well, we might," Laura said. "You, I'm guessing, will not be so easily bribed. Still, I hope living with us in the country won't be a complete bore and chore for you. And if you think of something that might compensate, even a little bit, you should tell us."

The offer feels so empty that Darby doesn't respond, and so they just listen to the radio plodding its way through the top forty. "Rocky Mountain High." "Loves me Like a Rock." Outside the car, fences run endlessly up and down hills of burned brown. Then, gradually, traffic thickens once again. Billboards spread their invitations along the road. Gas stations and shopping centers cluster more closely.

"Let's do some shopping," says Laura, out of the blue.

"Here?"

"There are a few hip stores in Santa Rosa." Laura is already taking an exit off the freeway. "Didn't you say something about getting a halter top?"

"Yeah…" Darby wonders where this is going. Surely Laura knows that Sibyl has ruled out halter tops in her ongoing campaign to suppress Darby's sexuality.

"Also, did you know that a milkshake is the perfect cure for a hangover?"

So she knows! Darby carefully brushed her teeth last night when she got home, and didn't say a word this morning about a stomach upset. But somehow Laura has figured out that she drank. What's more astonishing, is that Laura isn't judging her for it. Just offering to help. And by now the feeling in her middle has gone from discomfort to vacancy. Twenty minutes later, she finds that a hamburger and milkshake do, in fact, impart wellbeing.

And the purchases they carry back to the car an hour later fill Darby with a sense of triumph, only slightly tinged with guilt. Everyone else at school has a halter top by now. And the one she and Laura picked out, glimmering beige Lurex, with thin straps and a loose weave, shows off Darby's growing bust more beautifully than anything she's ever worn before. The only problem now: whether, and how, to tell mom.

"I'll talk to Sibyl about it," Laura says, as if Darby had spoken aloud. She puts the Rambler in gear. "I mean, she wears hot pants, right? So I'm sure she's not going to be hypocritical."

**

Suddenly Laura wakes up, remembering. The last pill she took was yesterday. Or was it Thursday, which would mean she's missed two? If you miss one day, then you should take two the next. Laura's pretty sure that's what Dr. Appledorf said. But what if you miss two days? Should you take three pills? Or is it too late? And if it's too late, what will happen? Because over the past six hours, Hiram has pumped an awful lot of sperm into her.

Oh, how could she have been so careless? It's just the way things are right now, all topsy-turvy; hard to remember to brush your teeth, let alone pop a pill every night. And it's especially complicated when you don't know where you've left your things. The only way into the master bathroom is through the master bedroom, and when Sibyl's in there with either man, it's awkward to get anything out. Laura doesn't even like to knock. She's got a toothbrush in all three bathrooms now, but she can't have an extra everything everywhere, and she's always forgetting things: her razor (until Hiram persuaded her to stop using it altogether), a couple of times her dandruff shampoo. And one Sunday morning that Sibyl didn't come out until 11 a.m., she left in the master bedroom the clothes she wanted to wear to the Women's Re-entry brunch.

Sitting up and leaning forward over Hiram's stillness, Laura can make out the green glowing face of the clock on the bedside table beside him. Five minutes after twelve. Chances are, Sibyl and Leif are fast asleep right now. If Laura snuck in, they'd never notice. She wishes Dr. Appledorf had been more explicit. Does every hour count at this point? Is it all the same if she waits another seven hours until Sibyl's up and dressed? Better not to take a chance. Laura pulls the covers back softly and searches on the floor for her clothes where she threw them in passion a couple of hours ago. Here are Hiram's underwear and his pants. Under them her own panties. No sign of her jeans, but her shirt is close by and she slips it over her head. Treading on the balls of her feet, she passes through the bead curtain that cordons off the former dining room. She heads for the stairs.

Times like this, Laura wonders why. Why should she and Leif sleep together at all anymore? Why should they even live together? His hands on her body are the hands of a scientist, cool, precise. Sleeping with him is like putting on a pair of shoes you find in the back of your closet; you remember as you force them over your heels why you never could wear them.

Last night at dinner, Laura and Hiram looked across the table and in his grin, she saw what they would do as soon as they got into bed. The whole evening was about the two of them. They snuggled together on the couch after dinner, reading. She was about to ask Hiram if he was ready, and then Leif put down his newspaper. "So Laura. You want to come over to my place tonight?"

Everyone's eyes shot up from whatever they were reading. To refuse him—her own husband—was to insult him and to throw the whole group into yet another big conversation. "Oh." She found Hiram's hand and squeezed it. "Sure, honey. Which place is yours?"

Leif chuckled. "My stuff is mostly upstairs right now." A moment later he got up and winked at her. She rose with the molasses motions of a child getting ready for school, bent to kiss Hiram on the top of his head, and followed.

Leif closed the door behind them. "I hope you don't mind. I just think it's better for everyone if we alternate once in a while."

How calculating, how theoretical! "You're probably right."

"After all, it's been, what, three days?"

"I wasn't counting."

"We don't have to do anything if you don't want to."

She mustered a smile. "We can. I mean if you want."

His mustache dipped. "My mistress of seduction."

"Sorry. I'm… tired."

He shrugged. "Then let's just be together."

They lay in faint embrace a few minutes, getting as near as they could to the way they used to talk, about Ivor's D in chemistry, about Matt's perverse decision to turn down the one birthday party invitation he'd received since first grade. It was both stale and comforting, this sliver of domesticity in the midst of turmoil. Then they rolled apart and fell asleep. But before that, before even getting into bed, Laura took her pill. Or did she? She knows she took it in that room, but was it that night, or the night before with Hiram? Either way, the package is sure to be in the master bathroom.

Laura pads up the stairs. Outside the bedroom she listens. A soft moan from inside. No, nothing; she must have imagined it. She twists the knob until the latch springs. The door eases open without a squeak. Wider. Wide enough to see inside and then to see, in the moonlight flooding through the window, that Sibyl is nude, kneeling at Leif's hips, facing the door. Her long hair hangs like a straw curtain that doesn't quite conceal what she is doing to his penis with her mouth. Sibyl's eyes flicker up to meet Laura's.

Laura jumps back, slamming the door.

***

As an experiment, Sibyl decides not to touch a brush or broom again until someone notices. Days go by as lint builds up in the carpet by the front door. Streaks of ketchup linger on the front of the stove. Sibyl can smell the bathroom down the hall. But nobody says a word. Then Jane Jummel calls to say she's stopping by for Sibyl's Hawaiian pork chop recipe, and Sibyl finds herself bustling around the house with the vacuum cleaner in one hand and a sponge in the other.

Walking down Market Street to her office the next morning, Sibyl spots something in the window of a poster shop that she just can't resist. Drawn in black ink, a longhaired woman is breaking a broomstick in two. "Fuck Housework," read the words at the bottom. Sibyl brings it home that evening and tacks it to the kitchen wall when everyone is coming in for dinner. "What the hell, Sibyl?" Leif asks her. "Are you trying to tell us something?"

"Yes, I am. I'm trying to tell you that I'm sick of being the only one to clean anything in this house."

Leif and Laura look at their plates, Hiram at the ceiling. Adrienne turns to catch Darby's eye, obviously wondering whether their mother, of all people, has really nailed a poster to the kitchen wall with the word "fuck" written on it.

"I mean, I'm working full time now," Sibyl says. "And I think it's the responsibility of all of us to clean up after ourselves."

Laura sighs. She certainly means to do her part. She sometimes spots a streak of grime on the bathroom floor and plans on attacking it first thing Saturday, but Sibyl always seems to get there before she does. And Laura has been busy with homework. It's not so easy, after so many years out of school, to write a winning essay.

It's Leif who responds. "You're absolutely right, Sibyl. I think we all owe you an apology. We've been so distracted with everything else that's going on, and you're the only one who has focused on what really needs to be done, the actual work of having a joint household."

Now Laura feels she has to chime in. "I'm sorry if I haven't done enough. Normally I'm very good about this stuff, but everything's been so topsy-turvy since we moved in. I'm just getting my feet on the ground."

"Me too," says Hiram.

"Me too what?" Sibyl asks.

"Me too I'm sorry."

"So next time the kitchen floor gets sticky?" asks Sibyl.

"I'll pick up a mop," says Leif.

"And you?" Sibyl looks hard at her husband.

He makes scrubbing motions. "Whatever needs doing." He grins.

The following morning, Leif studies Sibyl's and Laura's collection of cookbooks and, not satisfied, heads for The Tiny Book Shop for a copy of *Larousse Gastronomique*. His grocery shopping lasts into the evening. When Sibyl comes home from work, she finds cans of pate; truffles; three sourdough baguettes; a wedge of odiferous cheese; two-and-a-half pounds of fresh eel; a wooden pestle and a large marble mortar. "What on earth?"

"Quenelles," he answers, continuing to unpack.

"Those sort of puff-pastry things stuffed with creamed fish? They'll take you forever."

"They're well worth the effort, though. I had them in New York once; they were delicious."

"What about the cheese and bread? And pate?"

"Dessert. And appetizers." And he noisily gets out every pan and pot in Sibyl's cupboard, mixing and pounding until long after everyone is half starving. The kids, of course, won't touch the finished product when Leif calls everyone to the table at 8:47 (the boys have already snacked themselves full of peanut butter), and neither will Laura, a fish-hater. Sibyl has to admit it's pretty good, and Hiram praises it a little too much.

Sibyl's sieve, which Leif used to remove bones from the eel paste, will never be the same, and the kitchen will smell of fish for a week. She wants to give Leif a lecture about household economy and balanced meals—he hasn't thought about a vegetable. But of course she has to keep her mouth shut after the big deal she's made. So a couple of days later he dives into braised goose stuffed with chestnuts and sausage. After that, his cooking impulse plays itself out. He simply doesn't have time between finishing up the semester and the oenology courses he's taking.

Hiram points out several times to Sibyl that the oil in the Rambler needs changing. If she really thinks all the household chores have to be shared equally, then why isn't she on her back in the driveway with 10W30 dripping in her face? When Leif finally shows Sibyl how to do the job, Hiram responds by taking a stab at spaghetti—globs of sticky noodles and a sauce made from ground beef mixed with apparently unseasoned cans of tomato puree—a failure so abject that it seems calculated. No one asks him to cook again for a month. How can a man who creates fine wine be so helpless in the kitchen? It reminds Sibyl again how much he depends on her.

Or used to depend on her: The one person who becomes truly serious about cooking is Laura. Conscious of how backward her mother's Midwestern casserole and meatloaf recipes seem here in the Bay Area, Laura prepares Sibyl's Chicken a La King and egg fu young.

Then, assured of a bigger audience than she had the last time, she takes another whack at duck a l'orange. Thunderous applause.

Why is it, Sibyl finds herself wondering, as Laura's mint-garnished rack of lamb arrives steaming at the table the next day, that she can't join in the chorus of compliments? Why is it, she asks herself, while scouring burned grease off her best roasting pan, that she can't just relax and eat the way everyone else does? Why does it irk her so to find stainless steel spoons among the silver, or to come across a loaf pan inside a mixing bowl? Sibyl speaks quietly and politely to Ivor about the bowls encrusted with Cheerios he leaves on the kitchen table nearly every morning. She clenches her jaw when Matt cultivates mold on six different media in her grandmother's tea cups. Then finally the smell of burning soy sauce draws her into the kitchen where she finds Laura pulling a tray of scorched chicken legs from the broiler. Sibyl can handle a burned dinner, but the sauce has blackened all over the cookie sheet, the very cookie sheet that Sibyl bought four days earlier to replace the last one that Laura ruined. "Don't you even care?"

Laura doesn't answer. She scrapes off the chicken—which is less singed than a lot of barbecue that Laura has seen people rave about at picnics—and plunges the encrusted metal hissing under a stream of cold water.

"Not cold water!" Sibyl shakes her head. "You're going to warp it!"

Laura brushes back a lock of hair to reveal her scowl. "I'll buy you a new fucking cookie sheet."

"With whose money?" Sibyl regrets this last jab as soon as she utters it. But Laura's attitude has forced bluntness on her. Yes, Laura and Leif still have some of their own money; he is drawing a last semester's worth of pay from PVSU. But the Wrightsons are not paying a dime toward the Eisenbergs' mortgage. They haven't contributed nearly as much to the down payment on the Mendocino land. The furniture and dishes and kitchen utensils the Wrightsons are steadily demolishing were almost all originally Sibyl's and Hiram's. And it will be years before the vineyard makes any money, or before Laura finishes her degree and looks for some kind of work. If Sibyl were in Laura's position she would tread more lightly, show more respect. Express some gratitude.

Laura's face crumples. "I'm trying so hard." Her tears well. "You don't know what it's like living in someone else's house. Every day I worry I'm going to use the wrong silverware or dishes. You have all these rules. Don't use the sponge under the sink for dishes. Don't put wineglasses in the dishwasher. I can't keep track. Are we supposed to be guests? I mean if you don't want us here just say so!" Laura drops the cookie sheet clattering in the sink and runs, not stopping when Sibyl calls remorsefully after her.

Leif follows Laura's sobs to the upstairs bedroom. But his platitudes, "it takes time, we're all adjusting," bring on more tears, and she doesn't come down for dinner at all. Only Hiram, arriving home a half hour later, can soothe her. He runs his hand through her hair. "You have to understand Sibyl. She likes to feel she's in charge, and if you go along with her way of doing things then she immediately calms down."

"I'm trying to do things her way. Nothing I do can ever satisfy her."

"She's like this with me, too, with everyone. It's her way. Don't take it seriously."

"I can't take another day. I told Leif. We're going to move out. Probably next week."

He sits back on the bed, silent.

"I'm sorry, Hiram. It's just not working."

Wrinkles bunch his forehead.

"What?" she asks.

"I'd be so shattered."

She takes his hand.

He squeezes. "Please Laura. Give it another month. I promise you, I'll keep her tied down and muzzled."

Laura laughs, thinking she can never refuse Hiram anything. "One month."

***

Stepping slowly, Matt places his right foot as precisely as possible in the lower left-hand corner of a square of the sidewalk, heel at the X axis, arch along the Y axis. Then he places his left foot, mirroring his right foot, in the lower right-hand corner of the next square. Walking this way he comes finally to the curb where the school bus is waiting to take him home. Mrs. Henderson, the driver hasn't yet opened the doors, but when she does, Matt will be the first one in. Mrs. Henderson spends a mean time of 11 minutes, 34 seconds smoking on her break, and Matt knows the other kids will pass the time chasing each other, or playing catch, or sitting around talking. But he will stand here as long as it takes her because this way he can be sure of sitting, as always, in the third seat back next to the window.

They don't understand why he does it this way, and he can't explain it to them. However, there is a reason. The scientific method teaches you to eliminate the variables. If you can maintain a consistent process, you will obtain cleaner data. Eat each night a quarter pound of hamburger, a cup of cooked Uncle Ben's rice with a gram of butter and a half cup of peas. Go to bed at 11:00, get up at 7:00. For breakfast, eat two bowls of Cheerios and a glass of orange juice; brush your teeth with 0.25 grams of Crest toothpaste; walk to the bus stop by the same route. Be the first in line. Sit in the third seat back on the left, next to the window, and you have eliminated some of the noise from your results. How, for example, can you know the effects on your digestive system of eating a strawberry for breakfast (as Matt did this morning, in addition to the Cheerios) unless you change nothing else about your diet, your energy expenditure, your state of mind from one day to the next?

It's true there is no theoretical reason that sitting in the second seat on the left, next to the window, instead of the third seat on the left, next to the window should change anything about the digestion of a strawberry. But it is the unanticipated variables for which it is most important to control. In order to know exactly what would affect the digestion of the strawberry, Matt would have to know everything else about digesting the strawberry before eating it. He would have to know the results before doing the experiment.

Of course, it's not fully possible to control all the variables of one's own life; someone forgets to buy Cheerios, an English teacher is absent or Matt inhales an upper respiratory virus, and the data are polluted. Still, Matt can analyze any of these occurrences—in effect making any one of them the subject of a new experiment—if everything else remains constant.

Behind him as he waits Matt notices something out of the ordinary. He seems to overhear his name spoken two or three times in a low voice. It's best not to take notice because turning, questioning the speaker, or any other reaction can enchain a whole series of events that could disrupt his routine. So he remains in position.

Just as Mrs. Henderson (about 173 centimeters, 68 kilograms, middle brown complexion, Negroid features, 51 years) returns from her break, steps up into her seat and is about to signal to Matt that he can get on the bus, someone taps him on the shoulder. Reflexively, Matt turns to see JJ Arbust (176 centimeters, 52 kilograms, pale complexion, Caucasoid features, brown hair, 13 years) whose nearly elliptical face and oversized ears Matt has known by sight for many years. "Matt," says JJ "I need to ask you something."

"What?" Matt turns to enter the bus.

But now JJ has him by the arm, physically restraining him. "No, out here. I want to ask you here. It's really important."

"No," Matt says flatly, struggling to break free of JJ's grip. By now he can see from the corner of his eye someone stepping around him to go into the bus. And JJ won't let go without getting his question answered. "What?" Matt asks impatiently.

"Well, I was wondering…" JJ seems to draw out the question on purpose. A second person goes around them and into the bus.

"What?"

"Why do you always have to be the first person on the bus?"

"Just a habit," Matt says.

JJ releases him. But as he climbs in he can see that big-nosed, clownish Max Ferry (169 centimeters, 50 kilograms, red complexion,

Caucasoid features, hazel eyes, strawberry blond), and the slight, nervous Andre Olmov (168 centimeters, 42 kilograms, Caucasoid features, green eyes, black hair) two of JJ's friends, have taken the third seat to the left, Max by the window and Andre by the aisle. Matt can feel his heart pounding. All the other seats in the bus are empty. It would be one thing if this happened as an accident—he could ask them to switch, even sit in the second seat back for one day—but it's clear from the huge grins on the boys' faces that this is a set up, that they've been watching his routine and have deliberately decided to sabotage it for sport.

"Get out of my seat," Matt says calmly.

"*Your* seat?" Andre says. "What makes this *your* seat?" He turns to David. "Did you see a name tag on this seat?"

"No," says Max. "No name tag."

"I always sit here," Matt says.

"Not today," says Andre.

From his seat across the aisle, JJ laughs.

If he hadn't already eaten a strawberry today, Matt might be willing to sit in a different place. It could be his experiment for the day. And even though he has already started an experiment for the day, he accepts that random events can often interject variables which the scientist cannot control. Sometimes a set of data simply has to be scrapped. He accepts that this can sometimes happen because of human error.

What makes this event *un*acceptable, is that JJ, Max and Andre are *intentionally* fouling up his data. That someone could do this, could destroy Matt's routine out of malice, is the reason that Matt loses his composure and grasps Andre firmly by his T-shirt. Andre is a slight boy who hasn't gotten his adolescent growth yet, and Matt, who's already showing some of his father's size, yanks him so suddenly and violently that Andre tumbles into the aisle.

"Now move," Matt orders Max, whose forehead is already lined with sudden apprehension.

Before Matt can follow up, though, he staggers under the force of a shove by Andre from behind. Now Matt whirls. He finds himself hitting Andre again and again. Andre has to put up his hands in front of his face. Someone near the entrance to the bus shouts "Fight! Fight!" and Matt is surprised to observe himself hitting still, even after it's clear that Andre has capitulated. It's interesting that JJ and Max have not come to Andre's assistance; clearly this is more than they were expecting from Matt. So Matt is puzzled to find himself still pummeling Andre, to the point that a smear of blood now appears on Andre's lip.

At last Matt feels strong hands on his shoulders, pulling him back and away. Mr. Bennet (213 centimeters, 102 kilograms, 32 years, dark brown complexion, Negroid features), is half carrying, half dragging him off the bus.

***

Dr. Peter English, M.D., gestures for Laura, Leif and Matt to sink into his too-soft furniture. The carpets are double pile—even the acoustical tile looks soft—and everything's done in soothing colors of beige and olive so that Laura feels as if they've already been confined to a padded cell.

It's so embarrassing to have to go see a psychiatrist, and that's probably why Laura and Leif didn't do it before now. They could see something was wrong a long time ago. They knew Matt wasn't like other kids. He never really made friends, spent all his time absorbed in his own world. But to take him to a child psychiatrist suggests that they have failed as parents, or worse, perhaps, that they have given birth to a defective being. As long as he did well in school, as he always has, it was easy to reassure themselves that there was nothing to worry about. And Leif always scoffed at Laura's concerns. "He's not interested in GI Joes; he's interested in cell biology. It's just taking him some time to find other kids at his level."

And then—why not admit it?—Leif and Laura have been distracted by the big changes in their own lives. You can't be quite as attentive to your kids when your life is being reshuffled. And so they let the problem go, ignored it, really, neglected it, until they got the call from the school. As horrified as she was by the news, and as shocked as she was by the form it took (Matt? The scientist? Fighting on the school bus?) some part of her took it with relief, a kind of gratitude in knowing that it was in the open now, this fear that nagged her.

Now Matt sits with alligator calm in his armchair across the room from Laura, his gaze unfocused, blinking as she recounts his story.

"When," asks Dr. English, "did this problem start?"

Thin as a cracker, with an aquiline nose and nearly circular eyes, Dr. English glances from his notebook to Matt, from Matt to Laura, from Laura to Leif. Long strands of hair sweep across his bald crown. He wears the uniform of an academic—cardigan with leather elbow patches, black wool pants, thick-soled walking shoes.

"Matt's always been different," says Laura. "I remember when he was three, he used to spend hours staring at ants' nests. I mean hours, just watching ants. And when he was four or five, you could never satisfy his curiosity about anything. You would start with 'Why do plants need sunlight?' and the next thing you knew, you were trying to explain chlorophyll, then osmosis, and then you were running to the encyclopedia. And pretty soon he was reading the encyclopedia to himself; I mean the *whole* encyclopedia.

"We always thought this was a good thing, just a sign of intelligence, but by the time he was nine or ten it was all he wanted to do, reading endlessly, books about natural history and biology. It leaves him no time to make friends. Am I right, Matt?"

Matt's eyes shift to her in his immobile face. "Substantially."

"How do you feel about this, Matt?" Dr. English asks.

"About what?"

"Are you concerned that you're spending too much time reading and not enough time with friends?"

"No."

He and Dr. English gaze quietly at each other for a moment. "Okay," Dr. English says finally. "Maybe I could talk with Matt alone for a moment?"

Laura and Leif look at each other. There's a pause in which they communicate by their stillness that neither of them wants to get up, neither wants to surrender Matt to this thin, furrowed man; Laura because she wants to be present to seize any treasures of insight he might dredge up; Leif because he doesn't quite trust him. Then with a heave they rise simultaneously.

When his parents leave Dr. English's soft-surfaced room, Matt feels abandoned for a moment. And then, gradually, he regains his composure. Psychiatry didn't involve needles or scalpels, after all. And for a long time, Dr. English does nothing. He sits, gazing at Matt, as minutes tick past, both of them silent. Above his head, Matt notices the painting of a flower whose blossom fills the canvas. The artist has painstakingly reproduced each petal so that the eye follows its whorls down to the center of the canvas where pistol and stamen thrust delicately. It's the only decoration to break the texture of the beige walls, and Matt's eyes are drawn to explore it for long minutes while Dr. English still sits silently, studying Matt. Maybe the doctor is like those nineteenth century physiognomists who believed they could discern their subjects' temperaments from the shapes of their heads. Matt is ready to get up and leave when finally the doctor speaks: "Your parents are worried about you."

"Yes."

"Why do you think that is?"

"My mother doesn't think I have enough friends."

"Would you like to have more friends?"

"I'm not concerned."

Dr. English closes his eyes for a long moment, then suddenly fixes them on Matt again. "Your mother says you keep to a very strict routine."

"Yes."

"Why?"

Matt hesitates. Dr. English is a man of science. Can he understand, then, that Matt's approach to life was based on the scientific method?

Could he understand a daily routine based on the principle of eliminating variables? Surely not. Dr. English might understand the words. But he still would not accept it. The problem is that Matt has deviated from the social norm to an extent that most adults, and all children, find unacceptable. Society can only function if its members behave in prescribed patterns, and it will exert whatever power is necessary to enforce them. Matt has long ago reconciled himself to that fact. To allow Dr. English to scrutinize his thought processes is to invite intrusion into them. And that Matt can't allow. "Why does anyone have a routine?" Matt says.

"Would you say, though, Matt, that your routines matter to you more than most people's?"

"I haven't studied that."

Another long pause. Matt is beginning to interpret these silences as a signal that Dr. English has been effectively flummoxed, and to taste in them a faint savor of triumph. So he waits, determined not to speak again until Dr. English does. Then another factor intrudes. The Wrightsons arrived on time for their 11:30 appointment, but it's now 12:23, almost a half-hour past lunch time, and Matt feels hungry. And the hunger reminds him of the disorder that, as always, has been imposed on him from outside.

Still Dr. English says nothing, his eyes closed in rumination. Matt is wondering if he has gone to sleep when the doctor suddenly asks, "What time do you get up in the morning?"

Matt takes a deep, slow breath to calm himself. He forces from his mind the thought that this session, in addition to destroying his equilibrium and wasting his time, is costing his parents perhaps $40 or $50. He answers, "0700 hours—seven o'clock."

"Then?"

"I get dressed."

"What do you wear?"

"Pants and a shirt."

"What color shirt?"

"Green."

"Always green?"

"Always."

"Amazing," Dr. English comments. "Everything the same, every day. It must be an enormous effort. Why is it worthwhile to you?"

Matt feels himself sink even deeper into Dr. English's plush chair. Gradually it's dawning on him that he can't cut Dr. English out altogether. Unless he shuts his mouth now, refuses to answer another question, the doctor will gradually tease out of him the details of a life he has worked so hard to keep private. But to refuse to speak is too obvious a form of resistance. It invites more scrutiny, perhaps meetings with other psychiatrists, perhaps forcible efforts to alter his routines. Lies about what he did, the facts of his day-to-day existence, won't hold up for more than a few of these sessions. His parents will contradict him; inconsistencies will emerge. The only alternative to complete candor at this point is to offer a diversion. "Why is it worthwhile?" Matt repeated.

Dr. English nods.

"I don't know, really. The truth is, I've just been very confused lately with everything that's going on."

The eyebrows rise, sending ripples across the narrow forehead. "What *is* going on?"

"I don't know if it's supposed to be a secret."

Dr. English leans forward and spread his hands. "Matt, I promise you that everything you tell me is totally confidential. Totally. I won't repeat it to anyone, including your parents, without your permission."

"It's just been... chaotic."

"At home?"

"Yes."

The pencil moves on Dr. English's pad. "Chaos can be upsetting."

"Very," said Matt. "Disorienting."

"And what has made life so chaotic at home?"

When he finally emerges from Dr. English's office, Matt shows no

more expression than when he entered. And he rides silently on the
way home.

"What did Dr. English say?" Laura asks.

"He wanted to know about my social life."

She swivels in the front seat to see his face. "Did he have
any advice?"

"No." Matt stares out the window.

"Matt? You know he's trying to help you. We're all just trying to
help you."

"Then leave me alone. I don't need a psychiatrist. I can handle the
situation on my own."

"I'm not sure that's true. For a long time we thought it was, but
when you get into trouble in school then we have to wonder."

"I'm not in trouble." And that's the attitude he takes from that
moment forward, denying the obvious, fending off everyone who tries
to help. Laura is starting to panic by the time she and Leif return for
their second, private session with Dr. English the following week.

But at first, the psychiatrist has more questions than answers.
"What was Matt's birth like? Was he easily comforted as an infant? As
a toddler, did he adapt well to change?" Those are the easy questions.
After that, he wants to know about Matt's "environment." "How many
people live in your house, now?" Laura can't help wondering what Matt
has told him. "What's your relationship to this family, the Eisenbergs?"
Dr. English greets their disclosures impassively, as if a large portion
of his clientele were involved in extended marriages; then he sinks
his probe deeper. "What was your initial attraction to the Eisenberg
family? Would you say that it was mutual for each of the four adults?"
and even "What are your nightly sleeping arrangements?"

Leif's forehead pinches in irritation. "I have to say, Dr. English,
that I wonder where you're heading with this. Aren't we here to talk
about Matt?"

Dr. English thinks calmly for a few seconds before answering.
"Of course. But in psychiatry, we can't look at any individual in isola-

tion from everyone else. We're all parts of several systems—family, school, workplace, neighborhood, city, nation—and for most of us, but particularly for children, the most important of these is family. As a psychiatrist, my work is in large part to understand the dynamics of my patients' families." Leif, who has always argued that the foursome has nothing to hide, suddenly feels himself cornered in the glare of the doctor's searchlight.

And when, after a studied pause, Dr. English reveals his diagnosis, Leif rebels. "Obsessive-compulsive disorder! He's not mentally ill. He's just a little eccentric."

"That's how his behavior strikes you."

Leif flails. "I'm sure he doesn't meet the criteria."

Dr. English stands and draws a thick volume from the shelf of books behind his desk. "Repetitive, apparently purposeful acts are carried out in ritualized fashion," he reads. "Sufferers do not usually derive any pleasure from performing the activities but feel increasingly anxious if they try to resist the compulsions, or if their compulsions are interrupted by others. Hand washing, counting and checking are the most common compulsions. Compulsive acts may have to be performed so many times in a particular way that they seriously disrupt work and social life."

Laura's breath comes short and quick. Leif wants to beat the psychiatrist over the head with his tome.

"What causes it?" Laura asks finally.

"We believe it's a reaction to stressful or deeply disturbing events," Dr. English answers, taking his seat again. "It may involve irreconcilable conflict between social demands and an individual's fundamental urges. Sometimes these urges can be sexual in nature. For example, a person who masturbates but is taught that masturbation is evil may obsessively wash his hands in effort to expiate his feelings of guilt. A child whose parents push him to an unreasonable level of academic achievement may develop a pattern of checking and rechecking his schoolwork so obsessively that the work never gets completed. I'll have to spend a lot more time with Matt to understand his dilemma.

So far I have only formed a sort of working hypothesis."

Leif raises his brows. "Which is?"

"Matt is at an age when adolescents begin to define themselves as sexual beings and begin to seek relationships with the opposite sex. He can only do so by reference to the relationships he sees around him. Your marriage naturally stands in the foreground for him, and this rather sudden change in it has thrown him off track."

Dr. English raises both hands to ward off objections. "I'm not condemning the arrangement you've chosen. I'm quite aware that there are more patterns possible than the standard nuclear family. And it's certainly not my role to uphold any one system as inherently better than another. My point is simply that a child, particularly an adolescent, needs to pattern his own behavior after a clearly defined model. When you take one model and replace it suddenly with a new one, the result is confusion."

Shame wells up in Laura, spills out her eyes onto her cheeks. Leif's face hardens into a mask.

"Matt has experienced the events of the last year or two as chaos," Dr. English goes on. "He's trying to reestablish order. He can't control the larger circumstances of his life, and so he is asserting control over the minutiae. Obsessively. He wants to make sense of the patterns and rhythms in his life, and so he's doing it in the only way he can, through careful, repetitious routines."

A fresh gush pours down Laura's face as she thinks of poor Matt, overcome by the disruption in his life, frantically, desperately trying to save himself like some child piling pillows on his bed to climb above a flood.

"What's your prescription?" Leif rasps.

The long arm of the doctor plucks a box of Kleenex from the end table next to Leif and hands it to Laura. "Unfortunately, there's no quick and easy cure for obsessive-compulsive disorder. It's a long, painstaking process of slowly untangling desires, emotions, beliefs and expectations that have taken years to knot up."

"You're talking about psychoanalysis?" Leif asks.

"Loosely speaking. My approach isn't strictly Freudian. But in the general sense, yes; I mean that I, or someone else, needs to spend a lot of time talking to Matt, really listening to him, and helping him make sense of the conflicting signals he's trying to sort through. I should add that without treatment, the disorder can progress. Some obsessive-compulsives become totally unable to carry out normal activities such as getting dressed, eating breakfast, or leaving the house, because of the hours they spend repeating some trivial motion."

"What about us?" Laura's face is red, raw. "Since we did this to him, shouldn't we…"

"Stop?" Dr. English folds his hands. "Not necessarily. I can't speak for what's best for each of you; you have to decide that. But even if you wanted to, it may not be possible for you to go back to the way things were. It's been what? A year? Relationships aren't made of wire; you can't bend them one way and then simply bend them back again. Not to say you couldn't be monogamous again, just that it wouldn't be the *same* monogamy. I suspect the imprint of the Eisenbergs will remain with you for a very long time, even if you were never to see them again."

A panic crawls up Laura's spine. At the back of her mind, she realizes, she has always assumed that the foursome was revocable. It carried with it the flavor of a game. Now, too late, she sees what she was staking.

"Also," Dr. English goes on, "to split up with them now would be another dramatic change, wouldn't it? Again, speaking purely from Matt's point of view, that could be almost as upsetting as the first reversal in his view of male-female relationships."

"So you're saying there's nothing we can do?"

The desperation in Laura's voice seems finally to soften the tightness around the psychiatrist's mouth. "No. You've already taken an important first step in bringing Matt here. The important thing is that change is a lot easier at thirteen than it would be at thirty-one. We have time."

"And so… we shouldn't do anything differently?" Laura asks.

"Try to provide Matt some stability. Some predictability in his life. If he feels comfortable in knowing what he can look forward to, he may be able to relax his own grip on his daily routine. Try not to throw him any more curve balls." The lips of the psychiatrist curl helpfully upwards.

In the car, Laura can't stop crying. "I just feel so awful, so terrible that *we* did this to Matt. Oh god!" And her face disappears in her hands and her hair. *Obsessive-compulsive disorder.* Heavy with its nine Latin syllables, the diagnosis sounds impregnable. It might as well be *cystic fibrosis* or *myocardial infarction.*

Leif is silent, driving, until she finally turns to him. "So what do you have to say? Don't you feel anything about this?"

He exhales slowly through his teeth. "I don't buy it."

"What?"

"I don't buy it that the extended marriage did this to Matt. I'm not even sure I buy it that he's obsessive-compulsive. He sticks too much to his routine. He reads a lot of books. But I've known a lot crazier people being paid thousands of dollars a month to teach graduate students."

"But he fits the description. And this fight he got into. His teacher is concerned. The principal."

"He got into one fight with some boys who obviously picked on him. He gets excellent grades in school. He's passionate about biology. It's not considered normal in a kid. Other people have trouble relating to that, but it's not his problem."

Laura blows her nose, stares at cars, houses, trees without seeing them. "I can't believe you won't accept it," she says. "Dr. English is a psychiatrist. This is what he does. You're an economist. For you to say you know better than he does is just arrogant."

Leif sighs. "No. I'm not an expert. But as a social scientist, I know one thing. Most of what you'll hear from any of us—economists, anthropologists, sociologists, psychologists and yes, psychiatrists—is bunk. It's made-up stuff. Conjecture, theory and hypothesis dressed up in fancy language and passed off as fact. We like to pretend we have the same certainty about what we're doing as chemists and physicists, but we don't. We don't have evidence for what we say because we can't do experiments the way they can. You can't randomly assign a thousand kids to an extended marriage and compare them to a thousand other kids in a control group. You can't—"

"Leif."

"—prove anything. So what has Dr. English done? He's taken some speculation of Sigmund Freud and and tried to figure out if it would apply to—"

"Leif!" Laura turns on him. Maybe it's the success she's had in the classes she started this semester, all that she's learned, the degree seeming finally within grasp, that's narrowed the gap between them. Maybe it's the consideration that Hiram has shown her, the reverence in his touch, the respect in his voice that has given her new self-confidence. Or maybe she's just feeling the white instinctive rage of a mother whose offspring is threatened. Wherever it comes from, the power to talk Leif down surges in her for the first time ever. "This is Matthew, your son, we're talking about. He's not a theory. He's not a research subject. He's a boy who needs our help. If you can't see that because you're trying so hard to justify your behavior, then you're less of a human being than I thought."

"Justify?" Leif demands. "What exactly is it I need to justify?"

"I think you know," Laura answers. And for once, Leif can't seem to retort—a milestone in their marriage. But Laura is so focused on the problem of her son that she almost doesn't notice. She has already dismissed him in her own mind as an obstacle she'll simply have to work around. But where to go from there, how to help Matt, what to make of Dr. English's ambiguous prescription are questions she can't answer on her own, and so she turns to the person she is now closest to.

Holding her in bed that night, Hiram feels himself shaking. Doubt oozes like black pitch onto his pale pink conscience. What have we done? What have we done? God, what have we done? "Oh, Laura," he says. And then, "I'm so sorry. I know Matt's a little odd, but I never thought it would turn out to be something serious. Crippling. I'm so sorry." He tightens his arms around her, and after a long moment says, "It would kill me if I had to give you up. But if you think we have to stop being together, if that's what we have to do to help Matt, I would understand."

"No," Laura answers. She slides her fingers up into the tight-curled chest hair of this man who is ruining her for normality, who has changed, destroyed, corrupted the natural order of things with his kindness and decency. "No. Dr. English said we should stay together. Even if we didn't want to, we should do it for Matt."

"Whatever we have to do, we'll do it," Hiram says. "I'm sorry." Wide and doleful in the half-light, his face turns to her. "I feel to blame. We always said we were doing this partly for the kids, to give them the benefit of an extended family, more people to be with. But maybe we were kidding ourselves, believing what we wanted to believe. Maybe there's a price you have to pay for being as happy as I have been over this past year. With you. But it should be we who pay the price, not the kids. Not the kids."

"Stop it," Laura orders. "You're not to blame. If anyone is to blame, it's me and Leif. Matt's our kid. We knew what he was like going into this. I should have noticed what was happening with him and pulled back if that was necessary. I was distracted, a little." The back of her forefinger grazes his cheek. "No, it sounds like the best we can do is keep things as steady as possible. As unchanged. That sounds like fantasy, right now. But somehow maybe we can at least provide him whatever the other kids are getting. They seem all right. Ivor, Adrienne, Darby."

***

The light comes on in the kitchen, waking Leif. The faint jingle of jars on the refrigerator door, the slow squeak of a cupboard being opened carefully, the clink of glassware. One by one he discards the other possibilities in his mind: Hiram or Sibyl down from their room for a midnight snack, or Ivor getting a glass of milk. Matt with some kind of kitchen experiment that has to be checked every so often all night. No. Leif, propping his head on his hand, knows it's Darby.

And he knows it's up to him to go into the kitchen. Hiram loves his wine so much he doesn't think anybody can be hurt by it; he'll give a sip, even a whole glass to a child—a little wine with dinner, where's the harm? "Kids in France grow up that way!" As for Sibyl, sweet indignant Sibyl prides herself. She doesn't believe anything like that could happen to *her* children. Laura is too caught up in fretting about Matt to worry about anyone else. Leif, on the other hand, feels himself being challenged. He's always said to the others that they have to treat this marriage as a real marriage. He has always said that by taking more responsibility for each other—for each other's children—they can accomplish what as couples they could not. Did he mean what he said?

Another clink in the kitchen. In a second, she'll be gone. Leif swings his legs from under the covers, snatches Laura's bathrobe as he passes and strides silently into the kitchen. Splat! Standing by the sink as a precaution, Darby has thrown something into it and now is quickly rinsing her glass. In two steps, Leif arrives to arrest the spigot.

Her eyes roll up to him. "What?"

Drops are still splattered all over the basin. Leif dabs one with his index finger and raises it to his nose. The ripening. The crush. The fermentation. It's all there in tiny molecules wafting through his nostrils. He tastes it, tastes another. Yes, no doubt. He exhales a long sad sigh. "Cranberry juice!" Darby says.

Leif shakes his head slowly, the professor's authority in it. "Yes!" her voice is pleading now, but his face doesn't relent. "Okay, yeah. I had a half a glass of wine. My parents don't mind. You can ask them. Daddy gives it to us whenever we want at dinner. I was having trouble sleeping, I just thought it might help."

"Does it usually?"

"I guess." She catches herself. "For some people."

"Darby," Leif puts a hand on her shoulder, looks for her eyes. "Wine, beer—alcohol can be a lot of fun, but it can do things you don't even know it's doing. When you find yourself wanting it in the middle of the night, it's a sign that it's running the show, not you."

Darby steps backward, letting his hand fall. "I don't have to listen to this!" Her gaze flicks around as she remembers other ears. Her voice lowers to a seethe. "I don't even drink a tenth of what you drink every day, with your cocktails and your aperitifs and your nightcaps and your pinot whatever. You guys are smashed half the time."

Leif's lips purse. He has imagined himself working into this role. He was going to build a rapport, maybe start by teaching her how to play something by one of her rock'n'roll idols on the piano, or at least giving her a ride to a friend's house. But it's such a crazy time, so much going on, he just hasn't had the chance! Once he offered to help her with her homework and she sulked as if he were nagging her. And now this is what he must face. "If how much we drink upsets you, then let's talk about that. But, Darby, we're adults and there's a reason why adults are legally allowed to drink and teenagers aren't."

Darby flips him a finger. It's so casual a gesture for her it's like a toss of the head. She's already out of view, on the stairs back to her bedroom, when she says, "You're not my dad."

***

Sibyl would almost have preferred to see Laura sneering instead of biting her lip sympathetically. And there's Hiram, pouting with skepticism and jerking the rocking chair back and forth in agitation. Sibyl swallows hard. She isn't going to cry in front of them. She breathes slowly, gaining control. But she can never remember a moment of motherhood that hurt so much, not when Darby broke her wrist, not when Adrienne's fever raged over 104 for two days. This strikes her to the core. She has failed! Failed her daughter, overlooked what was in front of her eyes.

Leif rises from his chair and kneels in front of her. The shadow of an incipient beard darkens his chin and cheeks. His hair, too, has lengthened since he left PVSU. He gazes up at Sibyl and takes both her hands in his. "Remember you're not alone in this."

Laura leans forward on the couch. "Hiram said you were talking about breaking up the household, going back to the two separate families."

"Yes." Laura is waiting for Sibyl to go on and explain, but what can Sibyl say? Obviously this group experiment has caused this problem. It has disoriented everyone. And Laura's sloppy parenting has infected Sibyl's family. Sibyl held her tongue when Laura bought Darby a halter top, but she can't continue letting her rules be undercut.

"I had that impulse, too, when Matt got into his fight," says Laura. "And of course we'll move out in a heartbeat if you want it. If you really think Darby would be better off. But I think what Dr. English said may apply to Darby, too. Trying to go back to what was before is a kind of change, too. We don't want to upset things all over again."

"Exactly," says Hiram.

Leif squeezes Sibyl's fingers. "I think what's important is to keep a watch on Darby. She's been alone a fair amount. We can't let that happen anymore."

Sibyl extracts her hands from his. He's too kind to say it, but she can see what he's pointing out: that Sibyl returning to work left Darby by herself, or only with Adrienne, for months until the Wrightsons moved in. Could this be when she started drinking? If the two households split up again Sibyl would have to give up her job and stay home to monitor Darby. There's no way Hiram would take on that assignment. Sibyl feels a scream welling inside her stomach.

Leif shifts back on his heels. "From now on, Laura and I can make sure one of us is here whenever she gets home."

Laura nods. "Absolutely."

Sibyl exhales slowly. "I have to ask this. Have any of you given Darby anything to drink, besides a sip of wine at dinner?" She metes her gaze out to each of them, but can't help lingering on Laura. "Have you ever even known her to drink alcohol outside of that?"

Laura shrugs. "A couple of times I got the feeling she'd had drinks at a party. I didn't say anything to her because I didn't know how you felt about it. But I certainly never condoned her drinking, if that's what you're asking."

"I think we can all be very clear to her that she can't do it anymore," says Leif. "But we can't post a twenty-four-hour guard on the liquor cabinet. We should think about getting rid of the booze in the house."

Dump all the alcohol! It appeals to the anger in Sibyl to lash out at something. "Maybe so." And given Hiram's total unwillingness to help out, this may be the only answer.

"It's the only way she won't be tempted," says Laura. "If she comes straight home from school, or only to her choir practice, she'll get used to not having it around."

Hiram stops his rocking. "Whoa, whoa, let's not get carried away! Darby takes one drink in the middle of the night, and immediately we're talking about putting her under armed escort?" His tongue moistens his broad lips.

"It's not one drink in the middle of the night," Sibyl says. "I found a beer can under her bed. Leif thinks the vodka has water in it. She's been sneaking drinks for months. And when Leif confronted her, she said you allowed it."

Hiram shakes his head. "If she's really taking more than a sip here or there, let's ground her for a couple of weeks. But I don't see any reason we should punish ourselves by throwing out perfectly good wine and liquor because she has a problem."

Laura turns to him, surprise wrinkling her forehead. "Hiram! This is your daughter we're talking about!"

Sibyl reaches once more for Leif's hand.

Hiram glances from one to the other, as if he himself were the punished child. "Let me give the brandy to someone, at least," he begs. "I can't stand to see it go to waste."

Chapter Seven

RIDING in the back as usual, Darby doesn't notice what's going on at first. It takes a thump and a shout to rouse her out of a deep conversation about David Bowie album covers with Pence Thorne, who just moved out from Colorado. "Hold him down," someone says. Standing, she catches sight of Dave kicking. Is that? Yes, it is! As Dave draws his foot back, a flash of Matt's face appears: hexagonal glasses still in place, face red and jaws clenched. Remembering the last fight Matt was in, she has expected something like this to happen. Matt has no real friends at school, and that makes you a target for people like JJ and Dave. They've only given him this much space because he beat JJ so badly the last time. As usual, Mrs. Henderson, the driver, is off smoking somewhere. She scans the seats for Ivor. Adrienne is sitting up near the front, but there's no sign of Ivor; he must be at soccer practice. On her own, Darby can't force Dave to leave Matt alone.

"We have to help him," she tells Pence.

"What do you care?"

"He's like my brother, almost."

"He's so weird, though."

"Please? He's getting creamed!"

Pence pulls himself up from his seat. Not the fighting type, he is six inches shorter than Dave, slender, almost feminine, with shoulder-length black hair and a rock'n'roller's leather jacket. "Hey, Dave, give the kid a break," he says. Dave doesn't even turn around. Instead he delivers a kick that looks brutal enough to snap Matt's rib. Pence takes a deep breath and shoves Dave in the back, pitching him off balance. Dave whirls on Pence, who puts his fists up almost comically, like an old-time pugilist. Her heart swelling for Pence now, Darby stands next to him. "Yeah," she asks Dave. "What's your problem?"

"Butt out, wino," says Dave. He looks Pence up and down. "And you, too, pothead. Before I take one of your little dime bags and shove it up your ass." He feints with his left then swings with a right-handed blow hard that smacks against Pence's jaw hard enough to make his head turn.

At that moment, Adrienne screams. It's not a scream from the heart, not a scream of grief or terror, but more deliberate, like a siren. Perched in a seat near the front she sits up as straight as if she were in the school choir, chest puffed and mouth open, blasting the air with her single note for a full ten seconds. For a moment everyone freezes in surprise. Even after it subsides, there's a long moment while the combatants simply stare, deciding whether they're going to start up again. And in that moment Mr. Bennet appears at the top of the bus stairs, his eyes angrily summing up the situation. "You again?" He leans into the crowd and plucks Matt up in his lumberjack arm, hoisting him out of the vehicle.

Darby closes her eyes for a moment, as if not wanting to see the job in front of her. She has been putting it off long enough; now it's time to talk to Matt.

At home that night, Leif threatens to sue the school board. It's obvious that Matt has been singled out; he's getting two days suspension while the other boy gets off with a scolding. Laura, sobbing, tries to reach Dr. English on the phone while Hiram is hugging her. Sibyl tries to get Hiram to let go of Laura so she can make her phone call. Adrienne tends to Matt's bruises with ice. And Ivor promises to put a smoke bomb in Dave's locker.

It falls on Darby to dispense the practical advice. "First of all, you can't let them see you angry," she says.

Matt, rigid on his bunk, has no response for that. His ribs ache, his lip is cut, a tooth is loose. And nothing Adrienne can do soothes the pain. As far as he can tell, he has shown self-control in the face of completely irrational behavior.

"Whatever they say, you either laugh, or ignore them."

Matt swallows a trickle of blood. "He was in my seat."

"I know, Matt. And Dave Newmason is the biggest jerk in the school, second only to JJ Arbust. But it's a public bus. Everybody can sit where they want."

"Obviously. But if I give in to them, they will just keep trying to restrict my movements."

"They're going to keep after you even more if you try to take them on, one against two or three."

Matt has to accept that her conclusion is supported by recent findings. "What do you suggest?"

"Relax. Go with the flow. When you insist on being different, people think you're acting superior. They're going to hammer on you like the one nail that's sticking out of the board. That's number one."

"I can't be like them."

"So number two is find people you can be like. Make some friends."

"You sound like my parents. Ow!" Adrienne, spotting a laceration on Matt's left hand, has dabbed it with hydrogen peroxide.

"Sorry," Adrienne says. "I just have to sterilize it before I put the Band-Aid on."

Darby sighs. "Look, you're a cool dude in your way. You're smarter than anyone I know. You're actually pretty good looking, except for those glasses. And the clothes you always wear. They would not be so bad if you had some variety. And get longer jeans. The point is, it's not completely out of the question that people could like you. So get yourself some buds."

"Buds?"

"Buddies. Pals. Mates. You don't even have to like them. Just as long as you hang around with a group, JJ and Dave and turkeys like that are not going to single you out so much."

"Who?"

Darby was afraid he'd ask that question. "Like anybody. Other kids who like science. Andre Olmov maybe."

"He's friends with JJ."

"Right. Well, you and Adrienne could—"

"Darby," squeals Adrienne. "Matt is a *boy*." Adrienne's bunch are about the girliest girls in the school.

Darby closes her eyes a minute, trying to visualize a face that in any way resembles Matt's. "Can't you stick more with Ivor?"

"I don't play soccer."

"You should start." But Darby has to accept the impracticality of Matt integrating himself into one of the lunchtime pickup games. Ivor's world has no room in it for the non-athlete. Darby leans against the wall, taking a couple breaths before she makes the offer. "Okay, for now, and I mean only until you find someone more like you, you can hang out with me and Pence and Alexandra and everybody. As a favor, because I can't stand to see you killed in front of my eyes. But you need to get your own gang as soon as possible."

***

At lunch Sibyl walks over to Chinatown so she can buy whole-pod star anise and hot bean sauce. The rest of the ingredients she picks up at Safeway on the way home. But just as she's finished cubing the beef, into the kitchen comes Laura with grocery bags in her arms. "Oh," says Laura. "You're making dinner. Shoot. I bought fresh oysters. I was going to serve them with potatoes and stuffed squash."

Sibyl hesitates. She could at this moment wrap up the beef and put it back in the refrigerator. Everything she had planned could wait until tomorrow. But as Laura watches, Sibyl can't help herself from opening a jar of homemade stock and pouring it over the beef. Now it's too late to go back. "We're having Szechwan beef stew."

Laura droops. "I don't know how good the oysters will be tomorrow. I was going to serve them raw. On the half shell."

"I thought you didn't like seafood."

"Fish. I didn't like fish. But it turns out I do, if it's prepared right. And I love oysters."

"You could try freezing them." Sibyl sets a bunch of scallions on the cutting board and whacks off their root stubs.

"I don't think they'd be very good thawed." Then Laura brightens. "I know! I could serve the oysters as an appetizer. Does the stew have potatoes in it?"

They're completely different culinary traditions. And Sibyl had planned rice and stir-fried string beans as side dishes. But Laura is already taking the potatoes out of the shopping bag. "If you want," Sibyl says.

And so there are the two of them, butt to butt. What's particularly infuriating is that Laura never seems to crack a cookbook. A couple of months ago, she was still dishing up canned hash, and now here she is neatly twisting open an oyster shell with Sibyl's paring knife. "May I have the strainer when you're done?"

"Sure, but it's going to take me a while." Laura laughs. "I bought a lot of oysters."

"Well, don't be all night, if we're having them as an appetizer. The stew will be ready in half an hour."

"What's the rush?" Laura picks up another oyster, cracks it open a little faster this time. "Can't you let the stew stew?"

"I'll get the squash started. Maybe we could skip the stuffing, since we're pressed for time."

"But we're not really pressed for time, are we?"

"Only if we want to eat at a reasonable hour."

"Why is it always you who gets to decide when is a reasonable hour?"

"Somebody has to be a little organized."

Laura sets down her oyster and turns to Sibyl. "Meaning I'm not?"

"If the shoe fits." Sibyl finds the summer squash in one of Laura's shopping bags—along with a carton of milk that's rapidly getting warm. She stows the milk in the refrigerator and turns back toward the squash, unaware that Laura has stepped toward the sink to wash her hands. And so two bodies collide, oysters and garlic, soft and firm. Sibyl feels the impact on her left breast of Laura's shoulder. Laura takes a knee in the thigh.

"Ow!" they say in unison, and each of them puts a hand on the bruised spot. Their eyes find each other. And then Sibyl breaks into her low, hiccupping chuckle, and Laura's bubbling giggle quickly chimes in.

Hiram, ascending from the garage, smiles uncertainly. "What's so funny, you two?"

"We're making oysters on the half shell," says Sibyl.

"With Szechwan beef stew!" finishes Laura, as if delivering a colossal punch line, and both women giggle.

"Okay." Hiram rubs the back of his head, baffled. He retreats to the living room.

The meal that finally gets served up isn't the best effort of either woman. The stew waits too long while the potatoes are cooking and the oysters are being eaten. The kids won't touch raw oysters, and Hiram finds the beef too spicy. But no one dwells on the topic. Leif and Hiram want to try out the new lights on the tennis courts at Califano Park. "We could play tonight," says Hiram.

"You mean right now?"

"Why not? There may be a wait for a court if everyone's had the same idea."

And leaving their plates at the table, the men head to different bedrooms to change into shorts and sneakers. Kids scatter toward homework and hi-fi, and suddenly the two women are alone in the kitchen once again.

"The sink could be stacked up to the ceiling," says Sibyl, collecting up the plates, "and Hiram would probably go to a restaurant before he'd think of washing a plate."

"They wouldn't see them if they were stacked in the living room floor," says Laura, following with platters.

"Or the bedroom."

"Let's try it."

"What?" Sibyl stares at Laura, her soapy sponge frozen in mid-scrub, eyes widening.

So they actually stack the dishes on the beds in the adults' rooms, kiss the kids goodnight, and head out to the movies. It's the best time Sibyl and Laura have ever had together, taking in *American Graffiti* and then going for dessert. Sibyl finds herself basking in that glow that everyone loves about Laura. "So where did you learn to do all this fancy cooking all of sudden?" Sibyl asks her.

"Watching you," Laura says.

Sibyl sees she can talk, in a way she hasn't since college, about the thrill of doing work, real work, that your friends respect and that you get paid for; about how she might never have had children if Hiram hadn't insisted; even about the fantasy she once had, years before, of eloping with Sam Brower. "That's before I found out what he calls Nora behind her back."

"Tell me!" Laura commands.

"Mrs. Frigidaire. I think he's starved for sex, and he doesn't know what to do. He's desperate. He talks about her in a way I would never talk about Hiram behind his back."

"Oh, Hiram," says Laura, touching Sibyl's hand, "he wouldn't say anything mean about anybody because he doesn't have a mean thought ever." And Laura finds herself talking about Leif's small hypocrisies, his wanting always to be on top, in bed or in a conversation. Then, without transition, Laura is telling how sad she is not to have a daughter; since she already has two kids (your moral limit, according to Leif), she never will. "I love Ivor and Matt, of course, and girls are more and more like boys, these days. But whenever I see a girl doing typical girl things I feel a little pang."

"But now you do have girls," Sibyl says.

When the two women return, past midnight, they find that Leif or Hiram, or maybe the two together, have not only done the dishes and put them away, but mopped and waxed the kitchen floor.

Both are asleep, and Sibyl and Laura giggle because, without turning on the lights, they can't tell which man is in which bed.

***

Darby confronts a prickly pear, thin, menacing and defiant. Slowly she raises her broad-bladed hoe, then with a quick downward slash severs its stem. Another blow hacks it to the ground and a third plunges to its root ball. Behind it waits a bristling sow thistle, like a Gothic joke.

Hiram and Leif provided the kids with long-handled hoes, explaining that Mexicans have broken their backs with the short kind. Around each stake in the ground, there's a milk carton. The group, and their friends and relations, have been saving up milk cartons for months; they carefully cut the bottom off and flatten it until they can carry it up to the Property for a weekend, so each baby chardonnay struggling toward adulthood can be protected from the mouth of a rabbit or deer. They hoe around the cartons to knock out the close-by weeds which can't be gotten by Rototilling, because if you Rototill too close you break a stake or worse, take out a vine.

It's fertile soil. And so they grow: the cranesbill, dandelion, knotweed and tansy. The ragweed and curly dock, the mouse-eared chickweed, the thousand species of grass. It seems each weekend the weeds return to the row they hoed the weekend before. The air smells of crushed herbs. Darby splatters her pants with green. The August sun calls up the sweat from her scalp where it builds to an oily trickle down the side of her face. She feels an aching urge to throw down the tool, which is wearing blisters through her gloves, and to lie in the tall grass by the river. When her hoe hits a rock there's a clank and a spark.

Ivor's voice comes across the field. "How much did they say they're paying us?"

"Seventy cents an hour," Darby answers.

"And what's minimum wage?"

"Two dollars and something. But we're actually lucky, according to your dad." Her voice takes on Leif's lecturing lilt. "Ever since agricultural society began, children have worked on the family farm. It's no different from doing the dishes or vacuuming the living room floor. It's part of the work of the clan."

"The clan? What are we, cavemen?"

Darby snorts. "All my friends are going to the Eagles' concert." Where there would be beer. And wouldn't a beer go down well just about now? Slowly she sinks to her knees in the dirt. It's been so many months now since she's tasted anything alcoholic, Darby can hardly remember the flavor. They're all over her now, the adults. And this has turned out to be the worst thing about living with the Wrightsons, if Leif isn't home after school, then Laura is. For weeks they picked her up from school every day, as if she were in kindergarten, and even now if she doesn't come straight home or make a phone call, they send out a search party. She can hardly breathe without someone asking if she shouldn't rather be concentrating on her schoolwork. And now these weekends in the country. If it's not hoeing, it's cooking for everyone else, or cleaning house. It's beginning to look like she's got a choice between running away from home or living the life of Laura Ingalls Wilder.

"Desperado," Ivor sings, "Why don't you come to your senses! Stop making us hoe and fix all the fences!"

Darby can't resist a snicker.

Then comes Adrienne's voice. "I got a tired, sweaty feeling," she sings, "and I know you won't let me down, 'cause I'm already hoeing all around!"

When they've run through all the Eagles songs they can think of, Adrienne and Ivor move on to Beatles and Simon & Garfunkel, no longer tampering with the lyrics, just singing to sing. The rhythm seems to boost their pace. In a minute, they catch up to Matt hacking with stolid rhythm in the next row over. She and Ivor finish their rows in tandem and reverse course to head back the opposite way, running through folk tunes and camp songs, working from the most grownup to the most childish so that, by the time they pass Darby, stretched on her back in the middle of a row, they're singing, "Row, Row Your Boat."

"What's this," Ivor asks, pointing at her fallen tool, "a hoe down?"

**

An odd clacking rouses Laura from her novel. In the kitchen, she finds Adrienne stabbing helplessly with a paring knife at a mass of wet semolina.

"Are those lasagna noodles?"

Adrienne nods, unable to talk for sheer frustration.

"Did you put any oil in the water?" Laura asks. "Also, when you take them out, you have to separate them, otherwise—" She stops herself as Adrienne's shoulders begin to tremble. "Come here." She takes the girl in her arms. "Anyway, why are you doing this by yourself?" Over Adrienne's shoulder Laura scans the refrigerator door.

On the left side is the chore wheel, concentric disks with all eight names of household members on the small one and eight weekly cleaning jobs on the larger. Laura hated the idea at first. Was this why they took a plunge from the straight-and-narrow of domestic monogamy? To have their whole lives organized and posted? But after a few days, she had to admit that there were fewer arguments over whose turn it was to sweep, whose turn to do the dishes. And the house got a lot cleaner.

Next to come was the meal calendar; Sibyl laid the whole month out in advance, with one adult assigned as "cook" and one child assigned as "helper" each night to prepare and clean up after the meal. It is indeed Adrienne's turn to help, according to the calendar, but it's Leif's turn to cook. That's supposed to mean being there to at least coach the helper. Instead Leif has left a note: "Dear Adrienne, Sibyl and I are at the Morpetken Institute open house. Please make lasagna from page 259 of the Better Homes and Gardens New Cook Book. Ingredients in the refrigerator. Love, Leif."

"I'm going to have a talk with Leif," Laura tells Adrienne. "But in the meantime, let's see if we have some more lasagna noodles; I'm afraid these are done for."

Laura's hardly in the mood that night for the report that Sibyl and Leif, all flush-faced, bring back from Morpetken Institute. At this big house in Berkeley, two men and three women have combined syllables of their last names: Morrison, Peterson and McKenzie. The household makes part of its income by offering instruction in group living. "True, it's a little scary," Sibyl says. "These guys spend most of their free time analyzing their relationships. But we can at least make use of what they've learned and not repeat their mistakes."

Leif nods. "One of the suggestions is a sleeping schedule. That way you don't have all the tension around whose turn it is to be with which partner."

Laura grimaces. A chore wheel is one thing. But a sleeping schedule?

"It sounds a little scripted," Sibyl says. "But one of the things they talk about a lot is how to avoid jealousy."

Jealousy. That's what leapt up and bit Laura one night when she peeped at Sibyl and Hiram. Left to run its course, would this group marriage split into two couples once again? How would Matt and Darby cope if it did? To her own surprise, Laura realizes she'd miss living with Sibyl, Adrienne and Darby if the households re-divided. Over the past year they've become part of each other's lives in a way that can't easily be disentangled. She draws a slow breath. "Okay," she says. "For now."

***

There comes a scream, the kind that squeezes a mother's heart. Sibyl drops her briefcase to sprint for the stairs, dashes up, yanks open her daughters' bedroom door and beholds a nightmare. Darby stands in the center of the bedroom floor staring in horror at her own forearm. Blood covers the limb so thickly that Sibyl can't see the wound itself. More blood pools at Darby's feet; it stains the windowsill and drips from the shattered glass itself. Even as Sibyl watches, the arm gushes, and more of Darby's life falls onto the floor.

"Darby, my god!"

Darby looks puzzled at her. "I was trying to open the window.

It was stuck and when I pushed, it broke…"

"Come here quickly, to the bathroom!" Sibyl rushes her daughter to the sink, trailing blood everywhere, slopping it over everything, even Sibyl's new suit. Sibyl can't think about that; she can't think about what she was going to do today. A bath towel on the wound absorbs enough blood for Sibyl to see it: a gash from Darby's wrist half way to her elbow. Cover it up! Somehow, stop the bleeding!

Sibyl is wrapping the towel as tightly as possible around Darby's arm, trying to remember everything she's ever heard about first aid, when Leif appears at the door. "Sibyl? Are you guys okay?"

"Darby's got a little cut."

"Do you need anything?"

"No." Darby's blood is soaking through the towel. What should Sibyl do? And why does she turn away help when it's offered? "Wait. Leif? Do you know any first aid?"

Leif pushes the door wider. "Is it bad?" He sees the arm. "Ooh!" In a minute, he has Darby on her back with her arm raised in his hands, a second towel wrapped tight around the first one. He nods his head when Sibyl describes the wound. "Sounds like she'll need stitches. As soon as we get the bleeding stopped, we'd better drive her to the emergency room." Sibyl sits back on the bathroom floor and for the first time sees how much blood has soaked into her skirt and blouse. Leif catches the look. "Oh, that's right! Today's your big day, isn't it?"

Sibyl nods, her lips pressed together. The seminar was scheduled more than two months ago; lawyers are coming from all over the state, and now this. She'll have to cancel. Sam will have to fill in for her, improvising as best he can with whatever she can tell him over the phone. Why? Why did this have to happen today? Especially on a day when Hiram left at dawn to oversee a job in Sacramento?

"What's going on?" It's Laura now, peering through the doorway.

And before Sibyl can answer, Leif is explaining the situation.

"Okay. I guess we'll take Darby to the doctor." Laura sounds as if it were the most natural thing for Sibyl to trust her almost mortally wounded daughter into anyone else's hands.

Sibyl almost laughs at the idea. "No. I couldn't. She needs me to be with her."

Leif spreads her hands. "We'll call you from the doctor's office. And we can ring Hiram up as well."

"You'd better change," says Laura.

"I'm late by now."

"I'll drive you."

"I think Darby needs—"

"Mom!" Darby, who has been lying as if unconscious, opens her eyes. "You should go to your seminar. Let Leif take me."

"No, I couldn't—"

"It's okay." Darby peeks under the towels on her arm. "It's already stopped bleeding. I'll be Okay."

"Are you sure?" Sibyl gets up from the floor. "Thanks," she says to Laura and Leif. She heads back to her closet and finds another skirt, another blouse that will do. While Sibyl changes, Laura blots the blood off Sibyl's boots.

For the first time, Sibyl knows that four equals more than two plus two.

***

Leif, clear for so long, has blurred. Laura notices the change when she comes home from class one afternoon to find him lying on the downstairs bed, head propped in his hand, reading a textbook on oenology. His trim mustache has spread like black moss over his chin and cheeks, rounding and softening. He's not wearing anything under his bathrobe, and so it strikes her how cushioned the sleek flanks have grown.

He glances up, blinks. "Hi, sweetness."

Sweetness! The sharp Leif would never have called her that. Pet. Doll. Baby. Those were his terms of endearment in the years of their monogamy, and though Laura never objected to them, she sees now that they irked her. Pets, dolls and babies you take care of. Sweetness you crave.

When did he stop condescending? Ever since that day in the car coming back from Dr. English's office, when she shut him up for the first time, he doesn't interrupt so much. He's had to admit she was right about the therapy, too. Almost since the day Matt started, they've seen a change in him; no more fights at school and he seems to be making a conscious effort to alter his routine. Just this morning he came to breakfast wearing a red polo shirt and added a banana to his usual two cups of cheerios. Even though he weighed the banana first on a postage scale, Leif had to give Dr. English—and by extension Laura—credit for the change.

Nights when he's cooking dinner now, Leif comes as often to her as to Sibyl with his questions: Do you have to sift flour if the package says "presifted"? Do you put foil over a dish of enchiladas before baking? They've had whole conversations in the last week in which she has made points about Maslow, mitochondria and mimesis that he didn't dispute, didn't even attempt to qualify.

Last week, she asked him to read the first draft of her essay contrasting *Madame Bovary* to *Diary of a Mad Housewife*. For three quarters of an hour as he read it, she paced from the kitchen to the living room and back again, straightening books on shelves, scratching at globs of candle wax hardened on the buffet, opening and shutting cupboards as she thought about how she'd respond when he tore it apart. Valid criticism was one thing, but she wouldn't tolerate any put-downs. If he patronized, she'd point out that she was asking for his comments as a friend and not an instructor. His field, after all, was economics, not English. And she especially wouldn't let him insert any jargon. When he finally came looking for her, her hands balled involuntarily. "Laura," he said, "this is really..." when he paused, she nearly asphyxiated "...perceptive."

"Perceptive?"

"Yeah. I really like it, especially what you say about women's sexuality. It's thoughtful." He laid a hand on her shoulder, and the warmth in it radiated downward through her spine to unclench the muscles around her stomach. He had more to say, had circled whole paragraphs and drawn arrows, underlined words, written in the margins, but all this was to clarify, not alter. When she made herself listen, she could hear the earnestness of his intentions. She saw a man she'd never recognized, a teacher rather than a professor.

Now she lies down next to him. "Hi," she says, staring until he shoves his book aside. In the days of their monogamy, Laura rarely initiated their lovemaking. In the beginning there was a certain red silk camisole that always got the message across, or she might put something extra in a hello kiss. But after her body had swollen and burst with a second child, she felt too used up to want more from him. So weeks passed and then he was upon her, unable to restrain urges that seemed to have very little to do with her.

With Hiram, it's different. At first they made love whenever they got the chance; they'd fall into kissing and stroking almost as soon as the bedroom door closed. When the bracing shock of strangeness faded, they had moved on, emboldened to explore landscapes that had seemed fenced off in their marriages; they read *The Joy of Sex*, sucked and licked, faced in all directions, tied stockings and scarves around wrists and ankles, employed feathers, wax, vegetables, ice. Since then, gaining confidence in their access, they have fallen into calmer lolling and curling, into resting an arm across an abdomen, a leg across legs, a head on a chest. Sometimes all their caressing and holding flares into sex, sometimes it doesn't, and the wonderful part is that no one feels cheated either way because there is enough and will be enough, it seems, forever.

Sated by Hiram, Laura hasn't made love to Leif now in weeks. Months? It's hard to remember. They have slept side by side every other night for most of a year, and every kiss has felt to Laura like a throwback. This afternoon, it's not Laura's day to be with Leif at all, but in this moment that finds Laura and Leif alone (kids at school, Hiram and Sibyl at their jobs), the air smells different.

It's one of those dry, bright, cold California days when the sun outside glances off white stucco, infuses the pavement, endows every mote with a shadow, heats everything it touches but leaves what's shaded to shiver. It slopes through the windows over the bed, picks out the individual strands of Leif's hair, makes black-and-white patterns in the bedspread's wrinkles and folds.

Laura reaches a hand inside Leif's bathrobe. For the longest time, only his eyes register the touch as she runs her palm smoothly along his ribs (still so much leaner than Hiram's) around his shoulders, his sculpted chest. Her fingers trace, for the first time, the pattern of wiry wool around his mouth, along his cheeks. Then her hand slides slowly down his back until it reaches the impediment of the bathrobe belt. In a sudden motion, Leif pulls the robe off completely and stretches on his back, nude in the cool air. There's an erotic disparity now, a reversal that thrills both of them as Laura's hand finds its way across the hairless stomach, stubbled in goose flesh, to the strong thighs, and she employs the texture of her stiff denim skirt, filmy nylons, fuzzy wool sweater, even the ribbons of hair that spill from her head as she kneels astride him.

Chapter Eight

GENERALLY, Hiram has his best luck serving to Sam's backhand, and that's how he starts today. A good idea, it seems, because the balls bounce easily under Sam's racquet for an ace. Five love. Thwock! Same thing on the other side of the court. Thwock again. Satisfying, but by forty-love, Hiram begins to see that he can't take much credit for what's happening today. No matter where he puts the ball, Sam flails at it as uselessly as a cat batting at flies. As the game ends, he calls out, "Sam, you awake over there?"

Sam summons up a smile with such obvious effort that you can see he has swallowed some throttling beast. Awkwardly, he tosses the ball up for a serve and smacks it into the net. At the end of the set, in which Hiram has won every game, he calls for a break. The two settle on the stone bench by the side of the court where Sam begins twirling his racquet between his hands.

"Kind of you to boost my morale," Hiram says.

Sam nods, allows a flicker of a smile.

"You and Nora must have had some night last night."

Now Sam's face turns so leaden that Hiram suddenly feels his own head take weight. "What happened?"

Sam twirls his racquet. "Nora."

"She's sick?"

"No."

"Leaving you?"

Sam gives a quick, ironic sniff. "You're getting warmer."

"You're leaving her?"

Sam nods, still not looking up from his racquet.

"No!" Hiram says. It's not possible. When Hiram first met Sam at Alpha Delta Mu, Sam was the type who dated a lot but never got worked up over anyone. Nora, in their junior year, turned him into the romantic lover, hair tousled, eyes blurry. "This is the girl I'm going to grow old with," Sam said once, smiling into Nora's giggle. "Me and Nora rocking on the front porch of Easy Acres." Pictures fill Hiram's head of Sam and Nora, pressed together, dancing at their wedding, or bundled in the hammock of the beach house the Browers rented every year. He sees their kids, Michelle and Colleen, all giggles as Sam bounces them on his knees.

"When did you tell her?" Hiram asks.

"Last night." For the first time, Sam turns his face to Hiram and Hiram sees a kind of question written there that he's never seen before.

Everyone in the softball group has noticed the way Sam's been staring into the honey of the athletic travel agent from upstate New York, the softball group's only single girl, and Hiram has to ask. "Blair?"

"I know what you're thinking," Sam answers.

Cry, cry, cry, is what Hiram is thinking. He should find some words of comfort, of support at least. Or, since Sam's the one who is leaving, should he be offering congratulations? After all, Sam has found joy with a girl whose poise makes everyone on the field feel so creaky. Only as they sit there, in their tennis togs, backs against the stone of the Rose Garden, Hiram can't come up with anything.

"I'm sorry, Hiram," Sam says.

Which, under the circumstances shouldn't make any sense, but does in a queer way, because Hiram feels that Sam has somehow reneged. It's not just his marriage vows that Sam is betraying, the vows that Hiram witnessed and into which he followed. Sam is betraying the way of life he introduced to Hiram twenty years ago, the play-by-the-rules, work-hard-and-you'll-always-do-well credo he handed down by example. Sam bends his head, the thick eyebrows bunched as if in penitence. But then he draws back, his small lip-less mouth making a smile. "Well, I guess you know how hard it is to keep a marriage going, year after year, sucking it in. And when an opportunity comes along, you think, 'Life is too short to keep eating stale bread.' Am I right?"

This is a question Hiram can't answer. Yes, life is short. Yes, you need change sometimes. But there's another way. That's what Hiram has discovered in these last two years, what he has tried to tell Sam. You don't have to hurt anyone! In fact Hiram feels a twinge of responsibility here, because he defected first. He set the example for once, even encouraged Sam to follow. Only not this way.

"I guess we could have tried the sort of thing you and Sibyl are doing with the Wrightsons," Sam says, reading Hiram's mind again, "a threesome or what-have-you, but you know Nora. She'd never go for it."

"Blair would?"

"Blair…" Sam finally allows the muscles that were bunching skin all over his face to relax. "You have to know Blair. She would have done it for Nora, for me. She's… just incredible. Giving. Generous."

"It's not about generosity," Hiram finally blurts. "It's not charity. It's love, opening up to a new way of life. Maybe if you could get Nora and Blair to see it that way… Or maybe if you could balance it some way. Maybe there's some guy Nora has her eyes on."

Sam stares.

"Oh, come on, Sam," Hiram slaps a hand on Sam's narrow shoulder. "It goes both ways. Look, I'm not telling you how to run your life. I'm just saying there may be a way to keep everyone happy. If you want to. And Nora and Blair are both wonderful people."

"Right," Sam says. "You've certainly found a way to have your cake and eat it, too, haven't you?" His face slams shut. "Any hoo, I'm rested. What do you say we finish the set?"

So they go back to Hiram serving, and Sam missing with every swing, shirt untucked, disheveled, seemingly unaware, in his private haze.

All the way home, Hiram feels that he's holding himself together, that if he lets go his guts will spill onto his lap. He looks all over the house and finally finds Sibyl in back, on her knees dead-heading the cosmos. He tells her the news. She stares at him wordlessly, and then he walks over and kneels next to her. He will never do to her what Sam is doing to Nora. It's their silent pledge to each other, that what they have built together, this garden, this house, this life, will only be enlarged and never ripped apart. He pulls her into him and puts his face in her hair, smooth, cool, yellow.

***

Gently, Laura brushes Leif's hand from her breast.

His tongue stops lashing her navel. His voice comes muffled through the bed clothes. "Is something wrong?"

"It's sensitive."

His tousled face emerges. "You're not...?"

She can't deny it any longer, to herself, to him, to the others. The tenderness in her breasts, her sudden distaste for bacon, the lassitude: it all happened with Ivor and Matt, and now it's happening again. She has fought the realization out of her head for weeks now, because who needs another monumental complication? But she couldn't push it away forever. "I might be."

"Aren't you on the pill?"

For a moment, Laura feels too irritated to answer. Could he actually be wondering if she has a prescription? Or does he mean to ask whether she has been taking the pills assiduously enough?

He cocks his head in that condescending way he has. "Laura?"

"I may have missed a day. Or two." It's just as much his fault as hers, really. Has Leif ever checked to make sure that the tablets were in the bedroom where she needed them? Has he ever volunteered to knock on the door and disturb Hiram and Sibyl so he could retrieve them from the bedside table? He has not, and neither has Hiram. So how can he dare to accuse her of irresponsibility?

"Wow." Leif sits up. "Have you thought about what you want to do?"

"I don't know." And she realizes this is why she hasn't wanted to think about it. Abortion, to her, always seemed immoral. But how can this household take on the responsibility of a new person while still figuring out how the existing people can get along? Where would they even put another child? And even before that, she faces so many rotten months of swollen awkwardness, constant urination, nausea, exhaustion. What will it do to her school work? "What do you think we should do?"

"I'd have to think about it some more, but I think it could be a good thing." He rests his hand lightly on her abdomen. "I mean, it will belong to all of us, right? It's something completely new. A baby with four parents."

That, Laura, realizes, is what she wanted to hear, but hasn't uttered even to herself. The baby could be a symbol—no, an actual embodiment—of their union. A gesture of faith. A few months ago, she could not have felt this way. But in recent weeks, joy has mounted in the house, anxiety declined, like air displacing water in a submarine. The foursome feels less and less like two duos, more and more like a quartet. They have no need of a sleeping schedule now; it doesn't seem to matter who sleeps with whom, or how many days in a row. From all she can tell, the bullies at school are leaving Matt alone. He still hasn't made friends there, but Darby and Adrienne have become like sisters to him. And Laura herself feels closer to the two girls. Darby still complains about all the adults watching her so closely, but she has let Laura take her shopping for clothes. And Adrienne seemed to love the dolls' clothes they made together. Into this household, Laura could bring another child.

"We'll have to add on a new room to the house at the property," Leif says. "We've can't expect any of the kids to share a room with a baby. And maybe we'll have to move sooner, because it's pretty tight here already. But… a new baby. Wow!"

That's more or less how Hiram takes the news as well, the following evening. For a moment, he stares at her, just blinking. "Well it's… good!"

But when they are alone in the upstairs bedroom, he closes the door. "What are you going to do?"

"I think keep it."

"Amazing." He shakes his head and lies backward on the bed. "I never thought I'd have another child. Or… which night was it that you forgot the pill?"

"It was two or three times. Maybe more. Why does it matter?"

"I'm just trying to figure. Were you more likely to be with me those nights or with Leif?"

"Hiram, it doesn't work that way. There's no way of figuring out if it's yours or his."

The big lips are almost pouting.

"Just think of it as ours. All of ours."

He sits upright to hug her. "All of ours."

Sibyl asks Laura to take a walk with her. When they reach the park where all of them first met, she squeezes Laura's hand. "I just want you to know it's your decision. If you don't want to do this, you don't have to. Forget what Hiram and Leif say. They have no idea what it's like to be pregnant, to give birth, and everything after. They think they know. They think they were part of all that when their kids were babies. But you and I know who was up at 1 a.m., and again at 2:30, and again at 5."

Laura, glancing at Sibyl's svelte belly, knows what decision Sibyl would make. She knows what decision Sibyl thinks Laura should make.

But Sibyl goes on. "Knowing all that, if you decide to go through with it, you can count on me. It'll be like my baby, too. I mean, I would treat it that way. You won't be alone."

And Laura turns to give Sibyl a kiss on the cheek.

***

Pulling hard with his pliers, Leif finally dislodges the snap ring. He sets it aside and slides the crankshaft gear out of the Rototiller. Its teeth are worn and blunted. All he's got to do is replace this little gear, and the machine will probably hum along nicely. He'll have it ready by the next weekend, when all eight of them are heading up to the property for one of their work weekends. And Hiram thought it was beyond repair. "Fifteen dollars isn't cheap if it doesn't work," he said when Leif brought the used machine home.

Upstairs the phone rings. Then Darby calls to Leif from the kitchen. Leif finds a rag to wipe his hands and heads up.

"My name's Ben Flagon," says a soft, Boston-accented voice on the other end. "My wife's a friend of Andrea McGraw, your colleague from the university."

Leif hasn't heard from Andrea since leaving PVSU and didn't think he ever would again.

"Oh, yes. How is she?"

"She's doing well. Just had her and her husband over for dinner last week. Listen, I'm working on a feature about communes for *Personality Magazine*, and Andrea mentioned that you were involved in a sort of a wife-swapping arrangement."

Leif can't stand that sexist term and can't believe that Andrea used it. "Then she wasn't paying much attention. We're not 'swapping' anything. We're in an extended marriage. We've extended our marriages to encompass two men and two women."

"Sorry. Right. I knew that wasn't the right term. But it sounds really interesting. I mean right on the cutting edge. She mentioned that it's a really exclusive arrangement, which I think makes it especially interesting. And I was wondering if I could come by sometime and talk to you and the other members of the... marriage for my article."

Leif considers. *Personality* probably has one of the biggest circulations of any magazine in the country. It's one thing to stop sneaking around, to be honest with your friends and neighbors, and another to go public in such a big way. But lately Leif has been feeling that what they've got going is so good, it should be public. So much of what you read about the counterculture highlights the grubby, the violent or the absurd. Maybe it's time for the world to see that even clean-cut, middle-class suburbanites are expanding their definition of family. Still... "Isn't *Personality Magazine* more interested in Sonny and Cher than in social developments? Do they even print articles about non-celebrities?"

"Lots. I could send you some of the stories I've done. I interviewed one of your colleagues at PVSU who discovered a link in the human evolutionary chain. I did a story on a woman who's got a hundred turtles in her back yard because she's trying to save rare varieties from extinction. It's anyone—any *personality*—who's doing something worthy of note. And I think this whole group marriage idea is cool. It's absolutely fascinating, really trend-setting. I know people are going to want to read about it."

"Well," Leif smiles into the phone, "I'd have to check with the others, but I don't see a problem."

"Definitely not!" Sibyl, clearing the table, snatches Leif's dinner plate from him as if in punishment. "I don't need everybody at work reading about my sex life in a national magazine."

"Sibyl." Leif spreads his hands. "You don't have to talk about anything you don't want to. And anyway, this guy isn't interested in the nitty-gritty of what we do in bed. He's interested in the social ramifications of it. He sees us as on the cutting edge, and after all, we are. A lot of people who are locked into traditional, dead-end marriages could learn from what we're trying to do here. It could be an opportunity for us, not only to lead the way, but to talk about what's worked for us and what hasn't. What to watch out for. I think we have almost a moral obligation."

Hiram chuckles. "I wouldn't go quite that far. We're just bumbling along, and I don't know if I have any particularly good advice for anyone else who wants to try group marriage. But as long as he respects our privacy and doesn't pry any further than we want him to, I'm game."

Laura leans across the table to take Sibyl's hand. "I don't think we should do it if Sibyl's not comfortable." She sees Dr. English's pinched head leaning toward Matt. "And I'm worried about the kids. They may become the focus of some attention they don't want at school. You know, teenagers can be so cruel."

Leif nods. When he decided to bring the idea up to the others, he promised himself he'd drop it if anyone objected. Now he is caught up in the challenge of persuasion. "Okay, how about this? This guy, Ben Flagon, seems like a reasonably respectful person. What if we just agree on some ground rules up front—things he can ask about, things he can't? None of us will talk about what happens in bed, other than saying that both women sleep with both men—"

"And that it's very good," puts in Hiram.

Leif grins. "And that it's very good. And we won't let him use the kids' names."

"Any of our names," says Sibyl.

Leif shrugs. "Any of our names."

"But anyway, let's not do it now," says Hiram. "We've got so much going on. Can you put him off until after the wedding?"

"Of course." Leif nods, smiling.

***

The phonograph skips, making Marvin Gaye stammer. Drop lights and old kerosene lanterns sway on their hooks in the rafters so that shadows shift in patchworks. For a moment, Sibyl wonders if the pounding of feet will be enough to knock the whole barn down, the structure is so rickety. Filled with music this way, decorated with crepe streamers and balloons and filled with dancers, the place looks so festive it's almost seems a shame to demolish it. But in the daylight, Sibyl knows it's an eyesore, slouching at the foot of the hill, its corrugated aluminum loose on its sagging frame, rust-stained around the nail holes. Laura allegedly swept the loft this morning, but Sibyl can still see bits of straw tossed by the shuffling feet. There's just no way of fixing it up and certainly no way to clean it.

Building the new house here certainly makes more sense than halfway up the hill where the old one-bedroom farmhouse stands like a museum of mildew. Leif made a half-hearted case for both buildings, the barn especially, as an artifact of postwar rural functionalism, but Sibyl's not the only one who will be happy when they're gone. In place of the barn will rise their new house, plans for which have evolved into an octagonal wonder, designed especially for this double family by Hiram's architect brother. Four real bedrooms will each open onto a common area, so no one will have to go through anyone else's territory; Matt and Ivor get a room, Darby and Adrienne too, and then there will be the two bedrooms for the four adults. The roof, a geodesic dome, will include skylights for each of the four bedrooms, which will form a circle around the circumference of the second floor and redwood siding will blend the whole building into the hill "like the trunk of a big tree," Hiram said.

Sibyl had her doubts about inviting friends to serve as free labor to tear down the barn. But now she feels carried along by the celebration which somehow expanded in the planning from a barn razing to a hoedown. Even tomorrow's ceremony, which at first seemed silly and unnecessary, is beginning to feel right—the honest statement of what this foursome has become.

She has lost track of the kids. Duty and habit tell her she should check; just find them in the crowd and see that they're doing fine. The group resolved at first to serve only soft drinks at the party, but ever since the foursome rid their house of booze, Darby has shown no sign of drinking. The kids seem to take good care of each other. And when Sibyl last saw them, they were playing poker in the main part of the barn. How likely are they to wander from the hub of light—out into the fields where there are no street lamps and nothing to do?

They can't be far and everyone around here knows them and is a friend. That lets Sibyl's mind release its hold on her muscles and her body becomes limber. Her arms and legs swing to the beat. Over there, Hiram, Sam and Bob Eidler make an odd threesome twisting and shaking together for a few minutes, nodding to each other. It's a pity Nora wouldn't come. If only she and Sam and Blair would see it doesn't have to be that way, that love is not a limited commodity.

Now Hiram catches her look and dances his way over to her, a big grin widening his round face. A couple of years ago she'd have said she and her friends were all too old for this kind of dancing, this rock'n'roll freeform kind of thing, and now here they are. Her hair flaps across her face and she sweeps it back to catch across the circle a warm grin from Laura, her comrade, co-conspirator. Whatever doubts she has most of the time, right now, in this moment, she believes.

When night deepens, Sibyl cues up Donovan, Cat Stevens, John Sebastian. Couples glom together. Sibyl stands for a moment uncertain in the center of the dance floor until she feels Leif's hard arms coming around her from behind and she turns to lean against his chest. This now, this is very much like the dancing she did in college, pressed against a boy, thigh to thigh, in a way that's so much more intimate than rock. They hold each other, sway. Sebastian is singing: "So we left the truck and all our stuff and skipped across the sea. To emerald pools in paradise for four of us."

***

Birds are chirping, and Hiram's eyes flick open to the brightness. "Morning has broken!" He remembers singing that last night in the midst of the swirling. He never felt so tipsy in his life, but it wasn't the wine, it was the people, the occasion, that made him talk faster than he himself could understand and forget immediately what he said and to whom. Dozens of his best friends are here, and everybody he loves best in the world (except his brother, who's in Sweden. And his parents—now he wishes he had invited them because they'd certainly be carried along in the sheer joy) to congratulate him! To support him and Sibyl and Laura and Leif in their fantastic union: this brave, impossibly wonderful, new existence they have plunged into! "Praise for the morning," Cat Stevens sang, and Hiram sang along with him. "Praise for the springing fresh from the world!"

Quietly Hiram leaves the three motionless heaps in the grass and finds his way to the farmhouse to shower and shave. Laura and Sibyl discouraged him from his initial ideas of a tie-dyed T-shirt and cut-offs, or a Jewish prayer shawl, for the coming ceremony. So he long ago resigned himself to a brown flannel business suit he bought for a business conference three years ago and a new scarlet tie purchased for this occasion by Laura. Now, on an impulse, he steps outside to a doddering rose bush tangled in weeds in the back of the house and breaks the stem of an enormous red blossom he thrusts through the button hole of his lapel.

Down around the barn, guests are stumbling around looking for glasses and shoes, so Hiram gets the Yuban percolating where the pot-luck was served, with Styrofoam cups and packages of cold Danish. It's a short trek from there back uphill to where the knoll overlooks the neighbor's cow pasture, hills made bluish by distance and, far off, a glint of the Pacific Ocean. By then, Sibyl has cleared away the sleeping things, and Leif and Laura have set up a small table with five sandalwood-scented candles and the head of a sunflower. The others go to change while Hiram greets the guests as they find their way to the top of the hill, telling them where to stand. In an hour, everything is ready, and there's a murmur as Leif and Sibyl join Hiram at the makeshift altar, with Laura close behind.

The crowd has yet to comb and brush away the bleariness of late drinking or shake out the kinks made by curling to sleep in back seats. But the excitement of the occasion has charged the four who stand before them to an electric alert. Leif looks striking in tails with red tie and cummerbund. It's the same, remarkably well-preserved tuxedo he wore the day he married Laura some fifteen years before; the symbolism pleases him. Laura, on the other hand, couldn't possibly squeeze into her old gown, even if she could find it, and even if the baby weren't adding to her girth. Instead she clothes herself in a pale green dress with a swooping neck, the color, she says, "of new beginnings."

Sibyl knows perfectly well where her old wedding gown is and might possibly have pulled it over her still-slim thighs, but instead she prefers the smart maroon pants suit she bought for her second week of work, representative of her new status in life. She's pinned freesias in her hair to reaffirm her femininity.

For the first time in weeks, Hiram remembers his doubts about their choice of officiant. And now here he comes, hand in hand with Blair, last to arrive from the barnyard. Sam Brower is wearing a plaid jacket that Hiram's never seen before, his shirt open at the collar. "Bet you thought we wouldn't make it," says Sam, smiling to break the tension. Regret prickles Hiram for a second. He realizes there's a kind of quid pro quo going on here; in exchange for Sam's endorsement of the foursome, they're being asked to accept Sam's own new direction with Blair. Then the joy of the moment overpowers his hesitation. Sam is bound to see, just by looking at the four of them, that there's a better way!

Sam makes his way to the front of the assembly and, Caesar-like, raises one hand. "Can I have everyone's attention?" The whispering stops. "You all know why we're here. Hiram and Sibyl and Laura and Leif have embarked on a fantastic expedition. They are the new pioneers, my friends, astronauts of society, voyaging through space we thought was impenetrable to planets we never imagined. They've already glimpsed what lies ahead, and they tell me it's fucking groovy." A few chuckles rise from the crowd. "A paradise. We can't all go with them." The laughter swells. "But we can give them a proper send off. I think last night was a pretty good start."

"Ooh baby!" calls Jane Jummel.

Sam raises his hand again. "Now, this is the part where we listen to what Hiram and Sibyl and Leif and Laura have to say to us."

Hiram swallows. "Once the four of us were separate individuals, lonely and looking," he recites.

"When Hiram met Sibyl and I met Leif, we fell in love," Laura continues. She hesitates for a moment as nerves cloud her memory, then continues: "Each of us joined to another was much more than any of us alone."

"Then Hiram and I met Leif and Laura," says Sibyl. "We fell in love again."

"Now we're joining in something bigger and better still," Leif says. "The State of California won't let us call it marriage."

The crowd chuckles again. "Move to Utah," says Bob, getting louder laughs.

"And there's no other word in the dictionary," Leif says.

Then in unison, the four of them finish: "We call it happiness."

"These are the words of William Blake," says Sibyl.

"Children of the future age,

"Reading this indignant page,

"Know that in a former time,

"Love, sweet love, was thought a crime."

Silently, each of the four lights a candle; Laura's yellow, Sibyl's green, Hiram's red, Leif's blue. Together the four flames join to light the wick of the white candle at the center of the table. It flickers silently there for a moment, puny in the great wash of morning sun.

Chapter Nine

"YOU see, we do have spring in California." Laura points out the car window to an orchard of ancient prune trees, their black and twisted limbs set off against the pale grass and their own pink blossoms.

Anna Matteucci nods. At the end of a three-hour car ride with the *Personality* photographer, Laura knows nothing except that Anna is single, comes from Brooklyn and has been working as a freelance photographer for eleven years. She came to California because "you guys seem to be making all the news these days." Scrawny, with hair trimmed boyishly short and eyes planted close under overgrown eyebrows, she has spent the trip smoking Camels and tossing the butts out the window. She asks a few blunt questions, such as, "Isn't it illegal?" and "How do you know whose kids are whose?" then acknowledges all the answers with the same slow nod.

It's a sharp contrast to Flagon, the reporter, who turned out to be a tubby man, quick to laugh, with hair like dried pine needles, a swath of freckles across his nose, gold-rimmed glasses. On his first visit, he flourished what must have been a $25 bottle of St. Emillion, then apologized, because "of course you guys have plenty of wine with your vineyard. I should have thought of that." For a reporter, he at first seemed to have remarkably few questions, instead spinning stories of his own adventures sneaking into Elizabeth Taylor's wedding, getting roughed up by Huey Newton's bodyguard and being tear-gassed in Selma. It was only as the evening slid into night that his eyes seemed to focus more tightly. And when Leif said something about extended marriage as a concept that was sure to catch on, he pulled out a skinny notebook. "That reminds me." He warbled a laugh. "You guys have got me talking so much I almost forgot I'm supposed to be researching an article." Then Leif pontificated into the narrow notebook for more than an hour while Flagon made listening noises.

But Flagon is driving separately from his home in San Rafael for the journalists' weekend visit. To fill the pauses in her conversation with Matteucci, Laura made herself into a kind of tour guide, pointing out all the sights in the three-hour trip. "People say there are no seasons, but when you get out in the country, especially when you're working in the soil, you see that there are a definite summer, fall, winter, and now, spring."

Matteucci glances out the window. "In February, though?"

"I know," Laura says. "The early spring startled me, too, coming from the Midwest. The daffodils bloom in January. "

In a moment, the turn comes for the driveway, a long pitted dirt road. As they bounce down it in Matteucci's rented Skylark, Laura notices something new: a splash of red at the roofline of the farmhouse. Only when they're close enough to park does it become clear what she's seeing. A four-foot-high heart made from plywood is nailed to the eaves and painted red with white lettering that reads, "Hiram, Laura, Sibyl and Leif." By the time Laura has her door open, Matteucci is standing in the driveway with her camera trained on the valentine.

"It's not usually there," Laura says stupidly. She can imagine how the photo will look in the pages of *Personality*. "Just for Valentine's Day, I guess."

"Right." Matteucci backs up to get more of the house in her frame.

"Anyway," says Laura. "You can't use that because it has our names on it."

Matteucci lowers her camera, but before she can say anything, Hiram's voice comes from a hill above the house. "Hello! We're at the hot tub, come on up!"

As Laura and Matteucci approach, they catch sight of him show-ing off his invention to Flagon. When Hiram first described his hot tub idea to her, Laura pictured a wine barrel and couldn't see how more than one person would fit in at a time. What he meant, though, was half of an old oak fermentation tank, six feet in diameter, which he obtained free from a local winery that was converting to stainless steel. Hiram, Leif and Ivor half dragged, half rolled it to a spot with an enchanting view of the fields and hills beyond. He's been able to heat the whole tub, Hiram is explaining, by running a section of pipe from its bottom through a wood stove and connecting it again to the top of the tub.

"Where's the pump?" Flagon asks.

"That's the beauty of it," Hiram says. "It works by convection. The cold water from the bottom flows into the heater." He points to the section of pipe passing into the wood stove. "The heat causes it to expand, forcing it out of the top of the pipe into the tub. As the water cools, it sinks back down to the bottom, where it flows into the pipe and gets heated again. My biggest problem has been patching leaks, and as of today I think I have them licked."

Laura introduces everyone. Then Hiram pulls a thermometer by its string from inside the tub. "A hundred and one. We are ready to roll. Who'd like to be my first customer?"

Flagon laughs, and Matteucci crouches to get a better angle on Hiram with the thermometer.

"Hey," Laura says. "No faces in the magazine."

The camera sinks again to reveal Matteucci's scowl.

"I guess the message didn't get through," says Flagon. "I promised these guys we'd just take shots from behind or with their faces hidden or whatever."

Matteucci whistles low.

But now Laura is saved by Leif's voice hailing from below. "Laura? Sibyl?"

Heading back downhill, the four of them find that the Wright-sons' old Plymouth wagon has joined the Skylark and Flagon's

Mustang to turn the driveway into a parking lot. Already Leif has equipped himself with work gloves. Everyone shakes Matteucci's hand, and the photographer follows them out into the mud.

Whatever they've agreed to, or thought they've agreed to, Matteucci doesn't seem to pay much attention, snapping away from behind, in front, above, below and all sides.

"Don't worry," she says. "We can crop out whatever we want later."

Still, Laura can't help biting her lip. Maybe they should have gotten the agreement in writing.

"Ready for a hit?" says Flagon, who has come up behind them with a stake pounder in his arms. All morning, he has made ostentatious efforts to help out, pounding the odd stake, fetching tools and chattering away. Far from cloaking his opinions, the way Laura thinks reporters are supposed to, Flagon keeps bursting out with endorsements like, "I think it's so boss, this whole idea." And Laura wonders if the Eisenberg-Wrightson experiment fascinates him so much because he's frustrated in his own marriage. "Now, how did Leif put it to you exactly?" he asked. "My wife, Kathleen, rags on me if I help another woman put her coat on." "You keep up all this stake pounding, and we're going to have to pay you," Laura says.

"Hey, I see people slaving away, and I can't just kick back. Anyway, this stuff comes naturally to me. I'm an old farm boy from western Massachusetts. When I was a kid, some of our neighbors still plowed their fields with horses." Everyone stands back to let him drive the stake.

For lunch in the farmhouse, Laura and Leif serve chicken soup with sourdough French bread, salami, Camembert, persimmons, banana bread, imported pilsner. Flagon tucks in with gusto. Hiram shakes his head. "We're going to have to roll you home." Flagon roars as if it's the best joke he's ever heard.

All the merriment delays their return to the fields until almost two. That puts them behind the schedule Leif has laid out for the month, so it's already dark by the time they lay off. The little house fills with the aroma of baked beans from a big pot Hiram's got going in the oven. Flagon stopped at a winery on the way and has a whole case of cabernet that he's only too willing to share. Hiram agrees quickly, and no one mentions Darby, who, anyway, has been sober all these months. It's wonderful to be able to fill up a glass again without having to run to the wine house. The remains of the cheese and bread disappear. Flagon regales them with more stories of covering the civil rights movement. By now, Laura is so used to Matteucci's camera flashing that she's almost forgotten it.

Despite their parents' admonitions, Darby and Adrienne can't restrict themselves to ten-minute showers, and Ivor emerges from the bathroom still fully dressed to announce that there's no hot water left. "This is serious." He pulls back a pant leg to show dirt up to his knee. "I'm not going to bed like this."

"Good thing the hot tub's ready," says Hiram. And that starts them joking about everyone crowding in, under the stars. Before the meal is over, Hiram goes up the hill with a flashlight to rebuild the fire in his stove, returning with a satisfied report.

"You wanted the full commune experience," says Laura. She raises her glass in a mock toast and swallows its contents in a gulp.

The reporter opens his mouth then shuts it again.

Hiram lays a hand on Flagon's arm in mock reassurance. "What your wife doesn't know won't hurt her," he says.

"How far is the nearest hotel?" asks Matteucci, who has turned deeper and deeper shades of red since her second glass.

"Chicken!" says Leif.

"You're in no condition to drive," says Sibyl. Five bottles stand empty on the table.

"You mean," says Hiram, tipping his chair back on its hind legs, "you expect all of us to bare our souls while you won't even bare your asses?"

Matteucci scratches her head, causing flakes of vineyard soil to fall from her caked hair onto the table.

"Tell you what," says Leif. "If you two let us take a picture of you in the hot tub, you can use whatever photos of us you want."

Around the table, the giggling stops. "And names?" Flagon glances around the room. "Everyone's agreed?"

Hiram raises his index finger. "But no cheating. No bathing suits or underwear or anything."

As the six adults trek babbling up the hill, Laura laughs to herself at the silly bargain that it took to get the journalists to unbend a little. What are they afraid of, that the foursome is going to grope them? This has nothing to do with that! This is just a warm soak among the trees and the grass on a chilly night. Are they afraid that somebody's going to see their private parts? As if everyone didn't have more or less the same equipment! A hand touches her elbow, and Sibyl's face appears, pale in the darkness. "Laura?" Her voice is almost a whisper. "Are you sure you want to do this?"

"What, take a nude soak?" After all this time, Sibyl can still be so prudish.

"Don't be idiotic. I mean the photographs."

Laura stares at her, trying through the wine in her brain to sort out what Sibyl is referring to. Whatever it is, there's no reason for Sibyl to be insulting about it. She's afraid to have her picture in the magazine, is that it? Laura herself had been afraid, too, but at the moment she can't even remember why. Trust Sibyl to put a damper on the exuberant feel of the evening. "We have nothing to lose but our clothes!" Laura bursts with glee at her own sense of humor.

Sibyl smiles, swaying a little in the starlight; then her brow wrinkles, and Laura can tell Sibyl has had a few too many drinks to be quite as much of a stick-in-the-mud as she usually is. "Well, at least I'll get some towels," Sibyl says and heads back down the hill. By the time she gets back, Hiram has already stripped and climbed in, followed by Leif, white hindquarters mooning the moon itself. Laura can't wait to go in herself, rather than stand around shivering. And she's glad when she does. It's amazing how hot Hiram has managed to get the water with his little stove. After the initial shock, she feels her muscles unclench, her body lose its weight.

"Let me just get a shot of the four of you," Matteucci says, turning to retreat, but everyone yells and splashes until she and Flagon keep their promise. In they come, Flagon rueful, the water line just cresting the curve where belly meets chest, Matteucci, grim, crouching so that the water hides everything below her shoulders.

"Shit, I feel dizzy," Matteucci says.

"Better get out," Sibyl advises. "The truth is, you're not supposed to drink before getting into a hot tub. Something to do with the boiling point of your blood, I think. Probably none of us should be in here."

"You've fulfilled your end of the bargain." Hiram waves an arm magnanimously. Laura and Sibyl help the photographer climb over the edge to the stool Hiram has set against the side of the tub, and Sibyl points out the towels she brought.

"Jeez!" Matteucci says, teeth audibly chattering.

"Let me come down and get you set up with some blankets and a pillow in the living room," Laura offers.

"No, it's okay, I've got a sleeping bag in the car. I'll just stretch out in there." Her flashlight bobs down the hill for a dozen yards before it disappears behind bushes.

The view from here, even at night, is everything Hiram promised it would be. Below, the hill sinks out of sight into a silver-gray emptiness with trees, roads, buildings only faintly etched. Above, between silhouetted oak branches, an even greater void sparkles as it never does in the city. The hot water cradles Laura's body against the night air. The group's bantering subsides into reflection. Sibyl and Leif begin picking out constellations.

A flashlight gleams.

"Anna?" Hiram says.

Suddenly, blinding light blazes into the tub. "Say Camembert!" comes Matteucci's voice.

As their pupils shrink in the glare, they can make out the photographer adjusting the battery of floodlights she has positioned above the tub, an orange extension cord trailing back toward the house.

"Oh, come on, Anna!" says Hiram. "This is too much!"

"Fair's fair," Matteucci answers from behind her camera. She sounds more cheerful than she has since Laura met her. Click!

Sibyl crosses her arms over her breasts, and Laura finds herself doing the same. Click! Hiram is still shaking his head. Click! Leif faces the camera with leonine indifference. Click! Click!

"You don't want me in this," says Flagon, hoisting himself from the tub with unexpected agility.

Leif's arm comes around Laura's shoulder, and the four pose together an instant for Matteucci's eager lens.

After that, Laura tries Matteucci's own dodge, submerging herself to the neck. Then she turns her back to the camera. Finally she gives up and tries to ignore it. It's hopeless, though; with the light burning into the tub and the eye of the camera following her everywhere, the moment is shattered. In the face of Matteucci's click-clicking, Sibyl, Hiram, then Leif abandon their bath.

Matteucci finally flicks off her floods, and the world vanishes.

***

Leif bends over the hood of the rusty yellow John Deere machine. He's stripped to the waist of his cutoff jeans, feeling the sun on his back. Hiram is lying underneath with a wrench, only his strong hairy legs with their hiking boots visible to Leif, who is expounding on his favorite subject. "There are a few people who are looking at these sorts of social questions. Gary Becker, in Chicago, says that discrimination hurts the economy because employers aren't getting the best people for the job. So market forces, too, are working for integration, women's liberation. The next big thing is gay rights."

From inside the depths of the tractor comes Hiram's voice. "Did you ever want to try it?"

"Writing about discrimination in economics?"

"Making it with a man."

Leif freezes with the fan belt in his hand. For a second, he imagines himself and Hiram, lying in the dirt of this field, mouths pressed together, Hiram's round stomach against his, Hiram's broad fingers on his cock. He squints to clear the vision from his head. As widely as he has willed open the strictures of his Calvinist upbringing, he's never been able to admit, even to himself, that he could want such a thing. "No."

"No?" Hiram sounds skeptical.

"Did you?"

For a few seconds, only the clank of Hiram's wrench comes from under the tractor. Leif wishes he could see Hiram's expression. "I guess everybody fantasizes about it," Hiram says finally. "But since I haven't gotten around to it by now... Shit!" He bangs. "This thing is corroded solid."

***

Despite her condition, Laura still insists on the jogging routine she and Sibyl started months (it seems like years) ago. The least Sibyl can do is let Laura have the first shower. But this time Laura insists that Sibyl go first, only to find herself thumping on the bathroom door five minutes later. "Sibyl?"

"Who is it?" Sibyl's voice is muffled in her cocoon of water.

"It's me, Laura. Ivor's in the other bathroom and I really, really need to pee."

"Oh, sure. Come in!"

The room is thick with Sibyl's steam, the scent of Prell. On the toilet neatly folded are her castoff black panties, white bra, T-shirt and shorts, and next to them the maroon silk pajamas into which she will change. It makes no sense to Laura to fold what you're going to toss in the laundry, but she takes care not to undo the tidiness as she moves the garments to the counter by the sink. She pulls down her pants and sits. "Who's cooking tonight?"

"Hiram and Adrienne."

"Uh oh."

Sibyl laughs. "This time I am absolutely going to refrain from getting involved. When he was making pork chops with Ivor last week

I started out by showing them how to brown the meat and the next thing you know I was cooking the whole meal."

"I never go anywhere near him when he's cooking." Laura dabs herself but refrains from flushing so as not to affect Sibyl's shower. She realizes there's no point going out of the room in her sweaty clothes, only to come back in five minutes and take them off, so instead of pulling her shorts back up she slips them off. T-shirt and bra follow.

Sibyl turns off the shower. "You still here?"

"Yeah, I'm coming in after you, if you don't mind."

"No, no, that's fine." Sibyl pulls back the green plastic curtain and the two women face each other. Of course, they've seen each other nude before. As far back as Fallen Lake they beheld what there was to behold. They've visited hot tubs since then, been in dressing rooms together, and there have been summer nights when one or the other dispensed with her bathrobe on the way from bed to toilet and back. They just haven't ever stood quite like this, in such private and humid confines, nose to nose, breast to breast. Cunt to cunt. Sibyl is spangled with droplets, her hair slicked into a tawny tail, her chest pink from the heat. Laura is still salty from the run. A year, even six months, earlier they would have avoided such a moment and if it came, they would have fluttered and dodged away. Now they linger with half a smile on both faces. After a second, Laura shakes her head as if to say, "It's already too complicated." Sibyl lets out a soft hiss of amusement and reaches for her towel. Laura steps aside to let her exit the shower.

***

"Oh, this is cool," says Matt. "You hardly ever get to see this."

Darby leans down, hands on her knees, to peer into a shallow pool amid the weedy rocks. A pinkish orange starfish has wrapped two of its three crusty arms around a black clam.

"Are they hugging?" asks Adrienne, whose long hair hangs over her face as she bends.

Matt laughs. "You wouldn't want to be hugged this way. The starfish has suction cups on its arms. It's slowly pulling the shell open. When the starfish gets the shell open enough, it will insert its stomach and digest the clam right inside the shell."

"Its stomach comes out of its body? Eew!"

Matt nods. "Through its mouth."

"Amazing," says Darby.

Warmth pumps through all the vessels of Matt's body. Everyone is listening to him, everyone fascinated. At school for months now he has taken shelter in Darby's circle, so JJ and the others have left him more or less alone. But Darby's friends only tolerate him at her request. Here, at this moment, with Adrienne and Darby and Ivor, Matt truly belongs.

"I think that's what it would feel like if you kissed Mrs. Devereau," says Ivor.

Darby grins, picturing Ivor in deadly embrace with the most dreaded English teacher at Pleasant Valley Junior High. Mention of Mrs. Devereau reminds Darby how soon spring vacation will end, and a pang of wistfulness shocks her. Is it possible she doesn't want this to end? She started out the week feeling so resentful because the grownups had taken her away from everything and everyone to this beach house with no TV, record player or even phone, let alone booze. The first two days she hiked into town just to call Alexandra on the pay phone. But soon her money ran out. The beach here is usually too cold for sunbathing. And after hours of listening to her transistor radio, she got bored of that. Ivor disappeared on long jogs along the road. Matt and Adrienne went on hikes. Darby slept more than it seemed possible for a human being to sleep.

Then, out of desperation, on Tuesday night she organized a game of poker. The next day they played a raucous adults-versus-kids touch football game in the sand. Then they harvested and cooked mussels. There was a whale-watching trip. And a campfire on the beach with Laura playing the guitar, Ivor on harmonica. And Darby singing.

A chill wind whips across the water. A week ago if you told Darby she'd get up at five in the morning to look at fish, she would have laughed in your face.

"And the really amazing thing about this starfish?" Matt says.

"If you cut it up into five equal pieces, each one would regenerate into a whole new starfish."

"Damn." Ivor jumps over the pool, landing with a squish on a rock covered in brown sea weed. "That's exactly what I was planning to do to Mrs. Devereau if she makes me rewrite my *To Kill a Mocking Bird* essay. Can you imagine five Mrs. Devereaus?"

***

They all need ChapStick after a weekend at the beach, and Sibyl volunteers to run into the roadside market. Hiram, in the driver's seat of the van, taps rhythm to the Bee Gees song on the radio. He's in such an exquisite mood, even Darby's music sounds good to him. But he stops tapping when Sibyl comes out. She's reading a magazine as she walks, and there's something disturbing about her open mouth, her lowered eyebrows. "It's come out," she says when she reaches the car.

"What has?" Hiram asks.

"Here." She hands a magazine to him. "I got two of them."

It's been so many weeks since Flagon and Matteucci came up to the property, that Hiram has almost forgotten about the whole episode. Now he feels his face heating. The first thing you notice about the spread in *Personality Magazine* is the huge photo—stretching across most of one page and onto the next—of Hiram, Sibyl, Laura, and Leif naked in the hot tub. The four stand in a sheepish line with Hiram and Leif on either end, their arms across the shoulders of Sibyl and Laura, whose own arms cross to cover their breasts. White block letters set against the black of the night above their heads read, "THE MORE THE MARRIER." Beneath that, a smaller headline says, "Group marriage enthusiasts find monogamy just too two-dimensional. Their numbers are multiplying." At the bottom of the page, there's a photo of the farmhouse with the oversized wooden valentine nailed to it. Hiram flips to the article.

WHEN LEIF WRIGHTSON AND SIBYL EISEN-BERG FELL for each other during a casual softball game in the spring of 1971, both were already married with children. But where many lovers would have seen a curve ball, Sibyl and Leif saw a slow pitch in the strike zone. Both wanted to put into practice theories Leif had developed as an expert on polygamy at California State University, Pleasant Valley. Fortunately, their spouses were also smitten with each other, and the two families shacked up, joining a growing trend of such group marriages across the country.

The article goes on to give some statistics and quote other people in extended marriages before coming back to the Eisenbergs and Wrightsons:

But there are drawbacks as well, says Sibyl Eisenberg. "To connect four points with each other, you need six lines. That's how many relationships we're dealing with. So that means six times as much negotiating and compromising as in a normal marriage." The group is debating whether to live full-time on 400 acres it has purchased in the wine country. The move could derail the career aspirations of 40-year-old Sibyl, who recently took a job with the San Francisco offices of the U.S. General Services Administration.

Perhaps the most difficult challenge for the group is their collaboration in the rearing of Sibyl and Hiram's two daughters, Darby, 14, and Adrienne, 12, and the Wrightsons' two sons, Ivor, 15, and Matthew, 12. In theory, kids should thrive in group marriages because, "they have more grownups to spring off," says Hiram Eisenberg, 40.

But reality for this group has proved otherwise. Matthew Wrightson began seeing a psychiatrist last year to cope with the turmoil of having so many parents. And the household has had to ban alcoholic beverages to keep them out of reach of Darby Eisenberg, who calls group marriage a "bad trip." "I just want to have a quiet, normal teenager life," she says.

Obsessively, Hiram finds himself reading each headline and caption over and over. A heat of embarrassment washes over him. Everyone he knows will be talking about this for weeks. He wants to take it back, to hide the magazine away.

Darby has run into the store to get two more copies.

"We'd better get back on the road," Sibyl says finally.

"I just can't believe they did this to us," says Hiram. But then he realizes what's bugging him is not so much what the journalists have done as what the family seems to have done to itself. It's as if they all wanted to look as bad as they possibly could. He starts the van and pulls back onto the road.

Leif is silent, still studying the article. Matt, too, is unreadable. Laura looks close to tears.

Hiram holds back as long as he can. He doesn't want to get into this in front of Matt, but in the end, he can't help himself. "So, Darby. You made the big time. *Personality Magazine*."

"Yeah, I guess." Darby sounds bored.

"Making your parents look like monsters and yourself look like a juvenile delinquent." Hiram glances in the rearview mirror, trying to catch her eyes. "You know, Darby, there's an expression, 'Don't air your dirty laundry in public.' You know what that means?"

In the mirror, he sees Darby flushing. "You guys invited him to interview us."

"We did so expecting a little more respect and forbearance from him, and certainly a lot more maturity and self-restraint from you."

"It was a long time ago. I was just... tired of hoeing."

So this is her way of punishing everyone. Hiram can see it now. He sighs a long-suffering sigh. "I don't think you realize what you've done here. This is not your student newspaper. This is a national magazine. Everybody you know is now going to read that you have a drinking problem."

"I don't have a drinking problem. And I didn't tell him you guys threw out all your booze."

"You didn't?"

"He already knew. I thought you told him."

"What?" Hiram glances at Sibyl, who herself is twisting in her seat to read Darby's face.

"When did he ask you about it, honey?" Sibyl asks.

"I don't know. A couple of weeks ago. I answered the phone, and I was going to get you, but he said he wanted to talk to me anyway.

He said he was just following up on some stuff—what kids at school think, whether I'd ever want to be in a group marriage, stuff like that. He mentioned that he'd heard about the liquor thing and said he was once arrested for drunk driving. I thought he was just chatting. I didn't think he'd put it in the article."

Laura's voice is weak. "Did he talk to you, too, Matt?"

"Darby handed me the phone."

"And you told him that you..."

Matt hesitates. "He gave the impression you had already spoken to him about Dr. English," he says.

"It's not Matt and Darby's fault," Sibyl says. "We should have told the kids if we wanted them to be discreet."

Hiram can't let that one go by. "Like you were?"

"What's that supposed to mean?"

"You made it sound like we weren't getting along, like we were having big fights."

Sibyl's voice is steely. "I just said we have a lot of meetings now. I was trying to be honest."

Now Leif chimes in. "I did wonder, Sibyl, what you meant about not wanting to move. It gives the impression that you've got doubts, which I haven't heard you express to the rest of us for some time."

"You knew I wasn't crazy about the idea of quitting my job and moving someplace where I have to drive an hour to go to the grocery store."

"Oh god!" Laura breaks in. "Please can we not do this? Can we not tear into each other?"

"Okay, Laura's right," says Hiram, patting her on the thigh. "The question is, how did Ben know about this stuff?"

Everyone is silent.

"Leif?" Hiram asks.

"Not from me." Leif shakes he head slowly.

"Sibyl? Laura? Ivor?"

They all deny it.

"Adrienne?"

But Adrienne, still childlike in her innocence, has fallen asleep in the farthest back seat of the van.

***

Turning the corner, Darby stops. Parked in the street in front of her house, the van looks like something from a science fiction movie with its enormous arm reaching a saucer to the sky. Its engine rumbles softly as if it were poised to take off. A few steps closer, and the initials of the local TV channel become obvious. Dread pushes her back. She could turn now, flee, back to school, back to Roxanne's house. But curiosity pulls her like a conveyor belt.

Inside the house, huge white lights whiten her living room. Three men in jeans and a woman in a blue and red suit turn at the sound of her entrance. There's a cameraman, someone focusing lights and a third man holding a microphone on a boom over Leif's head. Leif offers Darby a half-smile. In the eerie brilliance of this scene, she can see her household has been transformed. All the colors are bleached pale, and all the space is filled with intruders. In this instant, she understands that her life as she knew it has ended. She wants to scream, to pick up the poker from the fireplace and smash these lights, smash this camera, drive everyone away.

The woman signals to a man with a camera, beams at Darby and rushes forward with her hand outstretched. "You must be Darby!"

"How do you know my name?"

"Excuse me!" Laura appears from the kitchen to take Darby by the arm. "We have a clear understanding. None of the children are giving interviews." Laura tugs Darby away from the lights, away from the people, but nowhere in the house can they escape the sound of the hum from the truck outside, the sound of Leif being questioned and giving answers.

Chapter Ten

LAURA can't stop looking at the red and clotted mess in the toilet. Gone! Perished before it had a chance to laugh or cry or breathe a lungful of air. Before anyone knew if it was a boy or girl, silly like Ivor or solemn like Matt. And why? Why did it come if it was going to leave so soon? Did Laura cause this? She let fears into her body: fears for Matt, fears for her studies, fears that the world outside will come down hard and destroy them. Deadly fears. And so she failed everyone. A sob comes out of her. This baby was their hope, it would have held them together no matter what happened.

"Laura, are you in there?" Sibyl knocks at the door. When Laura doesn't respond, she enters.

"Oh, sweetheart!" Sibyl dampens a wash cloth in warm water, helps Laura clean herself, follows up with a towel. With Laura's permission, she flushes, and soon the two are off to the doctor. In the waiting room, she keeps an arm around Laura's shoulders. "It's not your fault," she keeps saying. "Sometimes it just happens. More babies are stillborn than live."

"Then why do I feel so awful?"

"It was a life. It was inside you. And now it's gone."

***

Nothing else is certain for Hiram except that he must enter Laura, must fold himself in her, must lose himself. He strips himself, strips her. His mouth searches for hers. Then he draws back. Something has happened to her tongue. Someone pulled the plug; it moves so listlessly! Her hands flutter briefly at his chest, then fade.

He rolls back from her. "What's wrong?"

"Hiram, I'm sorry. I just can't. I'm all ripped up inside."

"Oh!" He strokes her cheek. "From the baby?"

"The procedure they did afterward. I feel like I've been Roto-Rootered."

"I'm so stupid! I should have thought. Forgive me!"

From the kitchen comes the jangling of the phone, and Ivor's voice summoning Leif. *No comment.* Hiram sends the message telepathically. *Just say, "No comment" and hang up the phone.* There's a pause, and then Hiram can hear Leif's resonant exclamation. "Delighted!... Only a few words... Absolutely vestigial... legacy of the agrarian economy..." He's at it again, and after what they agreed! Hiram wants to jump out of bed and wrap the phone cord around Leif's throat.

At this moment, to justify this, all the phone calls, the jeering of friends and the sneering of business partners, Hiram needs Laura even more. He needs to lose himself in her oblivion, to swallow her like a drug. But now the ghost of the fetus hangs over them like a scolding finger. It's his fault for not using a condom, for having so much sex with Laura, for wanting her so badly, for creating this whole group marriage with his will and his desire, his fault for daring fate with his happiness. If he had left Laura alone, she would not have gone through this pregnancy, Matt would have been a normal social teenager, and they would not have had their lives wrenched open by crowbar of the media, their insides pulled out for public inspection. "I'm sorry," he says again.

Her breath catches.

Through the darkness he reaches to take the tear from her cheek. "It hurts so much?"

"No, it's not that, I..."

"We'll wait until whenever you feel better. There's no rush."

"No. I mean I miss her."

"Who?"

"The baby. I miss the feeling inside me that someone is coming, someone important. I felt like I was carrying... hope."

***

Sibyl reaches for shoes in the back of the upstairs bedroom closet and finds the silver boots that used to get so many comments. The heels are only slightly worn, the scuff mark could easily be rubbed away; they've still got their shine. But it seems like another Sibyl in another time who took such pleasure in their outrageous hipness, who wore them with skirts and relished the attention. A pair of brown suede flats will do just fine for today. She's got slacks that match and a beige shirt. She looks in the mirror. The pouches under her eyes have faded, at least; she's had one good night's sleep since everyone agreed to leave the phone off the hook at night.

The calls from the reporters aren't the worst of it. After a while, you learn to deal with them like telephone solicitors. "Sorry, no comment." All except Leif, who for days insisted on giving interviews. He seems to believe that if he can just get enough time to explain, just put everything in the right terms, then everyone will understand, and the extended marriage movement will sweep the world. Part of her can't help admiring his faith, but the rest is consumed with fury, because as long as Leif keeps talking, the calls keep coming, night and day, from all over the world, not just from reporters, but from anyone Sibyl ever knew anywhere in her life.

The ones she loves are the hardest to face. "It's one thing to fool around in private," said her father. "Did you have to make yourselves jackasses in front of the whole world?"

Then Rose Eisenberg: "I can't go now to get my hair cut because there will be a copy of *Personality Magazine* with my son and daughter-in-law bare naked inside."

Colette, her best friend from her sorority, won't even take her call. All this time she thought she was being swept up in a wave that was washing across the whole country. Now she's being treated as if she invented group marriage.

Sibyl bends over Leif asleep on the bed. His beard has curled over his face like ivy on a monument. Finally last night he agreed to stop answering calls. "Just for six months," as Hiram put it. "Until things calm down." The fact that Leif's mouth has stilled makes him more handsome to her than he has been in the week since *Personality* hit the stands. Last week, as a peace offering, he said he would make breakfast for Sibyl every morning. But after weeks waiting around for eggs Benedict and buckwheat pancakes, her efforts to wake him in time to cook for her became half-hearted. Anyway, a bite of toast will suffice for breakfast this morning; Sibyl can't wait to get to work.

The only other person in the kitchen is Adrienne, quietly consuming corn flakes while reading *Black Beauty*. Sibyl gives her shoulder a squeeze. "Didn't you read that already?"

"Uh hunh." Adrienne alone, out of everyone in the household, seems unaffected by the turmoil around her. Every day she rises cheerfully, makes herself breakfast, gets herself to school, and makes it home or to her ballet lessons without fuss or worry. For a moment, Sibyl bathes in that calm; mother and daughter finish their meals in silence.

But when she opens the front door to leave for work, Sibyl jumps backward. Standing on the front porch, so close to the threshold he must have been peering through the peephole, is a man with hair down to his waist. His narrow, pitted face comes to a tip in a long beard. Instead of a jacket, he's wearing a blanket pinned at the chest with a Celtic broach. His jeans are patched; he's got no shoes and he's grinning. "Hey!"

Sibyl swallows.

"Are you Sibyl?"

Goose bumps rise along her arms and legs. Is it really possible that total strangers can now actually recognize her? "What do you want?"

The man smiles. "I just wanted to tell you that you guys are so bitchin'. I'm *from* Pleasant Valley, and this town, this whole county, is in the Dark Ages. When I heard there was a commune in my neighbor-hood, I had to check it out."

"This is not a commune." It disgusts Sibyl that someone like this considers her part of his gang. "And we're not even trying to be part of any movement." At least Sibyl isn't. She wonders what Leif, still asleep upstairs, would say to this visitor. *Go forth and spread the word?* "This is a very private affair. We only agreed to one interview as a courtesy. Thanks for dropping by, but I've got to get to work, so…"

Sibyl starts to shut the door, but her visitor blocks it with an out-stretched hand. "Don't be so uptight! Look, I've been sleeping in the park since my old man kicked me out. I just need a place to crash for a few days. I'm not trying to sponge—I can pay for it with grass if you want." He reaches into a woven shoulder bag under the blanket.

"I don't think you heard me. We're not taking guests. We're not open to visitors. And if you don't leave my front porch, I'm going to call the police."

A sour look twists the man's features, and he stops rummaging and turns back down the stairs. At the bottom, he looks up and sees her watching him. "Your karma is fucked, sister!" From the half-opened front door, Sibyl watches him climb into a rusty Oldsmobile with a broken muffler. Even after she can no longer hear the car's chug in the distance, she stands shivering in place.

It's a relief to finally arrive at the office, where she can put this insanity out of her head for a few hours. Her heartbeat slows to normal as she starts opening mail. The personnel director of the Glad-dis Corp. has written to ask if she can do a seminar. It would be her first presentation at a private firm, and she bounces up immediately to show the letter to Sam Brower.

"Sibyl," he says when she appears in his doorway. "I was just going to come find you."

"Look what just came in the mail." Sibyl hands him the letter.

He reads to the bottom, but when he lowers the paper, his little mouth is pinched.

"What's wrong?"

The letter disappears into the rat's nest in front of him. He leans back in his chair, folds his hands on his chest. "Sibyl, how would you feel about concentrating on desk work for a little while?"

"Desk work?" The idea is such a bolt out of the blue, she doesn't even know what he means.

"I need help with some reports. Employee surveys, entering data. How are you with a keypunch?"

"*Keypunch?*" Some part of Sibyl has been waiting for a question like this ever since she thought about returning to work. Standing in front of an audience of professionals, doling out lessons in aspect ratios and white balance, she has felt like an imposter who would someday be unmasked. Has Sam just now gotten around to looking at her resume? "Did I screw something up?"

"No, no, no. You've been doing a beautiful job. No complaints whatsoever. About your work." He smiles thinly. "But I got a call from Al Schmidt. He says he knows what you do in your private life is your own business. He's just afraid it will distract people at training seminars if they recognize you. Personally, I don't think it would be a problem. But you know how it is. Our whole livelihood pretty much depends on Al right now. Let's just wait a few months until the excitement dies down."

In the half hour since arriving at work, Sibyl has so completely immersed herself in this different world that the spooky incident of this morning has faded from her mind. Now the whole disaster of the past week, *Personality*, the phone calls, the harassment, has found her here, too. "A few months!" Her voice squeaks up an octave. "What about the mailroom and copy clerks presentation on the twenty-first? I've just spent the last six weeks getting ready."

"Irving will have to do it. Look I really could use the help." He gestures to the mess in front of him. "Dolly-Anne is useless with this stuff."

Sibyl opens her mouth. She wants to tell Sam how ridiculous this is, how unjust. It's none of Al Schmidt's business who she sleeps with.

Even if it were, what has Sibyl done to hurt anyone? She's not the one who snuck around, fucking a woman ten years younger and lying to his wife for over a year. Sam is the one. He left a woman who had devoted her life to picking up his underwear in favor of some long-legged travel agent. So who gets punished? Not this male chauvinist pig with his little eyes and wrinkled forehead. She nods, bites her lip, and backs away.

On the way home that night, everyone's eyes seem to follow her. Taxi drivers wink and nod. The clerk in the grocery store laughs behind his hand. Along the highway to the bridge, she half expects to see a billboard displaying her naked body in a hot tub.

★★★

Nothing Hiram can do or say can blot Laura's tears, nothing softens her mourning. Hiram falls as surely into her grief as for so many months—years!—he soared on her joy. After days of this, he turns to Sibyl, solid Sibyl for relief.

Only to find her weeping as well! And Sibyl weeping is something you never see. Hiram strokes her back, until she comes out with a story about Sam and typewriters and keypunch machines.

He pulls her to his side, smoothes her hair. "Oh, sweetheart. It'll all blow over."

But her fingers twist in his shirt, and all at once she says, "Sometimes I wish we could just go back to the way it was, before Laura and Leif."

Go back? Go back to that frozen life? Hiram feels spines along his scalp. Doesn't she remember how coldly they lived as a couple? Doesn't she see how dead she used to be herself, with her ironing board and her color TV? He can't help pulling away from her. She lifts a hand to clutch at him, and it looks to him like the claw of a creature from the grave.

At his office the next morning, Greta Dalminger stares down at him where he is working at his desk. The creases deepen along her jowls. "Hiram, I can't work here anymore."

He can only stare. More than the work-stained old building, more than the contracts on the books, more than the greased and coddled equipment or the guys with their stained coveralls, Greta *is* Jancorum. She has worked here longer than Hiram. And she never stopped growing. Especially in the last few years, his attention distracted, Hiram has relied on her to make bids, to close deals, stuff he normally trusts only to himself. "What are you saying, Greta?"

"I've taken another job."

"What? Where?"

"Quist & Sons."

He can't breathe; the blade cuts too deeply between his shoulders. James Quist has almost made a point of underbidding Hiram lately, as if it were some personal grudge. "I don't know what to say. I'm… I'm shocked. Are you not happy?" It's like waking up in the morning to find that the bedroom floor had disappeared.

"I'd rather not discuss it, Hiram. I'll finish up our bid on Tealhouse by Friday. May fifth will be my last day. That should give you time to get up to speed on the other jobs."

To get up to speed? "Greta, I know I've been out of the office a lot lately. A lot has fallen on you. More than I intended. But I do expect to be around here more in the future and take some things out of your hands."

"Thanks, Hiram. That's not my beef."

"What is it then? You want a raise? More time off?" It will not be possible to replace her. You can't hire someone out of the want ads to run your company. Hiram will have to work sixty-, eighty-hour weeks.

She shakes her head.

"Then what?" Hiram holds his hands out empty to her. "God damn it, Greta, you can't walk out after thirty-one years!"

"It was one thing when you kept your funny business inside your own house. Now you've put it in the newspapers and the television, everyone is laughing. Do you know what kind of phone calls I've been getting?"

Once or twice in the past few weeks he has heard her slam down the receiver in the next room. He hasn't paid much attention. But now he can imagine. Reporters. Suppliers. Clients. James Quist apparently calling to snigger and insinuate. It is like Greta to keep it to herself, until she reached the boiling point. When she warned him about her concerns months ago, he didn't worry. He was so confident he could keep his two worlds separate. God damn Flagon, the lying asshole, Matteucci with her prying cameras, Leif on his soapbox, Darby with her teenage vindictiveness, even Matt idiotically spilling all his secrets.

Laura is the only compensation for that. It has to be Laura. Laura, Laura!

***

Reaching out to grab her son, to save him, Laura wakes up. Doctors in blue masks and hospital scrubs were coming for Matt. Bending over Laura they reached for him with bloody gloves. She sits up in bed to clear her head, but the terror of it won't fade and deep within her abdomen comes the familiar ache. Today is it? Yes, today, the woman from Child Protective Services is coming to meet with her and Leif. Leif has assured her they're not going to take Matt away; if they wanted to do it, they would have done it at school where no one would resist them. But she can't rest easy. Ever since Matt told her about the visit this woman paid him at the junior high, Laura can't stop dreaming about it.

Even in daytime, she finds herself checking the clock obsessively when Matt is due home from school. Once she used to worry that he adhered so rigidly to a schedule; now she is grateful for it because she would know instantly if something were wrong.

She lies back onto her pillow, only to sneeze. The tissue box on her nightstand is empty, and she gets up to prowl for more. Her allergies, which virtually disappeared after she moved to California, have erupted again. At daybreak sometimes she hasn't slept at all. And Hiram won't leave her alone, hands always clutching as soon as they're in bed. It makes her want to be with Leif sometimes; for once his distance is relaxing. So many nights without sleep are clouding her head. On the last rainy night of spring, she ran a stop sign and crashed into a VW Bug.

There are no tissues upstairs, but some must be stored in the downstairs bathroom, so she descends. To get to the downstairs bathroom, she has to pass through the room that used to be the basement office. It's now the boys' room, the door marked with the triangular fallout-shelter sign that Ivor stole from somewhere. She eases the door open and pads in. There's a closeness in this room, so filled with Matt's laboratory equipment and text books, with Ivor's balls, bats, mitts, cleats. It smells a little of sweat and of formaldehyde. There at eye-level in the top bunk, his face made handsome and vulnerable by the absence of his glasses, lies Matt. Safe. Still in her possession. She brushes a lock of hair from his forehead. She wants to pick him up, as she could only a few years ago. Hold him, carry him.

Long ago Dr. English warned them not to make any big changes. Didn't he tell Child Protective Services this as well? That threatening to steal Matt away from his parents is going to make his condition worse, not better? A thousand times Laura has said to herself that if she could reverse the events of the last three years, and know that it would make Matt better again, she would. She loves Hiram with passion she never knew was in her, but she'd leave him tomorrow for the good of Matt. Dr. English has assured them that this is not possible. And watching Matt, it's impossible to say whether he's getting better or worse; he only seems more inaccessible, lost in his robotic world.

After the Child Protective Services woman interviewed Matt at school, Laura kept waiting to hear from her. Leif warned Laura not to call. "Let them forget about it," he told her. "They've got so many bigger fish to fry." But Laura couldn't stand it any longer. She needed to know! And since nothing could be said over the phone, she found herself scheduling this meeting. Pulling Matt's blanket gently to his chin, Laura climbs the stairs again, but she knows she won't get back to sleep. So she bakes cookies and spends the rest of the morning trying to study in the living room. One by one, the family rises. Hiram first; he's spending long hours at Jancorum since Greta left. Sibyl next, frantic to get to work. It's hard to get a friendly word from Sibyl these days; she seems angry at everyone. Then Adrienne, Ivor, Leif. On the dot of 7:05, Matt emerges in his green T-shirt. She's told him before about the appointment, but she doesn't want to upset him by mentioning it again. In fact, he shows no more than his usual care, measuring himself two cups of Cheerios, a cup of milk, a cup of orange juice. But then, after kissing her goodbye, he hands her something.

"What's this?"

"My tape recorder. Do you know how to use it?"

"I suppose. Why?"

"I want you to record your conversation with Miss Wlassowsky."

"Record it?"

"Obviously, it concerns me more than anyone. Since you've chosen to meet in my absence, this is the only way I can have a complete record of the proceedings."

"Matt, how... I can't do that!"

"You need to ask her permission. But it's fairly simple to operate."

And because she can't think of a strong enough objection, Laura allows Matt to run her through the buttons on the little machine. Then he leaves.

When the doorbell finally rings, she feels so fluttery she's afraid for a moment she'll collapse on the way to answer it. "Leif!" she calls down the stairs as she passes them.

With her short hair, John Lennon glasses and prim buttons, Miss Wlassowsky reminds Laura of a librarian. She seems, at least, less fierce than Laura imagined, and Laura throws herself instantly into wooing her. "Thank you so much for coming. I'm sure you understand why we were anxious to hear about your interest in our son."

Miss Wlassowsky declines tea, coffee, water, cookies and they both sit stiffly in the living room until Leif, stained in grease, finally arrives from the garage. Couldn't he at least have put on a clean shirt?

"I'm sure you can imagine that your case was quite an unusual one for us," Miss Wlassowsky says. She flashes her teeth at them, and Laura smiles weakly back. "We've never had to deal with a group marriage before, let alone such a highly publicized one, and so we needed to spend some time investigating. In addition to reading some of the articles about your case and meeting with Matt's teachers and the principal at Kennedy, we consulted our own staff psychiatrist."

"And?" Leif asks.

"Mr. and Mrs. Wrightson, I'll be honest with you. I don't think that your living arrangement is in the best interests of your children, any of them. In Matthew's case, his diagnosis of obsessive-compulsive disorder suggests that it's had a negative impact on his psychological well-being."

"That's one guy's analysis," Leif says. "I'm sure there are psychiatrists who would disagree."

"Not that we're disputing," Laura says.

Miss Wlassowsky's expression is grave. "It is not our policy to intervene in the sexual practices among consenting adults. But we are required to investigate when our office receives complaints. We've received more than one phone call asking us to investigate."

"From who?" Leif demands.

"I can't share that with you."

"People who know us, or people who just read about us in *Personality*?"

Miss Wlassowsky frowns. "I'm sorry."

Next to her on an end table sits the tape recorder. Laura hasn't given it a thought since Matt showed her how to work it, and it seems too late to pick it up now. "Are you going to take Matt away?"

"We will not take legal action to remove Matthew from your custody at this time."

Laura controls her impulse to leap up and embrace the prim figure in front of her. "Thank you!"

"However, I, or another social worker, will return to visit Matthew in three months to review his situation, and at that time, based on what we see, the agency will consider whether to take further action."

"So we're on probation," Leif says.

"Thank you, thank you, Miss Wlassowsky," gushes Laura. "I'm sure you'll see some improvement in Matt in three months."

Miss Wlassowsky takes off her glasses and polishes them. "You know, Mrs. Wrightson, this isn't the sort of case in which our agency normally becomes involved."

"No?" Laura says.

"But when you put yourselves in a national magazine, it was bound to elicit some calls. This is a fairly conservative county. In Berkeley or San Francisco, you might not have stimulated such a reaction. But, as you may be aware, our agency only serves *this* county. We don't have jurisdiction elsewhere, and only in rare cases do we attempt to contact agencies in other counties to which our cases have relocated."

"What's your point?" Leif asks.

"According to the article, you're considering a move to Mendocino County."

"Oh, I see." He laughs: a short, dry single-syllable. "You want to get rid of us."

Laura wants to cover his mouth. Here at least is an escape! They can flee! No one will bother them if they go to Mendocino, and clearly they must now, as fast as possible to get Matt out of the reach of the people who want to take him away. "Thank you, Miss Wlassowsky," says Laura. "Thanks very much for the advice."

Miss Wlassowsky stands, hesitates for a moment about whether to offer her hand, then simply heads for the door.

Leif shuts the door behind her. "You know, of course, that there's no way in hell they could get Matt taken away from us. There's no sign of abuse. They'd be in court for years."

Laura convulses in a sneeze.

***

Among all the letters Leif has received since the *Personality* article appeared, the one from the American Society of Psychological Economics stands out like a gold cup in a gardening shed. Five years ago,

when he submitted his article, "Polygamy in Middle Eastern Econo-
mies," to the society's journal, *Psychological Economics*, the comments
were excruciating. "The writer offers shallow evidence to support
doctrinaire conclusions," wrote one peer reviewer.

And now here is the president of the society asking him to speak
at its annual conference in New Orleans this June. "I regret the short
notice that this invitation affords," writes Nigel Anderssen, Ph.D.
"Your work has only lately come to the attention of the selection com-
mittee. However, the theme of this year's conference is Economics in
the Counterculture, and we believe your research in this area would
contribute valuably to the proceedings. Although most of the program
has been set for some time, there is sufficient enthusiasm here that we
would like to list you as an additional presenter…"

Anderssen! When Leif had approached him at the annual conference two years ago, the man had brushed him off almost rudely. And
now here he was, the president of the society, writing a personal invitation, effectively eating crow, except that Anderssen probably had no
memory of Leif. The *Personality* article has worked its peculiar magic
again. Leif wondered whether Anderssen himself read the article or
whether it was someone else in the society.

Or perhaps it wasn't the *Personality* story, but one of its doppel-
gangers that had attracted the society's attention. In the past month
alone, articles have appeared in most of the local newspapers. Three
radio stations have interviewed Leif, and the local TV channel. Before
the others gagged him, Leif was speaking out almost daily to counter
the misconceptions in the original article. There's still a sardonic note
in most of what gets printed, if not in the reporters' voices when they
call. Still, the interest is what's important. Across the world now, people
are paying attention. They've begun to see that love doesn't have to be
crammed into a little flowerpot.

But love requires sacrifices as well. And so, under pressure from
the others, Leif has stopped taking the calls from reporters. Now he
talks only to ordinary folks who are trying to follow in the Eisenbergs'

and Wrightsons' examples, and to the serious researchers, such as the graduate student who phoned yesterday from London. Maybe that's where Anderssen heard. Doubtless he thought a little controversy might boost attendance at his conference. Well, Leif is happy to play along if it means he'll finally get a chance to talk about these issues in a scholarly forum. So it's a little hard to hear Sibyl snort when he welcomes her home with the letter in his hand.

"Great," she says. "Now it's the psychologists. I suppose they want to do a study on us?"

"Sibyl!" It's hard to restrain his impatience. "Don't you get it? This is national recognition of the best kind. These are academics, not voyeurs. They're asking us—me—to talk to them about my research."

"I thought you'd given up on all that."

"I had, just about. But this is the kind of opportunity I've been waiting for all these years. This is the establishment reaching out to us. New ideas don't just dawn; they work their way slowly through the process of conferences like this, and research papers, and books, until eventually they become part of the mainstream. If anything is worth the stress we've gone through since the article came out, it's this. I mean, this is the whole point of the extended marriage."

"Is it?"

She stands there, one eyebrow raised, with the briefcase she hasn't yet put down, dressed in a pants suit of impeccably masculine gray. She wants so badly to blend into the corporate world! And for what? "Sibyl." He takes her shoulders in his hands and squares his face to hers. "These past two years have been the best of my life. I've loved being with you and Hiram as well as Laura; I feel as if I've had what I always longed for. But I would be the first to acknowledge that it has also been a struggle. We've all taken our knocks, one way or another."

Pink tinges the whites of Sibyl's eyes. He's never seen her so harried, so fatigued. As long as he believed the new job was helping her realize her potential as a leader and a thinker, Leif encouraged her in it. She told him once she would never have had the courage to work if he hadn't suggested it. Now Leif has to wonder if it isn't time for her to move on. It's tempting to remind her that she'll soon be done with Sam Brower and his business anyway. Once the family moves to the country, there won't be any need for pants suits and kowtowing. And moving seems more and more imminent given Laura's growing fear of Child Protective Services. But Sibyl is hooked on the ego boost she gets from Sam and his clients.

"I was harassed out of my job," Leif reminds her. "Hiram lost his secretary. Any time you get too far ahead of the mainstream, that kind of thing is going to happen. We may not have planned it that way, but we've ended up in the avant-garde, along with feminists and freedom riders. We're nudging the world along towards a better place. Sometimes the world is going to nudge back, and we have to stand strong when that happens."

Sibyl slowly shakes her head. "Don't you get it? This… this thing that you're rubbing in everyone's face. It's so private. Don't you understand that you're destroying it?"

"Damn it, Sibyl!" He wants to squeeze her head between his hands.

When they first met, her strength allured him. Rather than melting in his hands the way Laura had, Sibyl could stand cool and answer him back, kiss for kiss or slap for slap; she could make him crawl for her. He still loves that hardness about her, but why has she turned it against him? Why not against people like Hiram's secretary Greta Dalminger and What's-her-name Wlassowsky, the people who are really trying to tear the marriage apart? Why not against Sam Brower?

***

The realization hits Darby so suddenly that she sits up in bed. "It was you, wasn't it?"

"What?" They only turned the light out five minutes ago, but Adrienne sounds half asleep.

"You told that *Personality Magazine* guy that I'm a wino. And that Matt is crazy."

Adrienne says nothing, but this time she can't fool Darby by pretending to sleep. It all makes sense. None of the adults would have talked about it, even if they were drunk. They're all too ashamed. And Ivor is oblivious. He probably hasn't even noticed his brother is seeing a shrink. You can't exchange two sentences with him these days unless they're about basketball.

"What did that guy Flagon do? Offer you a plastic horse if you told him something embarrassing?"

"No!" Adrienne sniffles.

Darby cringes. "I'm sorry. I didn't mean to be mean. I know you didn't do it on purpose. It's just that things are changing now. A lot. I'm afraid of what's going to happen."

"Why?"

"Can't you tell?" Lately it's all Darby can think about.

"Because the grownups keep fighting?"

"Yeah. To start with." The four adults always had their fights, but ever since the *Personality* article came out, it's been endless. The phone ringing all the time. Mom coming home from work in tears. Daddy yelling at Mom, Mom criticizing Leif.

If it doesn't stop soon, they're going to split up. That's how it happened with Colleen's parents. Sam and Nora yelled and yelled, Colleen said, until one day she came home and all of Sam's stuff was gone. His clothes gone from their closet, paintings gone from the wall, even records gone from the hi-fi cabinet. Now he's in an apartment in San Francisco. Colleen and Michelle just see him every other weekend. He and Nora aren't talking to each other, so Colleen has to relay messages back and forth. She had to choose which parent to invite to her birthday party.

"Are the Wrightsons going to move out?" Adrienne asks.

"That's the thing. Haven't you noticed that Daddy and Laura hang onto each other all the time? I don't think Daddy wants to go back to just him and Mom and us two."

And strangely, Darby's not sure she wants that either. A few months ago, she could have listed her wishes in a home:

- Her own room
- A normal family that people don't comment about
- Fewer grownups snooping on her
- A well-stocked liquor cabinet, with beer in the fridge

She still wants her own room, but on nights like this, when she is worrying, it's nice to have someone she can worry with. Even a kid sister. What people say at school doesn't matter. Okay, it does matter but a lot of people's parents are getting divorced now, so they're not in a position to criticize. And that's worse. Faced with the prospect of what happened to Colleen and Michelle, this overfull, noisy, no-privacy household suddenly looks cozy, lively. Actually fun.

If the commune falls apart, who will she live with? Mom and Leif? Daddy and Laura? Too weird. It would be like grafting someone else's hand to your wrist. And which kids? What would she do without Ivor's jokes to crack her up in a moment of absurdness? Matt has become her project, her protégé, her encyclopedia, her math tutor. How can she come home and not find Ivor shooting hoops in the driveway, with Matt inside eating his bowl of Cheerios, in his green shirt and hexagon glasses. They're her brothers.

"Darby?" Adrienne has silently crossed the room. She touches Darby's shoulder. "Can I get in bed with you?"

Darby wipes her eyes and throws back the blankets so her sister can climb in. "We'll be Okay." She smoothes Adrienne's hair.

The liquor cabinet? It's been a while, but a glass of whiskey would do wonders in a moment like this.

Chapter Eleven

SIBYL rubs the back of her neck. "Acclimate" or "accommodate?" She can't read her own handwriting, and she should go in and check with Sam to see what he dictated to her, only she can't stand to be around her boss these days. She's just too tempted to punch him in the nose. "Acclimate." What difference does it make? Sibyl taps out another paragraph, then stops to roll her head. When did the pain start? Was it the first full day she spent sitting at this desk typing Sam's memos?

Or was it the weekend she spent by herself on her hands and knees replacing milk cartons over baby grapevines? Leif is at some infernal conference. But deer were eating the vines, and, clearly, if nobody did anything, they'd all be gone. Hiram, of course, has to work every weekend at Jancorum now, and Laura goes with him to help. If Jancorum fails, then they'll all go broke.

Sibyl tilts her head to one side, then the other, unable to ease the knot. Hiram and Laura, Laura and Hiram. Tonight the two of them are going to see *Hair*. When Sibyl was on her way out the front door this morning, Laura reminded her that Sibyl would be on her own to round up the kids, make them dinner. To Laura, it probably seemed very reasonable. How can she know, since Hiram obviously doesn't remember himself, that today is Hiram and Sibyl's fifteenth wedding anniversary? Sibyl has dropped a couple of hints. ("June! The month of weddings.")

But she wants to see if he remembers on his own. Anyway, it's awkward because Laura and Leif stopped celebrating their anniversaries around the time of the group wedding. Leif said it always made him think of kitschy silver platters and embossed doilies. Only as she had written the date of Leif's conference on her desk calendar did Sibyl realize she would be alone tonight. The more she tries to forget about it, the more it pops into her mind. The really significant occasion is the anniversary of the group wedding; she should concentrate on that.

Why is she the only one trying anymore? Ever since the article in *Personality*, Hiram has been sleeping only with Laura and Sibyl with Leif, but no one talks about it. The day Sam Brower pulled Sibyl off client presentations, Hiram had walked into the bedroom where she was trying to compose herself. She told him what had happened, and he waved his hand airily. "It'll all blow over."

"Sometimes," she said, "I wish we could go back to how it was before we started this whole thing." It was more of a sigh than a proposal. She thought he could understand her sentiment—she wasn't telling him he had to give up his lover—she was only remembering the simplicity of those days. But his hand flew away from her. He stepped backward, features tightening like the fingers of a fist.

Then Sibyl knew for sure that she was stuck. On that first night of exchanging partners, years ago at Fallen Lake, there had been an understanding. If anyone didn't like the way things were going, the experiment would stop. When did they pass the point of no return? There was no announcement along the way, no warning sign. And after all they'd been through together, all they'd shared and built together, Hiram could no longer offer Sibyl real comfort.

When it came time for Leif to fly across the country for his conference, she could hardly bear it. But she couldn't mention the anniversary either—it would seem so ridiculous to Leif—and she had no other argument to give. Only her need for him.

Sam appears in her doorway, his tiny mouth pursed. "Sibyl, you have to save us. This report has to go out to Al tomorrow, and it's lousy with typos. Dolly-Anne is hopeless." He tosses it on her desk.

"Thank god we have at least one real perfectionist in the office." Before she can answer, he's already turned his back, and Sibyl suppresses an impulse to throw the report after him. This wasn't what she was hired to do. She's tempted to quit, but without this job she would have no answer for Laura, who wants to move to the property this instant. Sibyl would do almost anything to delay the day that she'll be spending all her time scratching in the dirt, driving nails. Killing rats. A hundred and fifty miles from here.

As she pages through the report Sam brought back to her, Sibyl decides Dolly-Anne must have been smoking Mary Jane; it's going to take Sibyl hours to redo. She pulls out the memo she was typing and scrolls a fresh sheet of paper into the platen. It's five minutes before she looks at the clock and remembers with a shock that she has to leave right away to pick Darby up from school. A week ago, Darby went home with a boy from school and didn't come home until the next day. She claims nothing happened, but it was a clear violation, and everyone has rallied around; Leif and Laura take turns picking Darby up almost every day. But today, Sibyl's on her own. Well, she has a typewriter at home, and no one will be bothered if she's up all night.

In the parking lot, the Rambler's carburetor floods. The car is almost twelve years old, held together with chicken wire and duct tape, but with only Sibyl's and Hiram's incomes, they haven't been able to afford a new car (reason number 237 why Sibyl can't leave her job just yet.) When she finally gets the car started and makes it across the bridge, she finds Darby glowering at her on the front steps of the high school. They're late for Darby's choir practice and late also to take Matt to his molecular biology course. It's seven when Sibyl gets home to start dinner, perspiration overwhelming her deodorant.

***

Leif nods to a hand raised in the back row. "Why get married at all?" asks the hand's bald, fleshy-faced owner. Smiles spread across the faces of the little audience. "Why not just extend your extended marriage to include everyone in the whole country, or the whole world for that matter?"

Leif forces a laugh. Even after the calls from reporters began to trickle to one or two a week and researchers stopped phoning altogether, he had still imagined a healthy audience at this convention. He imagined hearty handshakes, requests for citations, business cards offered by the editors of journals. The truth began to dawn only when he stepped into the stifling room—apparently the only one in the hotel without air conditioning—and found it deserted just before his talk was to begin. Maybe if he had used the more colloquial term "group marriage" in the title, or even "polygamy," he could have attracted a few more people. It certainly would have helped if his seminar weren't pitted against such a major draw as "Female Workforce Participation: Trends and Projections" down the hall. Whatever the reason, he can almost count his audience on his fingers. And no sign of Anderssen. Three people left before he finished his talk. Now he wonders if he was invited here as a kind of freak show.

Impatience pitches his voice higher. "Marriage isn't dead; it just no longer has to be between two people. Commitment still matters. We still have to take responsibility for our children, responsibility for each other. You can't just leave it up to whoever wanders in off the street or some government bureaucrat."

A sallow man in a seersucker suit: "How many people did you say are doing this? Thirty in the whole damn country?"

"Thirty-three was the number of extended marriages Constantine and Constantine were able to document in 1970. We think the number has mushroomed since then. A survey in *Psychology Today* found that more than a quarter of readers would—"

"Was that peer reviewed?" A bearded guy in the front row.

"I don't—"

"I just wonder how many of those readers were in Californica?"

Everyone snickers. Leif might have saved himself weeks of trouble. No data, no example, no crafted argument can wedge open these minds. He draws a big breath. "Look, obviously anyone who wants to break such old taboos is going to have to fight huge social inertia, huge prejudices." He glances at the bearded man. "And so they're going to have to be unusually committed."

The day before he got on the airplane for New Orleans, Sibyl begged him not to go. Why was she so lonely? Laura and Hiram were there. She hadn't been able to explain. Leif had never seen Sibyl this way, her fingers working nervously over his collar, her eyes unfocused. He had already paid hundreds of dollars for the airfare and hotel; his presentation was listed in a program that had gone to every economist in the country; he couldn't cancel for no reason. Leif almost wondered if Sibyl was purposely testing his commitment to her, as if his research were somehow in opposition to that. Of course he loved her. He would call every night, twice a day if she wanted. Ever since he left her yesterday morning, he keeps seeing her inverted eyebrows, her twitching grimace. Why couldn't Hiram and Laura be company enough for three days?

Something is going on. Lately, it's Hiram and Laura all the time, as if everything they all had done in these years, everything they'd gone through, came not to four but only to two sets of twos. Don't they remember? What they have together, all their hopes and dreams, came about because they had climbed out of the flat world they'd inhabited for so long and burst into four dimensions. Two and two is not the solution; all the same old problems will reappear! Under pressure, everyone is falling into bad habits. He needs to get back. Can he find a plane tonight? Once home, he'll organize the group again, lead them on a retreat to the beach, to the mountains, somewhere. Soon. Soon!

"Many groups don't want to be identified," he says. "Disapprobation can overwhelm their resolve." He stares down from the podium at his audience. "It's hard to keep functioning in contradiction to everyone you meet at work, in school, in a restaurant or at a PTA meeting. That's why many extended marriages are going underground or heading for the hills."

***

Laura clutches the handle on the door as the van's wheels screech around a turn onto Market Street. Because he can't drink at home, Hiram drinks too much away from home. He insisted they stop for drinks on the way back from the theater. "I'm only good for about one glass," she reminded him, worried as much about the money as the alcohol. But that didn't stop him from ordering a second scotch for himself.

Now Hiram swerves around a double-parked car. At this perilous time, when he should be most cautious, he is becoming less so. At work, he's bidding aggressively on any job where Quist & Sons is in the running. Laura is just learning her way around the business, but she gets the impression the company could lose big money if it wins any of these contracts. "Are you too drunk to drive?"

He laughs. "I haven't had a drink since intermission. In fact, I was just going to suggest we stop for a nightcap on the way home."

A light turns red, Hiram jams the brakes and Laura pitches forward. "Please slow down."

"We're stopped." But as he says it, the light changes, and he zooms past a parked motorcycle cop who looks up quizzically. Laura can't see a police officer now without thinking of Matt. Even if Miss Wlassowsky hasn't reappeared, according to the fragmented reports Laura gets (more from Adrienne than Matt himself) the other kids continue to torment him. And not only kids: the most heart-breaking story was about his science teacher. After Matt gave a report on self-fertilization among nematodes, Mr. Thorkeimer asked how many human beings it took to reproduce. "Two? Only two?" he taunted Matt. "Then please remind your parents of that." Leif wanted to storm into school, but Laura knew the less attention they called to themselves, the better for Matt. As soon as possible, they must leave Pleasant Valley.

If Sibyl weren't so obsessed with her job, she'd understand how much moving would help Darby, too. The sooner they get her away from all her supposed friends, the fewer temptations she'll find. Everything will get better when they move. Laura repeats that to herself every night before going to bed and every morning when she wakes up, like saying prayers, and yet the day of actually moving doesn't seem to budge closer. At the property, the corner posts of the great octagonal house still stand naked. The little vines don't seem to grow, and weeds get higher by the hour. Sibyl and Leif still travel there almost every weekend, but with Leif preoccupied by his presentation and Sibyl so openly uninterested, it looks as if the group is stuck. At the back of Laura's mind, doubt is seeping like ink in a shirt pocket. Can they never get back what they had?

Hiram has become so possessive, wrapping his arms around her in front of the whole softball group, fondling her breasts whenever she wants to sleep. Why has Leif lost all interest? And why does Sibyl so often glower at Laura, like this morning when Laura reminded her about the tickets to *Hair.* If Sibyl is jealous, let her make her own date with Hiram! Laura wouldn't mind. Let her do whatever they have to do, let them all do it, but Laura can't live this way much longer.

"This is the dawning of the age of Aquarius!" Hiram sings. He glances over at Laura and laughs. "What's wrong, am I totally off key?"

"Not *totally.*"

It's impossible to really talk about any of this stuff to Hiram. He's under such pressure at work, all he can think about is Quist & Sons. Then on an evening like this, released from responsibility, he turns into a teenager. The group needs to talk all this out, but nobody seems to want to call a meeting.

Hiram sings, "Harmony and understanding, sympathy and just abouting." He stops. "What do you think they meant by 'sympathy and just abouting'?"

***

Laura laughs. More than anything about her, Hiram loves the sound of her laugh, water splashing on stones, and she rarely makes it anymore. He laughs, too, even though he doesn't see the joke, and he looks up from the road to relish her smile.

"Trust abounding," Laura says. "Sympathy and *trust abounding.* Not 'Just abouting.'"

"What's the rest of it?"

"No more forces of derision!" Laura has a gentle, clear alto. "Golden living dreams of visions, mystic crystal revelations, and the mind's true liberation!"

"Wow!"

"I can't believe you don't know it already. Adrienne played the album incessantly last summer."

"We should have put it in our wedding."

"Sung by naked musicians?"

He rests a hand on her knee. "Maybe for our anniversary. It's coming up, isn't it?" The realization hits him. "Oh my god! Is today the twenty-seventh? It's Sibyl's and my wedding anniversary. Our fifteenth wedding anniversary!"

"Are you guys still celebrating that?" It's not in Laura to be jealous, and Hiram can excuse the flat note in her voice. All four of them confuse which traditions they're observing and which ones they're not.

He sighs. "I completely forgot, but I guarantee you Sibyl didn't."

"And she didn't say anything? How typical."

"Don't be catty."

That shuts Laura up for the rest of the drive across the bridge from San Francisco. It doesn't take much lately to put her in a snit. Her mood has changed in the last few weeks, and nothing Hiram offers— food, wine, extra attention in bed—ever seems to cheer her. "Where can I find an all-night florist?" he asks as they speed into Oakland.

She doesn't answer.

He could wait until the morning, then dash to the florist in the Plaza, but Sibyl leaves for the office so early, she'll be gone before he gets back. And if he gives her a bouquet tomorrow night, it will be an obvious afterthought. Ever since that night when she said she wanted to break up the group marriage, Hiram has felt bad just looking at her. Guilt seeks him out every night, tracks him down in Laura's arms. If he brings something home tonight, Sibyl will at least know he remembered her on the day. Then he'll take her out some other night; they'll eat strange delicacies in Chinatown and find a concert of folk music. Hiram pulls off the freeway into downtown Oakland, but there's nothing open that remotely resembles a flower shop. He glances at his watch. Chocolates? Even the supermarkets are closed at this hour. Then, passing a hotel window, he catches a flash of color and skids to a halt.

Laura rouses from her sulk. "What are you doing?"

He hops out of the van. The street is still and gray in the lamplight. Downtown Oakland is sinking into decrepitude, but a few stately buildings cling to their dignity, among them this hotel with its gilded façade. Inside, black marble shines under Hiram's shoes, and an art deco mural fills a whole wall of the lobby. A huge bouquet sits in the front window, another on a side table, and the smallest—with red, white and gold gladiolas—decorates the front counter. The hotel clerk has no plans to part with any of them, but Hiram, who sometimes pays workers in cash on short notice, carries a big wad.

"A hundred dollars!" Laura says when he hands the vase to her in the van. "Do you know what our bank account looks like these days?"

He steers the van back toward the highway. Is there nothing he can do without offending someone? "I can only see the beauty all around me." He gives her a peck on the cheek. The van swerves.

"Hiram!"

The house is dark when he pulls into the driveway; even the porch light is out, which, since Sibyl never forgets anything, looks like passive aggression. Everyone is angry at him these days.

"I still can't get over it. A hundred bucks for this!" Laura holds the vase out to him, as if she hasn't noticed his hands are busy finding the keyhole in the dark.

The door finally comes open, and he finds the light switch on the inner wall. "They had another, bigger one," he tells Laura. "I could maybe get you some birds of paradise for a thousand."

There it is: the laughter for which he breathes.

***

Someone laughing? Sibyl wakes up with her head on the kitchen table next to her typewriter. She opens the door to the kitchen to find Hiram and Laura in the hall, silhouetted against the porch light. Hiram has wrapped one arm around Laura and is holding something in his other hand.

"Sibyl," says Hiram. "What are you doing up?"

She only stares, too sleep-fogged to answer.

"Well, I was going to give these to you tomorrow." Hiram comes to her, holding up bouquet of gladiolas in a glass vase. "But since you're up, here they are."

She takes the flowers in both hands. *I can't do this anymore.* Does she speak the words or only think them? It's as if she didn't need to move her lips, as if the thought itself were all there was in the little entranceway.

"For our anniversary," he says.

The vase is thick and filled with water, but her fury propels it so suddenly he cannot dodge. The vessel cracks on his breast bone, and a jagged edge slashes through his shirt. Water sloshes on his pants as the pieces fall, scattering petals and bending stems, to shatter on the rug. One shard rebounds, reflects a gleam of the porch light, and settles behind Hiram's foot. Another arcs back to land halfway between Hiram and Sibyl. Tinier fragments catch in the carpet's long twists, cling to Hiram's chocolate trouser cuff and Laura's apricot skirt hem, glance off his wingtips. One lodges on Laura's sandal between her largest toes. On Hiram's chest, blood surges in two lines.

Chapter Twelve

INSTEAD of taking Darby and Adrienne home from their tennis lesson, Sibyl parks the Rambler in the lot at Pleasant Valley Plaza. She switches off the engine, and sits still, not making a move to open the door.

"Why are we stopping here?" Darby asks.

They are both sitting in the back seat and can't see her expression.

"Hello?" Darby says. "Ground control to Major Mom."

Grass blades lie on the floor mats of the Rambler and there is a tear in the piping that runs across the blue plastic upholstery of the seat in front of Darby.

Sibyl sighs, slowly, as if forcing a great weight. "I have to tell you something."

Darby's hand clenches on the handle of her tennis racquet.

"What we've been doing, living with the Wrightsons, hasn't been working out all that well. So we may end it."

Darby looks over at Adrienne. Fear is breaking through her complacency. "Are they moving out?" Adrienne asks.

"We don't know yet. But the thing I have to tell you is that your father and I may not end up together."

"What?!" Darby's vision of divorce is of red faces and broken dishes. She has never once heard her parents raise their voices to each other, so what Mom is saying makes no sense. "Are you kidding me?"

"It's possible that we will separate. Live in separate houses." Sibyl's voice is level, but she still doesn't turn to face Darby and Adrienne. "Whatever happens, I want you to know that your father and I both love you."

Sibyl's last sentence hardly penetrates. Darby feels everything around her disappearing—walls, floors, earth, sky. She has come untethered to drift in a vacuum.

***

"I can't do it anymore," says Sibyl.

From the living room couch, Matt can hear every word through the partition of the makeshift bedroom in the former dining room. Until now, the adults always managed to keep their counsels private. But in the past week, it's as if they've stopped trying. Matt sets *The Human Genome* on the coffee table amid the clutter that has accumulated in recent days. A coffee cup holding cigarette ashes. Newspapers with last week's headlines. An orange peel giving off its odor of zest. How has Sibyl allowed this? But more than these changes in atmosphere, the tone in Sibyl's voice bothers Matt. It has risen in pitch, perhaps four or five whole notes above its usual range, and the tempo is slower, the words elongated. "I'm. Sorry. Hiram. I. Just. Can't!"

Hiram by contrast is speaking faster, his words running together. "Please Sibyl. We can't go back to being a *Leave It to Beaver* nuclear family. We can't reverse the flow of time."

"You mean you don't want to."

Hiram sighs. "Maybe I don't. Is that wrong? You said yourself— before the *Personality* article and all the reporters—you were happy. Happier than you'd ever been, you said."

"A year ago. And *you* just said we can't reverse time. Well, Leif is already out of work. The *Personality* article is published. Greta Dalminger quit. I've been demoted to copy clerk. We'll all be on the street if this keeps going."

"That's what's getting to you? Your job? You can find another job. The skills you have are high in demand. But this marriage is not just about you or me, it's the kids. It's all of us. We *need* each other."

"The kids? How can you even say that. They were fine before the Wrightsons moved in. Darby never drank. Matt had, if not normal relationships with other kids, at least peaceful ones."

Sibyl's voice lowers with this last sentence, as if she finally realizes she can be overheard.

But by now Matt knows what he has to do.

The ride to Dr. English's office is long. Matt has made the trip by himself only a couple of times because it involves changing buses downtown, then a long walk from the nearest stop. This part of town is older than the subdivision where the Wrightsons and Eisenbergs live. Matt estimates the age of the trees here at twenty to thirty years; their canopies stretch over the streets in places, giving shade from the afternoon blaze. Still Matt isn't accustomed to exertions like this, and his sweat glands are operating at full capacity by the time he arrives at the small house with its precisely trimmed lawn and cheerful carnations.

Dr. English shares the building with a chiropractor and an accountant, but he is the only one here on Saturdays, and no one notices Matt letting himself into the waiting room. A half hour passes before the doctor opens his door to say goodbye to a patient, and spots Matt waiting.

He stares. "Matt?"

"I need to talk to you," Matt says.

Dr. English's lips bunch on his thin face. "I have another appointment in ten minutes. But come in, we can talk until then at least."

Matt has wasted so much of his time in this office sitting in silence. Now he has to get to the point. "I lied to you."

"You lied?" Dr. English presses his fingertips together and leans back in his chair.

"Maybe 'misled' is a better word for it. When I first came here, I implied that my family's living arrangement upset me."

Dr. English cocks his head. "It didn't?"

"It had nothing to do with the behavior that resulted in my ostracization. I simply choose to live my life differently from other people. I prefer to control variables, to apply scientific method as much as possible. Very few people understand that. I didn't think you would either."

"Control variables?"

"It doesn't matter. The point is that no one liked me at school before we moved in with the Eisenbergs. The group marriage didn't change that. Unfortunately, I encouraged this misconception. Now it has spread to the news media. As a result my parents and their partners are making a decision based on a fallacy."

Dr. English blinks. "I'm not sure I follow…"

Suddenly Matt's trachea contracts, cutting off the air he needs to make words.

Worry lines appear on the doctor's narrow forehead. "Matt? Are you all right?"

Matt waves his hands to signal that he'll be fine. Dr. English offers him a box of tissues, but Matt shakes his head. He draws a slow breath, calming the smooth muscles in his bronchi. "I need them."

"The Eisenbergs?"

Matt nods. "Darby and Adrienne. We have to stay together. Tell my parents."

Dr. English leans forward. "These are very important topics for us to explore. I think you're on the verge of an important breakthrough. Let's arrange a time when we can talk at length and fully examine it."

Matt crushes the tissue box between his hands.

***

Hiram and Laura take the van. They take the syrup pitcher because it was in Hiram's family and the blue and white china because it was in Laura's. They take the bird's eye maple dresser, the bed, night-stands and lamps from the dining room; they take the cheese grater, the Lord of the Rings mugs, the Persian carpet, all the tools and the crystal pitcher.

Ivor takes his Catfish Hunter baseball glove and scuffed cleats, his Aerosmith poster, model airplane glue and free weights. He takes his whoopie cushion and his rubber vomit, the "I biked Yosemite" T-shirt

Darby once wore. He takes his mud, sweat and Irish Springs.

Matt takes the ant farm. He takes his crystal, barometer, specimen jars, butterfly net and raccoon skull. He takes his ferrules and filters and capillary tubing.

He takes one look at Darby and both look away.

***

"Sometimes we will still do things together as a family," Sibyl says. On Fourth of July she and Hiram spread chicken and watermelon on a blanket at Fort Point in San Francisco. They sit on opposite sides of Darby and Adrienne, like stone lions on a staircase. The fog comes in that evening so that they can't see the fireworks, only hear them boom, muffled over the water.

***

The dancers rush in raising their hands and retreat, lowering them. They turn, step in front, step behind. Across the circle, Sibyl catches Leif's eye and he smiles. It's not a full-face joy smile, but a lips-only "here we are," sort of smile. Or maybe it's an "I did this for you" smile. Folk dancing was her idea.

If Hiram and Laura were here, they would laugh and kick up their feet. They're not, and that's Sibyl's fault, she's the one—She stops this train of thought. Its tracks spiral endlessly downward, and coming here was supposed to be her way of getting off. She needs to forget herself for at least a moment, in the rhythm of the drum, the piping from another time and place. The dancers shift directions, and Sibyl focuses on footwork. It's a minute before she finds herself holding Leif's smooth strong hand. It doesn't give her the reassurance it used to. But that's not Leif's fault.

"Thank you," she tells him.

He raises an eyebrow. "For?"

"Coming here. Staying with me."

He laughs. "Where else was I going to go?"

It's true, he has almost become her dependant. The substitute teaching jobs aren't coming often enough. He diligently applies to private high schools, offers tutoring through classified ads, corrects papers for colleagues. And someday Hiram and Laura will pull together enough money to buy out Sibyl's and Leif's share in the Mendocino property. But for now, Sibyl is the primary breadwinner for the household of herself, Leif, and the two girls. Be careful what you wish for.

The dance separates them again and Sibyl finds herself holding the hand of an older man with thick glasses and five-o-clock shadow. He leers. She averts her face. Yes, she could do worse than Leif. If they are to stay a couple, she must learn to accept Leif's failings. And keep an open mind to his ideas.

An open mind is the only reason she agrees to go with him to Harmony House the next morning. In the front yard, four tomato vines sag with fruit. Sunflowers point their faces skyward. Sibyl and Leif make their way around a tricycle and a beach ball to the front door. As Leif rings the doorbell, Sibyl counts the minutes until she can excuse herself to pick the girls up from tennis.

He shakes his head. "You're already looking at your watch!"

"Sorry." She puts on a bright smile as the front door swings open.

"Hey!" A woman with waist-length hair and an ankh necklace steps aside to let them in. "It's not locked. We're not into that."

Sibyl extends her hand. "I'm Sibyl."

"I know!" the woman takes Sibyl's hand with the faintest grip possible. Apparently she's not into handshaking either. "I saw you on TV!"

Sibyl sighs. "And you're…?"

"Constellation."

"I talked to Starbuck on the phone," says Leif.

"He went to the co-op, but you can hang out in the living room if you want, or whatever till he gets back."

The two sit on a modernist couch, and Leif begins flipping through the pages of the Whole Earth Catalogue.

"Want some kombucha?" Constellation offers.

The tea tastes like fermenting fruit with a hint of mushrooms. Sibyl's trying to decide whether she likes it when a naked boy appears in front of her. "I want some." He points at Sibyl's tea.

"Help yourself," she says.

The boy takes her glass and drinks slowly. "Do you want to play cards?" he asks her.

"Sure, we'll play with you," says Leif. The boy returns with a deck missing several cards and Leif deals out hands for Go Fish. As they play, other members of the household drift through. Moon, a fifty-something woman showing cleavage practically to her bellybutton. A goat-bearded black man called Jupiter. More naked children. Starbuck never appears, but some of the others stay to talk and a gradual picture of the household emerges. Six adults live there with three children they are raising "in common." All the adults consider themselves to be married to each other, but over the years people have come and gone. The household now has room for one more man and one more woman. Two teenage girls would be welcome. The astronomical monikers are "just for fun." And so on. Sibyl loses track of the details, hoping Leif won't notice when she checks her watch.

In fact there is no danger of that. He leans toward Moon right now, zipping question after question her way. "Do you sleep according to a schedule? What about cooking? A formal process for decision-making?" Energy Sibyl hasn't seen in months sparks from his eyes. And suddenly she realizes that she is sinking into the couch, sinking away from this man.

A vision opens of the next several months. Leif won't move out right away. They won't fight about when or where or even whether to part ways. The arguments are mostly behind them already. Instead he will fade gradually from her life, returning for dinners and occasional sleepovers that will become less and less frequent as Sibyl begins to collect the implements, establish the friendships, build the routines of a single woman.

***

Leif takes the Grateful Dead albums, the Roszak, Maslow, Adorno and Marcuse. He takes the Beethoven sonatas he had helped Darby learn.

***

The moon wakes Hiram. For a moment he thinks it's morning. But no, the world has lost all color, depth and heat. Pine trees flatten themselves into black paper cutouts against the pinprick stars. Hiram's hands hover ghostly over his face.

Beside him, Laura draws long, faintly whistling breaths. He closes his eyes trying to join her, but this cold light has entered its energy into him. He didn't think of the moon when he and Laura decided not to pitch a tent. They expected only the stars and assured each other the mosquitoes would disappear with the sun. They took their ground cloth far enough away from Darby and Adrienne so that they could have their privacy if the impulse came to make love. Not long ago— just months ago, but it seems like years—that would not have been an "if."

He turns and props his head on an elbow. Even in these daguerre-otype hues, he still loves the bend and dip of her lips, the lush sweep of her hair. He still draws solace from her warmth. He admires the quickness of her mind, her willingness to try anything—to camp now when work is so pressing, to sleep under the stars, to plant tomatoes while waiting for the vines to produce. To try making a new couple out of the wreckage of the foursome. Does it really matter that they don't have intercourse?

No. Yes. Yes, the thought of her, open as she used to be, and visions of their revelation in these mountains just three years ago have made him stiffen and yearn. He reaches a hand to her arm, but stops before touching her. Let her sleep! She has suffered enough unrest in these months since the collapse of the group. He can be patient.

Shivering outside his sleeping bag, he quietly pulls on his jeans and boots. Twenty yards from the camp, behind a tree, he unzips to work on himself. But no; the erection is already gone, along with the images that inspired it. Instead he releases steaming pee against a tree. Down in the lake, a fish makes ripples in the metallic sheen of water. Hiram sits, watching for another. But all is still until Adrienne mutters in her sleep.

He had planned this trip for months as a way to revive his bonds with the girls. They won't ever speak their anger. They tell him by looking away when he smiles at them, by sitting silently in the car when he picks them up for a weekend, by refusing to share with him any of their sorrows or joys. He imagined sitting around the campfire and explaining. But how do you describe to your kids what was missing in your marriage to their mother? How do you talk about the flame that burns or doesn't burn, the cravings that are met or are not met by another person? When the group was together, he thought they could feel the joy. He hoped they could celebrate with him the expansion of love. But if they did, if they shared that with him even briefly, they must blame him even more for its dissolution.

Hiram gets up from his perch by the lake and follows the path to their tent, needing a glimpse of them. Through the netting he can barely make out their shapes like giant caterpillars in their sleeping bags. Through the odor of mosquito repellant, he catches the faint whiff of Herbal Essence shampoo. He loves them. That much he has uttered, on the phone, in the car, at bed time. Sometimes it is all there is to say. And silently he wills them to know it now, to feel it in their sleep.

A cloud passes beneath the moon, and Hiram yawns. Passing the fire pit, he picks up the whiskey flask. Maybe it will help him sleep. He unscrews, puts it to his lips and tilts back his head. He stops after the first swallow and blanches at the taste of water.

What happens next?

You can find out by visiting www.fallenlake.com.

Forty years later and all grown up, Adrienne Eisenberg has started a blog about the events in this book, and about her own life since.

You can communicate with her, with other characters in this story and with author Laird Harrison by visiting www.fallenlake.com.

On your mobile device, you scan this code with a QR code reader:

About the Author

Laird Harrison has worked as a freelance correspondent for *TIME*
and *People* magazines and for Reuters news service and has written and
produced video for many other national publications and websites.
Harrison teaches writing at the University of California, Berkeley
Extension. He grew up in Berkeley, California and lives in nearby
Oakland. This is his first novel.

11173678R00133

Made in the USA
Charleston, SC
04 February 2012